I0745489

ESCAPING DEMONS

BOOK ONE OF THE CASTILLIAN BLOOD SERIES

KILLIAN WOLF

Grim House
Publishing

Copyright © 2020 Grim House Publishing
All rights reserved. No part of this publication may be reproduced,
distributed, or transmitted in any form or by any means, including
photocopying, recording, or other electronic or mechanical methods,
without the prior written permission of the publisher, except in the case of
brief quotations embodied in critical reviews and certain other
noncommercial uses permitted by copyright law.
Printed in the United Kingdom.
ISBN: 978-1-951140-02-1

Editor: Claerie Kavanaugh https://www.claeriekavanaugh.com
Copyeditor: https://www.saltandsagebooks.com/
Cover design: https://miblart.com/
Formatter: Michael Davie

In memory of Frank Palenzuela III, who always put his family first and loved his father more than life itself. And to Raquel, whose heart was always filled with love, kindness, and generosity.

CONTENTS

FREE BOOK

Get the prequel free when you sign up for my mailing list at
http://killianwolf.com/

As a reaper my life is simple . . .

Go where I'm told, help the dead move on. No bonding. No
interfering with mortal affairs.

Collect, guide, rinse, repeat.

But when an escaped demon starts killing off a little boy's family
one by one and affecting the balance of the universe, am I
expected to stand by and watch?

Or should I save him, even at the expense of my existence?

PARADISE HOUSE

ADDISON

Nothing awakens a girl's inner demons like having to explain her choices to a man. Even if he is the perfect boyfriend, there's no excuse for calling me back to back like a telemarketer.

My phone vibrates for the twentieth time and I chuck it in the back seat of my blue Volkswagen Beetle, right after catching a glimpse at the caller. Carl. Again. Don't get me wrong, I love my boyfriend, but ever since I agreed to work as a live-in nurse, he has driven me up the wall. I don't know what his problem is; it's not like he's never going to see me again. Miami is only an hour and a half away.

Ding. I glance down. Another text message. *Dios mio,* he knows I'm driving!

Seagulls caw in the distance as my car approaches thick, green iron gates. No, this can't be right. A sad and over-grown, half-dead garden sorrows what appears to be a once lively estate. Does anyone even live here?

Unlike the wooden picket fences or hedges typical of the Florida Keys, these gates are black iron and fashioned to look antique. The iron bars curve inward into spirals at the top, resembling the type of gate you'd see in a storybook or in front of a castle. They open slowly and I drive cautiously inside.

The house is only three stories high, but each story is quite tall. My eyes follow the soft mustard paint of the house to the red terra-cotta tiles on the roof. Black iron bars protect four balconies and ivy covers more than half of the structure. What is a Mediterranean-style house doing in the Florida Keys? Dax didn't tell me he lived in a mansion!

I follow the driveway around a dried-up Spanish fountain, adorned with beautiful ceramic tiles of white, yellow, and blue floral designs, and park my car. I crinkle my eyes at the abandoned garden circling the driveway that runs all along the sides to where it seems to lead toward the back.

Staring at my reflection in my car mirror, I pass my hands over my hair, straightening it from the mess the wind created since I drove with the passenger window down for an hour and a half. I collect my purse and cell phone and step out of the car.

Ding.

Swiping up on my phone screen, I bypass the twenty-three missed calls, five text messages from Carl, and one from Ava, my best friend and roommate.

Carl: Addie please pick up. I'm not mad, I just don't think it's a great idea for you to move in with some guy you don't know.

Legit concern but this is work and he needs to trust me. Besides the fact I already told him I'd call him right when I got out. I don't know why he can't understand that I need this job while I wait for placement at the hospital. Not to mention, this is a great opportunity.

I ignore the rest of the messages and stick my phone

back in my pocket. Ava and Carl will have to wait until I'm finished with this interview.

A crow watches me enter through the front gate.

Well, that's creepy. I lift my fist to knock on the door, when it caws and flies down at me, trapping me inside the closed entryway. I jerk back and cover my head in panic. It misses me by an inch and lands on a branch of a nearby shrub leaning against the house. It caws again.

Crazy bird. Stepping back away from the crow, I reach for my phone to call Dax. The line rings a few times, but no one picks up. Then I notice the bird is still eyeing me with its beady black eye. "Well, what do you want?"

"*CAAAW.*"

"Jeez, What the hell is going on?" I've never had this sort of interaction with a bird before.

I lift my fist to knock on the heavy mahogany door when it slowly creaks itself open.

Through the darkness, I make out the details of the front entrance from the sliver of sunlight shining through a window from somewhere in the back of the house.

"H–hello?" Cold air smacks me in the face as I step out of the South Florida heat and into the foyer. I jump in place as the heavy door slams behind me.

"Hello?" I call but receive no answer.

The smell of wood tickles my nose as I stand inside the house and grip onto my purse. This feels kind of weird. Do I turn around and leave? Do I keep walking in? It would be rude of me to keep walking into the house, wouldn't it? But the door did open . . . My eyes wander around the foyer and stop at a tall painting on the wall to the left of the front door. A creepy little girl with honey-colored, curly hair and fair skin sits on a stone wall in a garden, holding a baby bundled up in a blue blanket. The girl's expression is serious, and her eyes follow me as I walk. I move over to my right, and the painting's eyes follow me. I walk over to the left and the same thing happens. Chills run down my spine. Like I said, creepy.

"My apologies." A man's deep voice comes from behind me and I startle.

"Oh, I'm sorry!" I spin on my heel and face him. "The door opened, so I walked inside." A strong aroma of Cuban cigar smoke fills my nostrils.

"It's quite alright. I'm Dax." He has a warm smile that stretches from ear to ear and a square, muscular jaw. He holds out a long-sleeved arm, in sorry attempts to hide the muscles protruding from its fit form. I shake his hand and hide a wince at how cold it is. His dark brown eyes sink into mine as he holds my hand in his. His eyes soften for a moment and stare into mine.

Not awkward at all.

"Nice to meet you." I politely take my hand back and rub them together. I clear my throat. "Wow, you like to keep the air conditioning running strong," I say in hopes of ending the awkwardness. My leg muscles quiver as I shift my weight.

Dax takes his hand back and chuckles. "My dad has always kept the temperature low. A stark contrast from outside, isn't it?" I laugh and shudder at his turtleneck sweater. I can't shake off the idea of something constricting my neck. I've had a fear of choking ever since I could remember. I push the thought from my mind and clutch my purse strap tightly in my hand.

"Shall we step out of the foyer?" Dax nudges his head to the other room, right outside the foyer. I offer him a grin. I'm relieved at his attempt to break the awkwardness. He leads me through a door next to the stairs and into a large red room with a red mahogany pillar in the center. My eyes glaze over the intricate details on the walls and ceilings, adorned with hints of gold, embellishments, and paintings.

"This place is so beautiful."

Dax turns his head and stares at me, searching my eyes. "Yes, my dad is to thank for the house itself, as he designed the plans for it, but everything else, the decorations, that was all my mom. She liked to call this room the Venetian room," he says, pointing into the room. "My parents loved to go antiquing on their travels and have their purchases sent back here. A huge hassle if you ask me, but they liked to live lavishly."

"I'll say!" Even the couches match the gold and red wallpaper. I tilt my head back at the dark, mahogany ceilings. The dark wood overlaps in a beautifully subtle way. It reminds me of a print by M. C. Escher. A design so unique, it wouldn't be seen in any other building or house. "He put a lot of thought into his design."

"Oh, you haven't seen anything yet." His eyes twinkle as he backs into the room.

"What are those three doors there?" I point to a set of matching mahogany doors facing each other and a third one in the center, facing the Venetian room.

"The one to your left is a dark room, although it hasn't been used in years. A bit old-fashioned, but it was an old hobby of my old man. The one in the center is a bathroom. And the one to the right is my room. But let's take a walk over here." He beckons for me to follow him in the opposite direction as he walks briskly to the other side of the Venetian living room.

I turn to follow him through another heavy door when I pause to face the double glass doors leading to a dark room. The pale face of a boy stares back at me in the reflection of the glass. He has dark hair with short bangs plastered against his forehead and dark eyes. I gasp.

"Addison?"

I stare at Dax, then back in the direction of the boy. He's gone.

"Are you alright?"

Where'd he go? Goosebumps ripple down my arms. "I umm . . ." I clear my throat. This is not the time to start seeing things. My new boss will think I'm nuts. I rush over to where he stands.

Dax disappears into the darkness of the room. "Wait there," he says.

Wall mounts light up the room, showcasing shelves upon shelves of porcelain dolls dressed in clothes of all kinds, from all over the world. They look so real they resemble small motionless children.

"Watch where you step. We haven't fumigated in a long time; there might be scorpions."

I shut my mouth, realizing it had been hanging open. My fists clench and I look down at the tile floor. I've never seen a real scorpion and I'm not sure I ever want to.

"Don't worry, they usually hide when the lights are on." He opens his palm and motions to the room. "So, this is the doll room."

My breath catches in my throat and my lips become dry. They're all staring at me.

Above an ornate table, is a large portrait of a young man wearing a pair of jeans cut at the knees and an open leather jacket, showing his bare, muscular chest. The man has long black hair, pulled back in a ponytail, and is looking straight at me. In his hands is a sword. He looks familiar. I dart my eyes toward Dax. A flush creeps over his cheeks.

"Er, my father had that made a few years ago."

"Oh, it's you? It's . . . eh . . . nice." I start to rub my arm out of nerves.

He clears his throat. "I was fifteen years old when the photograph was taken. The sword is right over there." He points to a sword adjacent to the painting. "It's actually a replica of Excalibur. From *The Sword—*"

"*In the Stone,*" I finish his sentence. "That's my favorite Disney movie!" I flash a wide grin and he relaxes his shoulders and smiles.

I turn to face the rest of the room and my eyes land on the collection of swords decorating the black-and-green-painted mahogany wood walls. The dolls' eyes move with me as I follow Dax to the far end of the room. I shudder before planting my eyes on a doll wearing a frilly peach dress. She has honey-colored eyes and wavy brown hair. Something about it seems familiar, but I can't place my finger on it. Nostalgia washes over me. I think I've seen it somewhere.

"Are you alright there, Addison?"

"Uh, yeah . . . this doll . . . it kind of looks like me. Just my imagination, right?" I let out a chuckle.

Dax's eyes fall to the doll. "I think it does," he says in a cheery tone.

He walks over to a set of heavy mahogany double doors.

"What's through there?" I say, forcing my gaze away from the doll.

"Nothing, just storage."

"Quite the woodwork for just storage."

I blink as he ignores my comment. *Shut up, Addie. Stop being so intrusive.*

"So, where are you from?" He says, breaking the silence.

"Cuban-American. And yourself?"

He cranes his neck to look at me and smiles. "I am too. Hey, so does your family live in Miami also?"

"My family?" I avert my eyes. Truth is, every time I try to think about them, or remember them, I'm filled with sadness and I wish I knew why.

"Yeah, do you have any siblings?" Dax continues as he sticks a key into the lock of the door.

"Nope, no siblings."

Dax hardens his face for a split second and yanks the door open.

"To be honest, I kind of avoid thinking of my family." My voice sounds more rigid than I intended.

"Why is that?" His voice is crisp as he speaks.

I inhale as my mind races for an answer. I don't want to tell him they died when I was young, but I can't remember them. I think my mind blocked it out. I know something traumatic happened to us but I just can't remember any of it. My whole childhood is fuzzy and I'm not sure it's a door I want to open. Silence lingers and I open my mouth to speak but Dax cuts me off.

"I'm sorry, Addison. You don't have to talk about it. Come, let's finish the tour." He walks into the next room, sticking a doorstop at the edge of the door to keep it open.

"This room is a bit of a cultural mix. My father liked to collect sword replicas. This one here is a replica of the sword belonging to Genghis Khan." He points to a saber with a strand of gray hair hanging from its jasper hilt. "That's real hair."

I lean in for a closer look and grimace. I look up and he's grinning down at me. I quickly fix my posture as I realize he's just messing with me. "That one behind you is a very good replica of the sword used by Alexander the Great."

I turn to look at what he's pointing at and gape at the

lapis lazuli hilt. "It's beautiful, but can I ask—what's with all the dolls?"

"Oh, my mother loved to collect them. She would buy one from every country they traveled to. My father used to say he wanted to design a house with a doll room just for her. And he did."

"Oh, that's so sweet. Where's your mother now?"

"She passed away a few years ago. Heart attack. Shall we go?" He spins on his heel and sweeps out of the room, intending for me to follow.

I bite my lip. I shouldn't have asked.

I scurry off behind him toward the dark room with the glass doors. I pause before entering, my goosebumps returning as the face of the boy re-emerges in my mind.

I shake it off and follow him as he flicks on the light. The room is long, with tall brick arches overlooking the backyard and dock, showing where the garden ends. "I'm sorry about your mother."

Dax softens his eyes at me. "Do not be sorry Addison. Anyway, this is my favorite room in the house." He walks to the built-in mahogany bar. "I guarantee you'll never find a bar of this quality anywhere in the Keys. Shall I fix you a drink?"

My eyes widen, realizing I did just enter a creepy old mansion and got too fascinated to stop and wonder if this gig is legit. "Oh, no thank you. It's quite early and I have to drive back a long way." Dax relaxes his shoulders and laughs to himself. "Of course. Shall I show you the rest of the house?"

I follow him up the stairs. "I brought my resume with me in case you wanted to see it again."

"That won't be necessary."

I swallow hard. He still hasn't even mentioned the position. Why would he be giving me a tour if I didn't get the job though?

I follow him up the stairs to a large family room with an enormous iron chandelier, surrounded by three big iron rings held up by chains. I gape at it, imagining what would happen if it ever fell. Each ring gets larger in size from the top to bottom. Lights resembling fake candle flames circle each ring. It is an impressive piece. An out of place chimney also decorates the far end of the room. What the hell is a chimney doing in South Florida?

The second and third floor are open-aired, allowing the third-floor corridors to be visible. I hold onto the iron rail as I stammer and take in every detail, from the silk wallpaper to the long drapes around double windows that reach the ceiling. The woodwork of the ceiling is also mahogany, even more detailed than the ceiling of the first floor; overlapping itself in a continuous square design. Again, different than anything I have ever seen. Paintings decorate nearly all of the walls. It's like being in a museum.

Addison.

"Hm?" I flick a look down the stairs then back to where Dax is standing.

He raises a brow.

"Did you say something?" I ask.

"No."

"Sorry, I guess I'm just nervous," I toss another look down the stairs before moving away from them.

"That's alright, there's nothing to be nervous about."

"This house is really something," I say as I set my purse down on a chair. I notice a picture frame on the coffee table next to it: Dax with long hair tied back in a ponytail, standing next to an older man. "Is this your father?"

"Yes. He's up in his room now. He stays asleep all day.

Only wakes up to eat and to use the bathroom. I'm afraid his dementia has made it dangerous for me to leave him here on his own, but I can't always stay."

"Right, of course. I'm sure you work and have to live your life." It's no wonder he needs help. I do a double take as I catch Dax staring back at me in silence. Did I say something wrong?

I hold my breath and scurry for any chance at a change in topic. I point to another set of mahogany double doors to our left. "What's in there?"

"That's the library." Dax turns his neck. "The pair of double doors on either side of the chimney leads to the second family room. There's a television in there, and a piano."

"Wait, a library?" Excitement overcomes me as I start moving toward it.

"Yes," Dax stammers, "but there's no point in going in there. It's very dusty and most of the books have been put away."

"Oh, that's sad." I was excited about an actual library being in a house. But then again, there's an entire room dedicated to dolls, so I shouldn't be surprised. "Shall we go see your dad then?"

Dax's face stiffens. "No, not today. I will have to prepare him to meet you next time."

I relax my shoulders at 'next time.' Guess I got the job. A smile spreads on my face, but it quickly drops as his brows furrow; he's brooding over something.

"Dax? Is everything alright?"

He breathes in as I break his concentration. "So, what do you think?"

My eyes light up. "About the house? It's like a museum. Bit too much for my taste, but it is gorgeous."

"A bit too much?" He furrows his brows again but then quickly relaxes. "Will you take the job, Addison? I want to hire someone I know he will be comfortable with and I believe that person is you."

One, I'm relieved he isn't a murderer, and two, he's being sincere. Everything else seems to fit into place, so why not? I need the money and the experience. It's a good deal. "I think I'll take the job."

I smother a chuckle as Dax tries to hide the excitement in his voice. "Great. When can you move in?"

I laugh. "Give me a few days to pack up my things."

We walk down to the front door together discussing house keys and payment. There is more to the house he didn't show me but there will be enough time for me to explore myself. The main thing is looking after the old man.

"Goodbye, Addison. I look forward to seeing you in a few days. Have a safe journey back; many deaths occur on that road so, be careful." His tone is icy as he says the last words.

The lights flicker behind us.

"I will—and thank you for showing me around." I turn to say goodbye, but he's already gone.

"DON'T FEAR THE REAPER"

AMBROSE

ix Months Ago

Had I a heart, it would be pounding in my chest. Reapers all over Earth don't think twice about the souls they collect. And normally, I don't either. But something about this one makes me hesitate. Usually, my scythe leads me to my appointments with enough time to figure out how and why they will die. But this one shouldn't be next. This untimely demise reeks of Abyzou, a demon who had been locked up in the deep dungeons of the lower levels of the astral plane, LLAPS for short. Last year, I'd saved a child from dying at her hand and I thought she was taken care of. We still don't know how she escaped.

There's a rumor going around that Abyzou's attacks were part of a larger plan organized by Azazel, the high angel of death. They say he wanted to trick a reaper into using their scythe to capture the demon, as doing so would somehow free him from his cage. If yet another person were to die unexpectedly, that would mean the rumors were true, and I fell right into his trap. As soon as I seized the demon, my scythe had glowed red. I had never seen that happen before; our scythes only ever glow blue.

The High Council was not happy with my choice to save an innocent child. I guess you could call me a rogue reaper, but I still try to do my job. Lest I want to end up obliterated.

The reaper in me wants to wait and collect his soul. But my newfound rogue demeanor is fighting it. If I don't follow orders, the Judge will have my head.

I dart my eyes around, looking for Abyzou. My scythe vibrates once and I hold it up, inspecting the blade. A red light sweeps across the metal. So subtle, I would have missed it had I blinked. Curious.

A motorcycle accelerates around the street corner. The Earth vibrates beneath my feet, and I grip my scythe in hand, ready to collect the soul. My hollowed eyes follow the bike as the man on it leans back and wheelies down the straight away, bunny hopping until he reaches the next corner. If it wasn't for my scythe glowing red, I would expect him to die in a crash. I start moving forward under my hooded cloak as I watch him lose control.

No! This isn't right! I stare at my scythe. It glows red. It's been hacked. Again.

My rogue side itches to save him, but I grind my teeth, willing him to rescue himself instead. Jump off the bike, you idiot, I think. There's a lawn full of grass right next to you. A few broken bones, and you'll be alright.

I don't flinch as the man tries his best to take control of the bike. The fact humans think they can overpower the mechanical creations they invent always amuses me. Don't they realize the metals and motors they put together can crush them faster than they can create them?

An earth-shattering screech shakes my bones as my appointment crashes through a wooden fence. I have to hand it to him, even then he still doesn't let go of the bike. The next hit comes harder. He crashes headfirst into a cement wall as he gets flown off the bike. Before the engine cuts off, it speeds forward, running the poor chap over.

I rush over to collect his soul, still unsure if this is how he dies. I wait over the man's body as blood gurgles out of his helmet. I can't do anything until he's at the very brink of death. As much as I want to put him out of his misery, my job isn't to kill. Although, I think my scythe killed him. No, I killed him. Perhaps if I had not been using this scythe, after it glowed red, a demon wouldn't have compromised it.

I look over my shoulder and spot a set of police cars turning the corner. Someone has most likely called an ambulance. It wouldn't be the first time someone's life gets saved and reapers get called out for no reason. A sudden desire to remove the helmet urges me forward.

What am I doing? I'm not supposed to meddle. I switch off that little voice for just a second. The man whispers something. I inch closer but don't understand him.

I extend a bony hand out to his helmet and pull it off. The helmet cracks into two pieces from the cement wall, having broken it upon impact. I take back my hand as the man chokes on his own blood.

For the first time ever, I feel panic. Anticipation washes over me as I lift the man's head to remove the rest of the helmet. I look over my shoulder for an ambulance, but I would have heard it by now. I take my scythe and gently twist a small dial close to the blade. I slow down time, just enough to give me a chance to think. What the hell am I doing? Time to think for what? I can't save this man's life! Can I?

The Judge would not be pleased. Despite this death being unnatural and caused by a demon, my scythe is clearly compromised. Think he'd understand? Damned if I do, damned if I don't.

Not even I know the limits to the scythe. Magick is magick, is it not? What harm could it do if I try and save this young man's life? The way I learned to reap, why not try and reverse it? With a tap of the blade to the man's head, I concentrate on the energy coursing through it.

Did it work?

I reset the dial and unfreeze time. Sirens wail about a mile away, followed by police officers. I lean in, but to my dismay, blood gurgles out of his throat like a clogged fountain, and he lets out moans of pain. No, this can't be. I've made him suffer more! I drop down to my knees and lift up his head.

"I fixed you," I say. "It's going to be okay."

But as I hold his head, blood drenches my bones. I turn him over and find sharp pieces of heavy plastic stuck deep within the confines of his skull. I twist out a piece and he starts to convulse. I've made a terrible mistake. I set his head gently down on the ground and my scythe starts to glow. I commence reaping to rectify my mistake, but after a second, it flickers, its light dimming. What's going on?

The man forms a fist, and I take it as a symbol he's fighting for his life.

Does this mean there is hope? A paramedic runs through me. I stand as my scythe no longer glows. Maybe the magick takes a little longer. Maybe he'll survive. I follow them to the hospital.

Invisible to anyone around me, I stand in the corner of the emergency room, scythe in hand, ready to collect the poor soul who is suffering through a painful death. As a reaper, I have the ability to observe Earth from inside the veil and step out if I deem it necessary. I watch idly as nurses try to save the man's life.

I take a few steps forward and extend my arm. Normally, my scythe would glow once to commence my reaping, but it isn't yet. Why does this keep happening? I lower my eyes to the blade and peer at my own reflection. Nothing's happening. My eyes flick back to the room and my surroundings are frozen. The doctors and nurses are frozen in time, and so is the clock on the wall. It stopped at 2:22 a.m. A low vent sounds right behind me and from it walks a tall woman with straight red hair, wearing a black suit. I recognize her immediately as she moves in from the portal. A visit from her is no social call.

"What are you doing here, Deacon?" I ask, as the Judge's right-hand reaper stands beside me.

"Ambrose, the reaping authorities have been alerted that you tried to interfere with the natural order. Again."

"That was no natural order. The moment I got to the scene, I didn't have any information on how he was going to die. I only intervened because I suspect there is a demon once again in our midst. But he is going to die anyway. I did nothing for him."

Deacon arches her brow at the word demon, but then puts on a straight face. "The problem remains. Something in you has changed. You've been spending more time than allowed on this plane and are experiencing empathy. As you know, that is detrimental to our kind. What's more, you delayed this young man's time of death, which still sent a ripple through the fabric of their universe. I am here to retrieve your scythe and collect this soul myself."

Refusing to look her in the eye, I give her an icy cold jaw. Handing over my scythe means certain death. It's not like we can just stop doing our jobs and do something else. No, I will be beheaded in front of the council by the Judge's gold scythe, my bones disintegrated and released into the universe. This is something no reaper has ever been faced with, but it's also something that wouldn't bother a reaper. Except for me. I don't intend to turn myself in. "Deacon, what part of, 'This man was not supposed to die' do you not comprehend? Has it occurred to you that if a demon actually is behind this, then this man's death could be the scheme of some evil plot?"

Deacon scoffs. "And which demon do you presume is behind this?" she says, crossing her bony arms out in front of her.

"You know very well about the rumors."

"The Judge has stated the rumors are false, Ambrose."

Arguing with a reaper about whether or not one should question The Judge of the High Reaper Council is admitting to thinking outside the rest of the operatives, even though we normally do have our own suspicions. We know better than to question anything out loud. "What about my scythe having glowed red when I apprehended Abyzou? And just now—"

"You'll have to take it up with the Judge. It was probably acting from your insubordination. You have to come with me now, Ambrose."

An urgent need to run shoots through my bones like electricity. My eyes dart to Deacon, moving in to collect the soul. This is it, my moment.

I open a portal and jump through, my human shape turning to bones beneath my cloak. Deacon, unused to reapers making rash decisions, jumps in after me.

When not guiding a soul to their next stage, portals can work like a stepping-stone from one scene to the next; there is no in-between unless you step into the bridge of the astral abyss.

It's only a matter of minutes before Deacon catches up to me. I need to outsmart her.

I open portals everywhere, jumping from cities, to deserts, to forests, giving her a run for her money. But Deacon is one step behind me each time.

I open a portal within a portal, so it looks like I'm walking into another desert, but instead I'll be walking right into my chambers inside the astral dimension. I close the portal behind me and drop my scythe on my mantle. I think I finally lost her.

"It's worse than we thought. Why did you run? You knew how this would end." The echo of her voice resonates in my ears.

My jaw drops and I spin around to meet her gaze. "I suppose I just wanted to see if I could outrun you." A smirk creases my face.

"You know what this means."

I take a step toward my scythe on my mantle. "If I give up my scythe, what will become of me? Can I be sent back to the mortal realm?"

"That is impossible," she says.

"I've spent centuries as a reaper. I've never faced the inevitable human experience of death, Deacon. Wouldn't you run?"

I don't want to be zapped out of existence. I can't even imagine it. The human spirit has more in store for them. Not even I know what becomes of the death of a reaper.

"You should know the answer to that, Ambrose. I never would have done what you just did. However, had a mistake like this happened to me," she scoffs again, "then yes, I would gladly give up my scythe."

A heavy sigh escapes my chest. Deacon makes a valid point. As a reaper, I am not supposed to care about what happens to me. Keeping the order intact is the only important thing.

Perhaps I have fallen short of my abilities due to me spending a lot of time on Earth. Perhaps it is for the greater good of the council that I just accept my fate and correct the order with my execution.

The Judge told me once before it is not up to me to make decisions on the fate of a human, even if an outside source, such as a demon, is behind it. I am still meant to just collect the souls and let him correct the rest. But I did not listen. And maybe it is true, maybe it is my fault for feeling this way because I have been spending more time on Earth than allowed. But with my newfound knowledge, maybe I am just able to think outside the box. And maybe, I'm right.

"You are right. I broke the law and now must face the consequences."

"Thank you for complying. Now hand over your scythe," Deacon says as she reaches for my blade. I extend my scythe for her to grab it, and just when she reaches over for it, I raise it, swinging it over toward her neck. Her scythe clashes with mine as she blocks me. I shield my eyes as my chamber room gets filled with a bright light.

I push myself up from my knees and straighten my back, readying myself to take on the Reaper Council. From the center of the courtroom, I scan the many reapers staring at me from their seats. My eyes land on a pair of black, sullen eyes belonging to the grim, hooded Judge sitting in the high podium.

They say if you look deep within them, you can see the end of your existence. I stare right at him, refusing to move a muscle. If I'm to be executed, I refuse to show fear, or regret.

Without an ounce of sympathy in his voice, he leans over his stand and says, "Ambrose, I hereby sentence you to death for delaying a human's time of death and thereby causing unnecessary pain and fleeing your bond. Hand over your scythe and step up to the podium, where you will be vanquished from existence."

I curl my fingers around my scythe. "Would you at least allow me a few final moments to tell my story?" Reapers in the courtroom gasp. I can feel Deacon's eyes burning into me.

"I doubt it'll do you any good." He straightens his spine. "But go on. I'll be curious to hear how you arrived at such a spontaneous turn of events."

I turn to face the courtroom. Dozens of reapers watch me in utter astonishment. Reapers are known for obeying orders, understanding the laws of nature need to be abided by, and they never meddle in the affairs of humans. Voicing opinions isn't a common occurrence in this realm either.

I clear my throat before I begin. "As soon as I reached my appointment, I knew the man on the bike wasn't supposed to die." I turn to the audience. "My scythe didn't glow."

All hollowed eyes are on me as reapers gasp throughout the courtroom. The Judge slams his gavel. "What's this about your scythe not glowing?"

Curious that the Judge doesn't know. He normally keeps a watchful eye on all of us. "Just like when Abyzou was sending children to their untimely deaths. My scythe wouldn't glow then. I got to the scene and had no inkling on when my appointment was going to meet his death."

"I hope you're reaching your point soon."

My eyes dart to the side of the courtroom as I reflect on how I approached the dying man. I look back to the Judge, whose permanent frown on his skull is impressive, as it doesn't move. "Now, please do not assume I was ignorant of our inabilities or arrogant. I know we do not have the ability to bring anyone back from the dead, but since this man was dying and not dead yet, I couldn't shake the feeling I should try to save him. What if the rumors are true? What if . . ." I look around the room. "What if Azazel has escaped?"

Gasps sound from around the courtroom. Reapers are not in the business of saving people either.

The Judge slams his gavel on the mantle. "That is ludicrous. Ambrose, I have already had this discussion with you. Do not go around making the rumors worse."

"Fine then, if not Azazel, then perhaps some other demon escaped." I turn to continue my story.

"The ambulance had not arrived yet. The only one around was a police officer who had watched the whole thing and called it in. But he had not left his car yet." I spread my hands out in front of them.

"I admit my mind was made up. I was going to try and save this man."

"But that's against the rules," someone shouted from the benches.

I turn to face them. "Yes, I meddled. I used my scythe to try and heal. I figured, magick is magick, isn't it? There was blood all over the pavement and the wall. I leaned over the stranger and with a simple tap of my scythe, the man opened his eyes. This is when I realized I had made a grave mistake. I did not understand why he was still in pain. I, a grim reaper, found myself standing in front of a man in between life and death and it felt . . .awkward. Never had I ever hesitated before."

"This is preposterous," someone says. Deacon shakes her head and then lowers her gaze to the floor. I shift my weight and look back at the Judge as incoherent chatter spreads through the courtroom.

"Order, order." The Judge slams his gavel on the podium and motions toward me. "I want to hear what he has to say. Go on."

I take a deep sigh of relief, spread my arms, and continue.

"'It's okay. I fixed you,' I told the man as I removed his helmet. Blood stained my hands, and I immediately realized the helmet had caved into his skull from the crash. He'd suffered irreparable damage. I felt saddened. I had made a terrible mistake. I should never have intervened. While empathy is not something we are permitted to feel, I could not control it happening to me, Your Honor."

The Judge rests his skull on his skeletal hand. "Yes, it is curious that this did happen to you. I myself have spent years down on Earth reaping and collecting souls. I looked human in order to comfort them as well. Still, I never felt empathy. So, tell me, why did you run?"

"Your Honor, if I may. None of us have ever faced nonexistence. We're meant to be immortal. I was simply afraid."

The crowd gasps again.

"When the ambulance arrived, I followed it to the hospital. I stood in the corner of the emergency room with my scythe in hand. When it was time, I moved forward and, when my scythe didn't glow, I knew something was wrong. And here we are."

"Yes, here we are." The Judge sits back in his chair. "A very moving story indeed, if I were human." Reapers in the crowd laugh at the suggestion. Deacon shifts in her seat behind me. "The problem still remains, Ambrose; you broke our laws and caused irreparable damage. How are we to fix the cause and effect of delaying a timely death? You have changed the course of human history."

Someone coughs in the background. I turn around to look at Deacon standing up.

"If I may say something, Your Honor."

"Yes, go ahead."

"Empathy is scorned because it affects how we do our jobs."

"Precisely, which leads to actions such as these."

"Yes, but it is not illegal. And as Ambrose said, he had no control over what happened, doubtful as it may be that his scythe actually glowed red, he did try to rectify his mistake. If a demon is lurking, Ambrose only did what he thought would salvage the order. Perhaps it wasn't empathy at all."

The Judge leans forward in his chair. "What are you getting at, Deacon?"

"Instead of sentencing him to permanent termination, why not re-train him? Losing an operative would make us short one reaper. We don't often produce more."

The Judge rubs his jaw for a few seconds in contemplation. "Yes, Deacon, you are right. What's more, you can be his partner."

I purse my lips together as Deacon shifts uncomfortably in place. It looks as if Deacon's insufferable need to always report the facts has finally caught up with her in an inconvenient way to herself. Yet, beneficial to me.

Deacon's mouth drops. "Wait, what? No, that's not what I meant. Please, I don't want to babysit. I don't even like being in the human world. I hate humans. I'm more useful to you as your right hand!"

"Yes, but you've reaped before. You have eons of experience. Frankly, there's no one more qualified than you, Deacon."

"But—"

"And, just to make sure you do the job, Ambrose will hold the scythe key that will enable you to return. So, you must always be with him if you want to get home, Deacon. You have to ensure Ambrose does not go rogue nor break any more laws." The Judge turns his gaze back to me. "You have to complete a number of assignments given until we determine you're fit to reap by yourself again. Failure to comply will lead to your termination." And without waiting for a response from either of us, the Judge slams his gavel.

I'M NOT READY

ADDISON

"I'm only taking what's important. I'm not leaving my room here barren, so don't worry." I take some of my clothes off the hangers and throw them into my suitcase.

Ava takes them out one by one, folding them neatly and repacking them, shaking her head. "I'm going to miss you being here." She fumbles with her blouse, making sure her Santeria beaded necklaces remain unseen.

"I'll come back; I swear. And I'm sure you can visit me at the house. Oh, Ava, that place is gorgeous. You couldn't even imagine. It looks completely out of place in the Keys, like it belongs in Spain or something. I can't help feeling like I have to work there."

Her body sags against the wall, picking up a pillow to hug close to her chest. "Well, I am happy for you and I hope it goes well. What's that Dax guy like?"

I pause. "He's intense. I mean, he seems kind and funny too, but there's a seriousness about him. I guess that's normal for a boss though. He really cares about his dad."

"How old is this guy? How old is his dad?"

"I didn't get a chance to meet his dad because he sleeps most of the time and Dax didn't want to disturb him without preparing him to meet me. Dax must be in his twenties. He's around our age." I zip up my suitcase and make my way to the bathroom to collect my toiletries.

"Woah, I expected him to be a lot older. Is he cute?" She calls after me.

I smirk. "I wasn't looking, but . . ." I scrunch up my face. "He's kinda handsome. You know, the tall and muscular type."

Ava throws the pillow she was hugging at me. "Oh, I'm definitely visiting you at work."

"Did I mention the house also has a built-in bar?"

A knock comes at the door and a butterfly releases in my stomach. "That's probably Carl." I jump over a pile of clothes on the floor and run out to open the front door.

I peek through the peep hole to make sure it's him. It's Miami; one can never be too safe. Then I swing the door open. His smile shows his perfect teeth and I pull him in for a kiss. His soft, full lips brush against mine.

"Woah, Addie, careful with the pizza."

I chuckle and take them from him, setting them down on the counter.

"I got you your favorite." He opens the grocery bag, letting me take a peek before he sticks it in the freezer. "Mint chocolate chip ice cream."

"You're the best!"

"I also brought wine for when we're at the beach later."

"Could you be any more perfect?"

He takes my hand and swings me around, pulling me into his chest. He lifts my chin up and dips his lips to mine.

"Ahem."

I chuckle into his mouth. "Sorry Ava."

"Give it a rest, jeez." Ava shifts her weight to one foot. "It's not like she's moving away forever. She's keeping her stuff in here just in case it goes south."

"It won't go south," I fire back. "But yeah, exactly. And you both can come visit me."

"How pissed do you think your new boss will be if I move in too?" Carl lowers his eyes but keeps his smile.

I scoff and playfully slap him on his chest.

"I'm kidding, relax. Come on, let's eat so we can get to the beach to watch the sunset."

My head rests on Carl's chest as we watch the waves crash in front of us. He lets out a heavy sigh as I dig my toes into the sand and gaze out into the sunset. He stares into the distance, keeping his posture rigid.

"You're terrible at relaxing." I nudge his side. He raises his eyebrows and moves my hair from my eyes as the wind picks up.

"I don't feel comfortable with you moving to the Keys for work."

"You act like I'm moving to another state or something. I'll only be an hour away. We will see each other, I promise. It's not like we hang out every day as it is."

"Exactly my point, Addie. And also," worry lines crease his forehead, "I was hoping . . ."

"What?"

"I was just hoping maybe we could move in together."

I gulp. It isn't that I don't want to be with Carl. My eyes dry up and I rub them, sitting upright. I just pictured moving in with someone after I had been a bit more settled in my career. Not to mention, I like living with Ava.

"Oh . . . Don't you think it's too soon?" I say.

"Too soon? No, I don't. Addie . . . I love you."

It takes everything in me not to cringe at his face. It's not like it's the first time we've said those words to each other, but it's the first time I mutter them back to him, not knowing if I truly feel the same way. One thing is for sure, I certainly don't want to move in together yet.

His eyes dart away from me and I know my hesitation just hurt his feelings. "I'm sorry. Maybe I am moving too fast. I shouldn't have said anything. You're right, we will spend time together." His voice cracks. "Are we okay?"

I gaze into his hazel eyes and nod. I can tell he's nervous and that somehow sends a shiver down my spine. All he wants is to be with me, what more can a girl ask for? "We're fine. Don't worry. I just need some time, but I will get there." I lean in and let him wrap his arms around me, pulling my frame into his. His hands caress the small of my back as I part my lips to kiss his chest. I dig my fingers inside the top of his shorts pulling him even closer. He raises my chin and meets my lips with his. I kiss him back, despite my stomach flipping over.

"THE ENCOUNTER"

AMBROSE

The ground vibrates beneath my feet as a breaker slamming repeatedly into the pavement nearly fifty feet away rings through my bones. I close my eyes and concentrate on deafening the outside world. A pelican flies above me as a baby starts to cry. All at once, police sirens go off and an ambulance drives by. Then, finally, there is silence.

"That's better."

"What?" says Deacon.

"Earth is noisy."

We reach the back of a grimy gas station, beside a door labelled Women Only, before it turns into a crime scene.

Deacon holds out a bony hand giving the command. "We'll wait here. This one should be entertaining enough."

I lend her a side look and adjust my collar.

An unkempt man with piss stains on his trousers cowers before another man who stands holding a knife to his throat. He has a durag on his head and has a teardrop tattoo on his right cheek with a neck tattoo that reads 'Trust Noi.'

"You stole ma shit, gimme it or I'll cut you."

I squint my eyes as I watch the man raise his arms above his head in defense. It doesn't do him any good. The one with the durag jabs his knife into the man's throat and pulls it away sharply. "Dead men tell no tales," he hisses as blood flows from the victim's wound. He reaches for his throat as he starts to cough, cupping his mouth with a shaking hand as blood sprays out from his throat. His head lands on the ground like a sack of potatoes.

"It's time," says Deacon. Our scythes glow as the assailant checks the man's pockets for what looks to be a small plastic bag filled with a white substance.

The door to the woman's bathroom opens just as he stuffs the plastic bag in his pocket. A twenty-something-year-old girl with wavy brown hair comes out. I squint at her. Something about her reminds me of someone, but I cannot put my finger on it. The girl stops in her tracks. She looks down at the homeless man covered in blood on the pavement and opens her mouth to scream, quickly fumbling for something in her purse.

My eyes dart at the man with the durag as he lunges toward her with his knife. She starts to run, but the man grabs her by the strap of her purse and she screams. He grabs her from behind and cups his hand over her mouth.

The man I tried to save . . . That's who she looks like. Maybe I can save her while there's still a chance. While she isn't dead yet . . .

Deacon moves forward to the homeless man. "Quickly Ambrose, this is your reap." Her mouth drops open and she grabs for my arm. "Ambrose, what are you doing?"

I switch off the invisibility cloaking on my scythe and rush forward, at full reaper speed. "Let go of her," my icy voice hisses in his ears, making him drop his knife.

"Where the fuck did you come from?" the man says.

"I do not like to repeat myself. Let her go." I push the man from his arm, halfway forgetting my own strength as he lets go of the girl and flings her toward the wall of the gas station. I press my blade up to his neck, even though I don't want to kill him. "You've done enough killing for one day. Leave here and don't come back."

The man's chest pounds so hard I heard it thudding inside my head.

"Yeah man, okay. Got it."

I take a fist full of his shirt and jerk him forward, causing him to stumble before running off full speed. I turn to the girl. Her eyes meet mine as she picks up the purse she must have dropped on the floor after I apprehended her assailant.

"Are you okay?" I ask her.

She rubs her chest and I notice a red aura over it, showing she has a rising ailment. Hopefully, I've given her enough time to enjoy the rest of her short life. "You–you came out of nowhere . . ."

I swallow. I made my decision in the spur of the moment and hadn't considered the possibility of scaring the wits out of her. I flick my eyes to the side, in case Deacon was beside me in her full-blown skeletal figure. But she isn't there. At least Deacon is still in the veil. By the looks of the struggling homeless man, she's waiting for me to come back, and probably judging me.

"I'm glad you did though. You saved my life."

I meet her big brown eyes. She has a glint of a tear at the corner of one of them, but I can tell she's struggling to keep it intact. Despite the scare she just had, she's probably trying to be strong. For some reason, this brings a smile to my face.

"I'm Addison," she says.

"Hi Addison. I'm glad you're okay. Be careful out here,

these roads are kind of . . . empty. You never know who or what may be lurking."

She raises an eyebrow and gives me a side smile. "Yeah, I uh—" she clears her throat. "Was just headed to my new job and needed to stop for gas."

"Of course," I say sheepishly. "Well, Addison, it was a pleasure to meet you. But I must be getting back to work now."

"Yeah . . . me too." She starts to back off and waves at me. I mimic her wave and watch her turn around to leave. I wait until she is out of sight, on the other side of the gas station, where I presume her car is parked before I cloak myself again.

"What were you thinking?" Deacon spits as I enter the veil, now cloaked to any human.

My jaw tenses. I know I messed up. To be honest, I wasn't thinking. "It would have been an unnecessary death—"

Deacon holds her hand up. "Just stop; take care of this one. We're already late."

The homeless man who had just been slaughtered opens his eyes and peers up at me and Deacon, eyes bulging.

"You let him get away."

"I'm afraid there's nothing we can do about that. It's okay to stand up now," I tell him. The man's eyes gloss over our black suits. "You some kinda fed?"

"No."

Deacon lets out a raspy sigh. "If you get up, you'll see you're no longer in any pain. Now, we need you to come with us." The man does as he is told and looks behind him. His jaw drops as he sees his body on the ground—lifeless and covered in blood.

"Truth is, if he hadn't killed you, you were on your way to an overdose." She pulls out her pocket scythe and turns the blade. I roll my eyes.

In a flash of light, we leave the scene.

Deacon and I step onto a wooden dock. The smell of fish and saltwater fills the air.

"You didn't have to be so short with that last one."

Deacon tightens her face. "I'm not here to be their therapist. They had enough time for that while they were living."

"I only mean, a little bit of kindness can help their transition go smoother. Help them to understand what's happened."

"Since when did you start caring about the wellbeing of these degenerate souls?" she spits.

I take a deep breath. "You and I have two very different ideas about what our position entails."

Deacon stops and turns to face me. "Written by whom?" She combs her straight, red hair behind her ears, showcasing her sharp cheekbones. "I'm not happy about having to babysit you. You have a reputation for going rogue and I'm the one in charge of the list. Not you. I work fast, and preferably alone. We are not here to save lives, Ambrose. What were you thinking, showing up in front of humans like that?"

"She wasn't scheduled to die," I say, keeping my voice as steady as it can be.

"Accidents happen with humans. And now I too have to suffer."

"You're just upset I'm the one with the scythe key."

Deacon clenches her teeth and I try my hardest to hide a smirk. "We have work to do."

We walk among the crowd, only visible to the dead or dying, and reach a small restaurant on the water. Inside, a cook struggles to prepare her orders as she hovers over the cutting board in pain.

"Where's my group order?" a waitress calls out.

"Get Sam to take over. I can't stand up."

"Tammy? What's the matter?"

"It's my stomach again. This time it's really bad."

A waiter runs over to her to help her ease down against the wall. "Maybe you should just call it and go home."

Tammy closes her eyes and nods.

"Come on, I'll help you to the office chair."

Tammy starts to get up but collapses back to the ground.

"I've seen that look on humans before, the look they get right before puking their life away. I heard the room starts to spin. What do you think, Deacon? Do they mean that literally?"

"Let's go," says Deacon, ignoring my inquisition.

The waiter is shouting for someone to call an ambulance, but we know it won't do her any good. We move in and approach the young cook.

"I'll do the talking this time, Deacon."

She rolls her eyes, but steps to the side.

"Tamara? You're okay now. You can come with us." The girl sits up and gapes at the people running around her body, lying lifeless on the kitchen floor. Nearby, an ambulance approaches, and firefighters come rushing in.

"W–what happened to me?"

"You died from a severe bowel obstruction. I am sorry," I say as I soften my voice.

The girl starts to weep. Deacon sighs behind me and I ignore her.

"But how? I'm young and healthy. I've even been to the doctor for my pains."

"None of that matters now. But you do have to come with us. You can't stay here."

"Where do I go now?"

"The only thing I can tell you is your journey has not ended." Tammy takes my hand and walks with us into a portal Deacon opens. After sending the spirit off toward its path, we step into the next scene.

We arrive at a streetlamp just minutes before witnessing a black Dodge Challenger racing a yellow Camaro. The winds are heavy, and the humidity in the air declares there is going to be a storm soon.

I wait for the cars to race in and chafe my chin. "Why do you suppose humans take such risks with their lives, knowing their dire mortality?"

"I stopped pondering that question centuries ago," Deacon says. "Here it comes."

One of the cars peels into the corner and it flips itself over, crashing against a wall. I sigh and shake my head. Just like the motorcycle accident. I start to move forward, and Deacon stops me.

"Hang on." I look back at Deacon, who is staring at her hand scythe. "Something's happened; a law has been broken. We need to go retrieve a soul. We're going to have to make this one quick." I let Deacon retrieve this next soul and have a portal open to save time.

My eyes narrow as a tall figure emerges from my portal.

"Now you've done it." Deacon says.

I glance at her and then back at the portal as the Judge steps down and shuts the portal behind him. This is it. The Judge is probably going to disintegrate me right here and now, without a trial. I open my mouth to speak. "Your Honor, I can explain," I start.

"Silence," he holds up a hand. He turns to Deacon, then

his hollow eyes meet mine again. . "Ambrose, you have been on Earth for six months. Enough time for you to have learned your lesson, but I see now that all of that time has been a waste. You've defied my orders." He switches his attention to Deacon. "Both of you."

Deacon's mouth drops. Before she can get a word in, he cuts her off. "You were late to collect that soul." He turns to me. "And you saved a human. How hard is it for you to understand that you must not get involved?"

"You're right," I say. Deacon shoots me a stare. "I defied your orders, but Deacon didn't. Please don't punish her for what I've done."

The Judge grimaces and clutches his gold scythe. "Feeling empathy toward your cohort, although admirable, coming from you, makes me wonder about your empathy in general." His head turns slowly to Deacon as he speaks to her, his voice calm and eerie at the same time. "Deacon, I do not care how long I've trained you. I do not care that you are my prodigy. I will exterminate the both of you and start over. I cannot have this be a lingering factor with the Reapers of the Veil."

Deacon pushes her scythe forward. "I accept my fate, Your Honor. But first if I may, something has happened in the Florida Keys. I think it requires our attention. If you give us some time, I will prove to you that Ambrose's foolish actions were only due to his insufferable inability to not meddle. There is no empathy forming here."

The Judge eyes her intently while chafing his jaw. "I have grown fond of you, Deacon; it would be a pity if you let Ambrose take you down with him.

"Seeing as I do not want to afflict a domino effect upon another reaper's path to put them on this job, I will allow it. You have three days to retrieve the soul."

"Yes, Your Honor," we both say.

Right before walking back through a portal, he turns back to us and says, "And Deacon? Don't disappoint me."

Deacon's eyes narrow toward me as the Judge disappears from sight.

"CUBAN CIGAR"

ADDISON

I'm still shaken by almost being killed by that thug. As I stand in front of the door to the mansion, I take a deep breath and straighten my hair as best I can. I'm okay, I tell myself. Shit like this happens all the time with much worse repercussions. It could have gone way worse if the guy with the wicked fighting skills hadn't shown up. I didn't even get his name. But God, was he gorgeous! Okay, get yourself together, Addie. I'm about to step inside and make a good impression on my new boss. Besides, gorgeous or not, I have a boyfriend.

I shut the door behind me and meet Dax's brooding gaze as he inspects my small suitcase and backpack.

"Is that all you have?" he asks.

Fumbling with my hair caught beneath the strap of my backpack, I yank it out and stop myself from fidgeting, trying my best to not look unruly. "Yep, this is all I need." Maybe it's the drastic change in temperature from walking into a cold house, or the eyes of the painting following me when I walk, but I can't shake the feeling of being watched from the moment I stepped back into the mansion.

Overpowering tiredness sweeps over me, replacing my shock factor from earlier. I decide it's the effects of the painting and look up at Dax's pale face. "Ready when you are."

He glances at my messy hair and gives me a brief smile. "First, let me show you to your room, then we can go up and meet my dad," he says, turning as he leads the way.

"Has he woken up at all today?"

"Only to take his medicine this morning."

I inch closer to the windows to try and catch the warmth from the sun beaming through. Why are all the curtains closed? It's a beautiful day outside. "Hey Dax? Mind if we open up the curtains, let in some sun?" After a few seconds, my stomach drops. Did he just ignore me or did I not speak loud enough? "Dax?" I say a bit louder.

Yep, completely ignored me. Maybe he's a vampire . . . I chuckle to myself.

"What's that?" he asks.

"The curtains! Can I *open* them?" I quickly lower my voice, realizing I probably sounded rude just then. He arches an eyebrow at me and gives a nod but doesn't reach for the curtains. I pull one to the side and let the beautiful sunlight in. I furrow my brows as he steps away from the light and walks up the stairs. Well, that was weird.

Maybe he *is* a vampire.

Following him up to the second floor, I notice the detailed blue, yellow, and white Spanish tile work on the face of each step. The house has so many intricate details; it would take hours to study.

The sun shines through the mauve curtains, giving the bedroom a pink glow.

"I hope this is okay," Dax says.

I walk in and a sense of familiarity washes over me. The

room reminds me of something. As if I've been here before, but I know that's impossible. "It's lovely." I set my things down on the floor and follow him out of the room.

"Instructions are as follows. My father needs to take three pills in the morning and three at night. He never eats breakfast and doesn't get up to eat during the day very much but ask him anyway around lunchtime. You'll have to make sure he does wake up to eat dinner." He turns around mid-step on the half-spiral staircase leading to the third floor. "I can't stay around long, I am sorry. I know it will get lonely around here."

I follow him up to the master bedroom. Loud snoring emanates from the French double doors.

"Pop?" Dax gently taps on his father's bed sheets. "Pop? I've brought someone I want you to meet." His voice gets louder with each word.

I stand politely at the foot of the bed as my eyes wander around the room. A picture on his nightstand catches my eye of a beautiful blonde woman with green eyes looking over her shoulder. Something about her gentle smile feels familiar, but I can't put a finger on it. Dax has the same smile, so it must be his mom. An elaborate wooden desk decorates the room, in the way of the balcony. On it sits books about birds, a brown globe, and a pair of binoculars. He must have many hobbies. One leather bound book catches my eye. I make my way over and squint at the title. *Dragons of the Planes*. Oh, he likes fantasy. That's cute.

"We can come back later if you like?" Dax asks gently.

The snoring stops. "Hmm? What?" Orlando opens his eyes and sees his son looking down at him. His eyes immediately brighten as he struggles to sit up. "Oh, my beautiful son. What time is it?"

My heart melts at how sweet the old man is when he sees Dax.

"It's three in the afternoon. I want you to meet Addison. She is a live-in nurse who will be helping me to watch over you." Dax waves for me to get closer. Orlando rubs his eyes and gazes up at me with a lost smile.

"Have I ever met you before?"

"No, sir. I don't believe we've ever met; my name is Addison." Poor old man. I move my hair behind my ear and smile back at him, trying to make a good impression. Dax's eyes bore into me. He's probably observing how well I can interact with his dad. Or how his dad responds to me.

"Pop, would you like to come downstairs for a walk around the house? Now that Addison is here, she could take y—"

"No, I just want to go back to sleep." Orlando scrunches up his face in discomfort.

Dax raises the covers up to his father's neck and turns to me. "I always ask if he will at least come downstairs, even though I know what the answer will be." I follow him back out of the room.

"Well, I must disappear." He turns to face me outside the bedroom door, smirking as he speaks. "I trust you will find everything you need in the kitchen. Please make yourself at home; this is your house too now."

I relax my facial muscles as I realize I must have been making a face as he arches an eyebrow and places a hand on my shoulder. "He looks a lot more intimidating than he is."

I let out a soft chuckle. "Thanks, I'm sure I can manage," I say as I wrap my arms around myself and swallow my guilt about calling him a vampire in my head. I never expected a boss to be so warm and friendly, despite the freezing temperature of the house.

Down in my room, I unpack my belongings. I take out a scrapbook of herbs and flowers I've been working on and set it on the vanity table.

Turning toward the balcony window, I peek through the curtains to the overgrown garden and place my hands on my hip. With such a big house, I'm surprised they don't have a gardener. Maybe Dax will let me work on it while I'm here. Gardening has always been one of my favorite pastimes and by the look of that yard, it is in need of some major tender love and care. After all, learning about herbs and medicinal plants is what got me interested in healing the sick in the first place.

I turn to the remaining articles of clothes sprawled out on the bed and grab a few shirts. I pull open the closet doors by their gold handles and nearly drop my clothes on the floor.

Four little red eyes stare back at me from the dark closet.

I shut the doors again and swallow hard. Pull yourself together Addison, there's nothing alive in there.

I grip onto the door handles with both hands and count to three before swinging them open.

Four hideous, fixed red eyes stare back at me threateningly, as if protecting the closet.

I let out a long sigh of relief as the bedroom light reveals the eyes belong to two mermaids. Nothing but a set of dolls; one blonde with a blue, shimmery tail, and the other a redhead with a green tail. They are pretty, apart from their menacingly red eyes. These are odd toys for a child. Could age have changed their color? What could have done this?

I toss the dolls on the closet floor so I won't have to look at them and hang up my clothing. I change into a pair of black scrubs and a sweater and turn to leave the room.

Just as I reach to close the door behind me, the bedsheets lift and stretch out. I still. Did that really just happen?

Carajo, I'm definitely sleep deprived; I need some relaxing tea or a brandy. I wipe my face and spot a white butterfly sitting on the railing of the balcony and walk over to have a closer look.

Pink and orange seeps through the clouds as the sun takes its break for the night. Shivers run down my spine despite the sweater I have on, so I pull in the curtains and turn to leave the room.

Snoring echoes from Orlando's bedroom through the cathedral ceiling. Right, his medicine. I have to get that ready. I set out to do just that, as well as set all the alarms as instructed by Dax.

I set the dimmer on the large gothic-looking chandelier, just to give myself enough light to walk around without having all the lights turned all the way up. Unfortunately, it gives the mansion somewhat of a spooky ambiance. The light flickers from its fake candles, dancing upon the paintings, making it look like they are coming to life.

A bang sounds from behind me and I jump a foot in the air, letting out a high-pitched shriek. What the hell was that? I set all the alarms, didn't I?

A child's laugh echoes throughout the cathedral ceiling of the family room. Chills run down my spine as I quickly search for something heavy. The only thing I see is an empty vase, so I grab it. My heart thuds in my chest. I inch toward the family room, fighting to keep my breath steady.

The double doors next to the chimney slam shut as a kid races out toward the stairs. His mocking laugh sends shivers down my spine.

I have to grab onto the wall as I nearly fall backward and set the vase down on the table. Nice going Addison, it's just some kid, *not* a ghost.

"Wait! What are you doing here?" I run after him as he scurries down the stairs. Where did this kid come from?

"Freeze!"

The boy stops in his tracks and turns to face me. He looks shockingly familiar, but I can't place him, so I push the thought away.

"I know the alarm code," he says. "I'll show myself out."

"Ah, Dax failed to mention that to me," I say, leaning against the wall and scratching my forehead. "So you come in whenever you want? What's your name?"

"I'm allowed to be here." He quickly turns and disappears down the steps, his loud footsteps thudding along.

I grab my hair and pull it as I stand, bewildered at the fact that a kid was hiding in the house and just scared the living crap out of me. If this kid knows the alarm, why wouldn't Dax tell me? This is a huge liability . . . I mean, isn't it? Maybe he just forgot to mention it.

A few minutes later I'm still staring down the steps and realize I haven't heard the alarm, nor the door close. He's still here. I start down the stairs to find him, and this time I intend to have him call his parents.

"Hey, kid?" I search for him in the Venetian room, then the bar area, calling out, but I don't see him anywhere. Great. What's with his parents letting their young kid play in this creepy mansion by themselves? Unsupervised. People in this neighborhood must be really trusting. Not far from a dangerous city like Miami no less! Screw it, he isn't here and I'm tired. Either he's still in the house or is just very quiet. Either way, I'll deal with him if he pops up again. I walk back up the stairs and grab Orlando's dinner and medication.

Inside his bedroom, the temperature is even colder than the rest of the house. "Orlando?" I set his bowl of soup down on the table next to him and lightly tap him on the shoulder. He stirs awake and stares at me. "Hi, it's time for your dinner."

I help him eat his soup, making sure he doesn't spill anything on himself. I keep smiling at him as he stares at me. "I'm your new nurse, Addison. Remember?" I'm not sure if he remembers our last encounter but he doesn't even respond. He just sits there, squinting his eyes at me as he eats his soup. I have a feeling Dax was right, this job is going to be lonely as heck.

After I give him his medicine, I turn off all the lights on my way back to my bedroom. The familiar smell of Cuban cigar fills the room. I guess Dax is home. The sound of a guitar playing coming from his bedroom confirms it. My heart flutters as he plucks the chords beautifully. I walk over and notice the door is cracked open and I gently tap on the wood.

"That sounds beautiful, can I come in?" I ask, ignoring the voice in the back of my mind telling me it's probably too late and inappropriate.

The playing stops.

"I didn't mean to interrupt; you can keep playing." I slowly nudge the door open but to my surprise, the room is empty.

I push the door open wider. "Dax?" The room is dimly lit by a single lamp on his bed stand. The beige laced wall-paper placed from the ceiling to the mahogany border bounces beautiful, intricate shadows around the room.

Beside the lamp sits a picture of Dax with a pretty girl with shoulder length hair. Probably his girlfriend. Across, is a bookshelf filled to the top with comic books. I totally did not peg him for a comic book nerd.

My eyes flick around the room as the music has stopped and the cigar smell has dissipated. Where is the guitar? My eyes skim over to the door in his room leading to the garage. It's obvious he's hiding and doesn't want to be bothered. I turn to leave the room, feeling rejected and alone.

I don't remember falling asleep. I stand at the entrance to the doll room looking at the vast collection of marionettes and porcelain dolls. A chilling tune starts to play as I take a step into the dimly lit room. It is the theme to the play *Phantom of the Opera*. I look over to where it's coming from. A figurine of a little monkey wearing a red hat sits on the mantle, mocking me. He rhythmically claps his castanets together as the song plays. I walk over to the strange little monkey and lean in for a better look. What made this thing go off? Suddenly, it stops, and the monkey's eyes narrow at me. My heart stops, and my eyes widen. I quickly straighten my back and notice that to the right of me, the facial expressions of the three marionettes change into menacing glares and are now looking straight at me. The lights of the doll room suddenly shut off, leaving me in blinding darkness. Blood drains from my face and my stomach turns to ice. This is the end. Why did I come to this house in the first place?

A high-pitched cackle comes from behind me. I close my eyes. No, I can't turn around. This cannot be real.

"HAHAHAHAHA," the cackle calls out once more.

"No! Go away! Go away!" I am frozen in place. I want so badly to run but I'm blinded by darkness and fear.

The cackle transforms into a screech. I spin around to a garden gnome running toward me at a vibrating pace, its grotesque face covered in bite marks. The hideous creature screeches, showing its mouth full of fangs.

I wake up covered in cold sweats. It was nothing but a dream. I reach over for my phone. Still no texts from Carl. I haven't heard from him since that day on the beach and I hate playing games.

I rub my eyes, trying to rub away the nightmare I just had but if it wasn't my phone, what woke me up?

A tiny screech comes from outside the balcony and I dart my eyes to the right. Was that a real sound? I listen for it again. A tapping coming from the balcony doors makes my head spin. I don't remember there being a tree that close to the house?

"SCREEECH."

"What the hell?" I turn on the lamp on the nightstand. The tapping continues.

"Screech."

I get up from under my sheets and walk over to the balcony. I move the curtain over to the side. A large pair of yellow eyes glare back at me. I stumble back. After the disturbing dream I just had, and the odd-looking dolls, I am in no mood for anymore creepy eyes. I swing the curtain all the way to the side, revealing a small owl.

"Screech."

"Wow, hello." I've never seen an owl this close before. I unlock the balcony doors and open them just enough to get a better look, but not wide enough for it to fly inside. The owl flutters his wings in shock.

"Oh, it's okay. I won't hurt you. Beautiful bird, please don't bite me. You woke me up from a nightmare. Thank you."

The owl gives a quiet hoot before shaking his wings and flying away.

"HYPNOTIZED"

ADDISON

My nose twitches at the hint of an all too familiar smell, and I can no longer fight the morning sunlight brightening the room. The wonderful scent of Cuban coffee is all the motivation I need to get my ass out of bed. I check my phone again, and there it is. A "Good morning, beautiful," text from Carl. My lip curls upward as I send him a good morning text back. Clearly, I overreacted last night, and he was just asleep. I put on a pair of scrubs and head out of my room.

Half expecting Dax to be sitting at the kitchen table, I am surprised to find only a steam pitcher filled with coffee sitting invitingly on the kitchen island. Assuming it's left for me, I pour myself a cup and wander the house while sipping before heading upstairs to check Orlando's vitals and to give him his medicine.

The house is silent.

My eyes follow the black railings that trace the half-spiral staircase up to the third floor and border around the open floor space. The master bedroom, where Orlando sleeps, takes over one of the entire sides of the wall. Next to it, on the wall adjacent, is a single door leading to a terrace. I stand there sipping my coffee, admiring the marble belonging to the chimney that reaches all the way from the top of the third-floor ceiling to the bottom of the second floor. Orlando was one hell of a talented architect. This house must have taken ages to build.

I walk past the chimney and through the French double doors, into a long bright room full of windows. Oh, this room is much brighter! I find dark houses depressing. Relieved, I go in and spot the piano and walk up next to it, taking a seat by the window to finish my coffee. My phone vibrates in my pocket. I take it out.

Ava: Hey, surprise! I'm meeting some friends for the lobster festival by Tavernier. That's where you're working, right? You in?

I roll my eyes to the side and shake my head.

Addie: I wish . . . But I have to work, duh. Meet you for coffee nearby?

A large cloud pushes itself over the yard, blocking the sun. Oh great, awesome weather Florida, thanks. I start typing back before she responds.

Addie: Not really lobster festival weather, is it? Lol

I lean toward the window to see if it has started raining yet and spot someone lying down on the dock. The small boy from last night is flat on his belly, looking down at the water. Ah shit, it's the kid again. I turn to go downstairs to get the kid to go home when I meet my face to Dax's chest.

I stammer backward and catch my balance.

"I didn't mean to frighten you." Dax curls his lips upward. "I hope you enjoyed your coffee? It's been a long time since I made any."

I inhale, catching my breath. "Yes, it's great, thank you. Is it okay for that boy to be out there by the water?"

"Oh, it's quite alright. He comes and goes."

The lines in my forehead crinkle. It's not my business to care about their liability issues anyway, at least now I can stop worrying about it.

"Yeah, he's just the neighbor's kid. He does whatever he wants. Sorry if he scared you. I don't make an issue of it, he's harmless. Kind of brings joy around here sometimes in my opinion."

I relax my face and straighten out the edges of my black scrubs. "Well, if you're sure. He scared the living daylights out of me last night."

"I'll have a talk with him." He smiles curtly at me and I smile back. Something about him makes me feel comfortable. I look out the window again and find the boy is gone. The clouds overhead fully cover the sky and it looks like a sea storm is about to strike at any minute.

"Good thing I'm staying indoors today."

"Yes, you'll be safe inside. Working—from the storm I mean. It's going to get bad very soon." He clears his throat and I resist the urge to laugh.

Thunder roars overhead. Just then, an owl flies next to the windowsill and lands clumsily.

"Oh, I met him last night too! Wait—I thought owls were nocturnal. What's he doing up this early?"

Dax chuckles. "This owl is special. He visited you last night, did he?"

"You know him? Yeah, he woke me up from a terrible dream I was having. It was *weird*."

Dax nods. "Crowley has a way of appearing when you most need him."

A loud giggle escapes from my throat. "He has a name? *Crowley*?"

"He became a familiar, or pet, that visits my dad. There's

an old hawk's nest on the roof of the house my dad built when I was a boy. The hawk only comes once a year, but Crowley here has taken the liberty to make it his home." We stand watching the owl make himself comfortable for a few minutes before I break the silence.

"Would you like something to eat?"

"No thank you, just focus on my dad." He says nothing else and leaves me to my work. My phone vibrates and I check it. It's Ava again.

Ava: I'll brave a storm for lobster, girl! Have you met me? And coffee tomorrow sounds like a plan! Xx

I tuck my phone away in my pocket and go to work.

I tap lightly on the door of the master bedroom. "Mr. Orlando?"

I can hear his snoring coming from inside the room. I silently push down on the brass handle and open the door. The snoring continues.

"I brought you your medicine." Remembering how Dax raised his voice when he talked to him, I approach his night-stand and put down a tray with breadsticks for him. "I brought you some breadsticks. Your son told me you like them sometimes," I say, raising my voice. Orlando's snoring cracks. He lets out a loud yawn and opens his eyes.

"My son? Where is he?" Orlando struggles to sit up. Oh, he's talkative today.

"Hi. I'm, um, not sure. He left a little while ago, I guess." I hand him his medicine and a glass of water. He tosses the pills in his mouth all at once, and with an unexpected surge of strength, he slams the glass of water right onto his face, spilling water all over his chest and sheets.

"Oh, no, Orlando. I'm *so* sorry. I should have been more careful." I take the glass from the old man. My hand trembles as someone whispers in my ear.

"*Addison.*"

"Orlando? Did you say something?" His eyes gloss over me, smiling as if not understanding what I'm saying because he can't hear me. It had to be him though—at least he remembered my name! That's a good sign.

I set the glass down and run over to the master bathroom, passing a small hallway of walk-in closets on either side. I stop for a moment and gape at how the bathroom is decorated with dark green and white marble tiles outlining the terra-cotta tile on the floor. This is no time to admire the bathroom, Addie! I find a hand towel with his initials, O. C., on it and grab it, making a dash back into the bedroom. To my surprise, Orlando ignored the water and had already gone back to sleep. How can he go back to sleep? He's all wet! I approach him and gently soak up the water. His clothing appears a lot dryer than I originally thought.

"*Addison,*" the whisper rings in my ear again. I spin around to an empty room. Okay, definitely not Orlando, he's asleep! A shudder tingles down my spine.

"Where are you?" I say.

"*Kill him.*"

My mouth drops open. "What?"

"*Addison . . . Pick up the glass . . .*"

My eyes gloss over and my body moves involuntarily. I pick up the glass cup.

"*Good girl, now smash it over his head.*"

My arm raises above my chest as I near Orlando's bedside.

The sudden, high-pitched siren of the house alarm goes off, causing me to drop the glass on the floor, shattering it. I shake out of my gaze. "Ugh! I'm such a klutz. Why is the alarm going off?" I start to run out of the room when I pause and turn to Orlando. He is still asleep, unaware of the shrilling noise around him. Surely, if he could hear me mention his son, he could hear the alarm? The loud ringing of the alarm nearly burst my eardrums; I dash out of the room and run all the way to the first floor.

When I reach the bottom of the stairs, I spot the alarm square with a flashing red light. Panic surges through my body. "How do I turn you off?" I start hitting numbers, knowing the action is illogical. I try blocking out the disorientating sound with my hands. "Where's Dax when you need him?"

"Press star and then nine." A child's voice comes from behind. I spin around to find the kid standing there staring at me. I do as he says, and golden silence returns. I take a deep breath. My ears are still ringing.

"Did you set this off?" I ask. He shakes his head. I don't believe him, but there is no point in arguing. "How come you're still here? I thought you went home."

He stares back at me and shrugs.

"What's your name?"

"I didn't set off the alarm."

"Alright, fine. I believe you. I didn't even realize it was put on in the first place. Okay, kid, I have to go back to work. Are you going home or are you sticking around?"

The kid shrugs again.

"So, you're not going to tell me your name?"

He smiles, showing his teeth.

"Alright, fine. See you around." I set off to clean up the glass from the master bedroom.

Even when I reach the third floor, my ears are still ringing. Damn, that alarm is loud. Might be a good idea for me to download an alarm app before I leave. That way I'll know if I have to come back. I spring the door open with a dustpan in hand. "I'm so sorry. Orlando. I don't know what hap—my eyes squint to the floor. Where's the glass?" The broken glass that littered the floor is nowhere to be seen.

I search the floor and I even sweep just to make sure. Nothing. No water, no glass. I stand there dumbfounded. Is someone playing a trick on me? The kid? No, can't be the kid. There's no way he could have gotten here this fast. I flick my gaze to Orlando. "Orlando? Did you clean up the mess?" I say, half joking. He responds with heavy snoring. I shrug. Must have been Dax. He probably came up to check on him when he heard the alarm and I just didn't realize he had come home.

"Dax?" I shut the bedroom door behind me. No one answers. Finally convinced he isn't around, I decide to get on with the day's work.

Later, I get a head start on checking Orlando's vitals and preparing his dinner. I sit over the stove reading a cookbook on healthy soups while stirring the pot when someone calls out my name.

"*Addison.*"

My nose twitches at the sound of the whisper. "Yes?" I put down the ladle, step out of the kitchen, and listen. "Dax? Is that you?"

Silence.

I scratch my head and go back to preparing Orlando's dinner. I want to make sure everything is ready since I agreed to meet Ava for coffee.

"*Addison.*"

"Yes? I'm in the kitchen."

"*Addison . . . Addison . . . Addison.*"

I take a deep breath. "What's going on?" I turn the stove off and walk out of the kitchen. "I'm coming."

"*Addison.*"

This time the sound of my name makes me stop in my

tracks. That is *not* Dax's voice. It's more of a loud hiss. But . . . it sounds familiar . . . *"Addison, Addison, Addison."*

I tread lightly to the top of the stairs leading to the ground floor. It is dark. The rain is finally starting to ease outside but the clouds still cover the sun. I reach for the light switch. A child's laughter springs out in the direction of the first floor. Oh, you've got to be fucking kidding me. Is the kid trying to screw with me? I tiptoe down the stairs in order to catch him. He thinks he can scare me? Well, I'll scare him first.

"Addison." The voice is coming from one of the rooms. I creep into the Venetian room but it is empty.

The laughter continues. It appears to be coming from inside the doll room. I swallow hard. There's no such thing as dolls coming to life, Addison; get a grip. I walk over to the door and grab the doorknob.

"Addison."

I stop. The hairs on my arms stand upright. The voice is coming from behind me. But how? I could have sworn it was coming from down here. I stay frozen on the ground floor a minute longer to listen for the voice. This time, it is coming from upstairs. I arch an eyebrow and look up at the ceiling as if I have somehow acquired x-ray vision. With a deep breath, I start walking up to the second floor until the voice becomes louder and louder.

"ADDISON," it roars.

I run to the third floor and stop at a room with a soft beige curtain tightly covering the glass windows. I move the curtain to the side and peek inside. There is a single bed with a headboard in the shape of a large steering wheel of a pirate ship. Still, the room appears empty.

"Addison."

I jump.

The voice sounds like it's right behind me. It has to be the boy. He's going too far with this. "Okay kid, you can stop now. It's *not* funny."

I spin around, expecting to see him standing behind me with his goofy smile. But there is no one there. Chills run down my spine.

"Addison."

Now it's coming from the second floor. I dash downstairs and listen at the foot of the stairs. I look over to the library. That's it. That's where he's hiding. I don't know how he's doing it, but now he's going to tell me! The library doors are locked. "Hey, open the door. I know you're in there; I can hear you."

"Addison." The voice is louder than before.

It's definitely coming from behind those doors. He must have locked it from the inside. I'm about to give up and leave him to his games when a burgundy tassel catches my eye behind an elaborate-looking lamp on the furniture next to the doors. I discreetly pull the tassel out as if someone is watching. It's a key. I stick it in the lock and turn it to the right three times. It works. The sliding doors are heavy, but I manage to pry them apart.

Passing my hand over the wall, I find the light switch and flick it on. What the hell? The room is empty. I walk over to a couch and peek behind it.

Nothing.

Well, I feel stupid. I squint my eyes at an altar in the corner of the room. On approach, I notice a thick book with gold trimming. It reads:

The Lesser Key of Solomon

Goetia

Edits by Aleister Crowley and S. L Mathers

Curiosity overtakes me and I look over my shoulders;

the coast is clear, so I open it to the front page. A giant snake with a scripture on it circles around four hexagonal stars, with a diamond shape in the center. I flip through a few pages and read the words: "*Preliminary Definition of Magick.*"

Woah, magick? Is this a spellbook? I spin around and take a closer look at the book spines on all the shelves. The library is stocked with books upon books of spells.

I hold a hand up to my mouth and gasp, sending a tremor of excitement up my spine. I don't believe it! Wait till Carl hears about this. Or maybe I shouldn't tell him. He doesn't exactly have an open mind about these things.

My phone vibrates in my pocket. I slam the book shut and turn the lights off. I quickly push the doors together and lock them before Dax gets back. He was stern about me not coming in here, and now it's clear to me why.

I reach for my phone. It's Ava. I already forgot all about the voice calling my name.

"EVERYONE PRACTICES SOMETHING"

ADDISON

Rain trickles down through the South Florida afternoon heat. I, of course, having forgotten my umbrella, make a dash through the parking lot to meet Ava.

Metal and wooden wind chimes ting as I pass through the open-aired entrance of the shopping center soaking wet. My feet crunch the pebbled walkway while I rush through dozens of wall mounts adorned with vibrant metal works of salamanders, fish, and sea turtles, all crafted by local artists. A piece of driftwood hangs from a post on the side of the door with the words *"The Rain Barrel"* painted on it. I flutter myself dry near a glass sculpture studio and make my way to the coffee house in the back. The sounds of the rain hitting the large philodendron leaves give me the illusion of being in a hidden village within a rainforest.

I spot Ava sitting at a table beneath shelter and run up. "You're not going to believe what I saw."

"Oh good, you're here. I should have listened to you about the weather! Not exactly festival appropriate, is it?"

She pushes my latte toward me. "Vanilla latte, topped with cinnamon, just how you like it."

"Never mind the weather. I think Orlando is some kind of wizard," I say, taking my latte.

Ava gulps her coffee down hard and starts coughing. "What?"

"I'm serious. Today, this kid who is always at the house was pulling a prank on me. Well, I mean I still think it was him. No one else besides Dax hangs out at the house. Anyway, I chased his voice all the way to the library, which is always locked, and Dax had been all serious about me staying out of it. But I found the key and went in."

"Woah, stop. Slow down. What?" Ava scrunches up her face.

I take a deep breath and explain everything slowly from the beginning.

"So, you're telling me you were hearing voices and never found the kid? That's creepy, Addison."

"Oh, never mind that. I know it was him. Who else could it be?" I take another sip of my coffee. "You don't think it's cool that Orlando practices magick?"

"This is South Florida. Everyone practices something." Ava takes a swig of her coffee and rolls her eyes

I scoff. "Not everyone! I don't."

"Okay, well, a lot of people down here do. But by the sounds of the description of the book you found, it sounds like he was into some dark stuff. I would be careful, Addie. That type of magick can be dangerous."

My phone buzzes. It's the security app! Since the house doesn't have any cameras, all it can tell me is there was movement after I turned on the alarm. Could Orlando have gotten up? Unlikely. And if it were Dax, he would have just turned the alarm off. "Oh no."

"What's wrong?" Ava is on the edge of her seat.

"I have to go. I think the alarm might be going off again."

"Again?"

"Yeah, it went off earlier, but it was definitely the kid. He probably walked in after Dax left." I gulp down the last bit of my coffee and grab my purse. "I hope he hasn't set it off again." When I look up at Ava, her eyebrows are raised and she's tapping her foot on the leg of the table.

"I don't know, Addie, I'm serious. Let me know if you want me to call my grandfather to find out what's going on."

Ignoring Ava's words of caution, I fumble for some cash and set it on the table, preparing to dart into the rain. "It'll be fine. Have fun at the festival."

I pull out from the pebble-ridden driveway and hit the gas, gunning it toward the neighborhood. I slow down once I'm in to check that I'm going the right way. I could have sworn there was a coconut tree just at the corner of this entrance. I drive a little further and spot a manatee mailbox I have seen before, except further on. Some of the houses look familiar, but it's like they are in the wrong order or something. Or, are they facing the wrong direction? Did I somehow make a wrong turn? Everything looks different, but it is hard to tell because the Keys-style houses and decor all look similar. "What the hell did I do?"

I make a U-turn and drive back to the entrance of the community. I type the address into my GPS, just to be sure. I draw my eyebrows together and clutch my phone, waiting for a signal. For all I know, the alarm could still be going off and something terrible could be happening.

The phone refuses to get any reception. My breath quickens. What the hell is going on? I turn my phone off and on again, but there is still no signal. How can there be no signal? I try to force the GPS to work by typing the address in again and waiting—but nothing happens. Oh, this is no use. Okay, I don't need my phone.

You know how to get there, Addison, come on.

I turn my car around and proceed to drive in the same direction I always have. I pass the stupid manatee mailbox and continue down the street for what seems like an age, until I find myself right back at the manatee mailbox! Did I just drive in a complete circle?

I stop the car and take a deep breath. This is ridiculous. Okay, I'm going back to the entrance and retracing my steps. I put the car back in drive and try again.

Once out of the neighborhood, my phone buzzes. The signal finally came back, and I'm able to get my GPS working. I follow its directions all the way back to the house, passing the manatee mailbox one more time. I don't understand. I drove this exact route! How the hell did I end up *lost?*

I race into the driveway, relieved to actually find it. I'm also relieved the door is locked and no one has broken in. I run to the alarm to punch in the code. But it hadn't gone off.

Could the app have malfunctioned?

I run up the second floor to check on Orlando and stop at the foot of the steps to find an angry face waiting for my return.

Dax's eyes are narrowing down at me and his jaw is stiff. "Where were you? My dad was having an episode. Something could have happened," he snaps.

"I'm sorry. I went out for some coffee, to get some fresh air. My app sounded off and I hurried back, but I guess I was so nervous, I couldn't find the house." I hurry over to Orlando's side. He is sound asleep and breathing steadily. His vitals appear normal. "I wonder what could have happened? Looks like you being here possibly calmed him down."

Dax lifts his chin. "Maybe. I'm sorry I yelled. I was worried. You are free to go out for lunch." He relaxes his shoulders.

"So, what happened? Did the alarm go off again?" I shift my weight.

"No. What do you mean by *again*?"

"Well, I saw the light flashing on my app, so it must have gone off."

"App? What app? The alarm didn't go off."

I look up slowly from my phone and show him the app. "I didn't just leave your dad defenseless. I have an app connected to the security sensors in case anything happens."

Dax squints at it. "Yes, I uh . . . actually, yes I did forget to turn off the alarm when I got in. I forgot. Yes, it did go off. Maybe that's what startled him."

"So, it was you who set it off?" I tip my head to the side.

"Yes, yes, yes I did. Sorry." He attempts to walk out in dismissal and I follow him out of the room.

"Wait. We should have someone come in and check the alarm then, to make sure it's working properly."

He arches an eyebrow. "The alarm is fine. I just said it was me who set it off."

"Right, but yesterday it went off on its own. I mean, it could have been the kid, but he swears he knows the alarm code, so . . ." I roll my eyes to the side.

"Right, fine. Can you call?" It's obvious he is trying to avoid the discussion completely.

"Well, I don't really live here . . ."

"Please, I'm busy. I would appreciate it if you called."

"Well, okay sure. One more thing."

"Yes?"

"I think that kid was trying to prank me today. He had me running all over the house calling my name."

"I'm really sorry, just try to ignore him."

"Well, the thing is . . . I thought about it and it just doesn't make any sense. I heard him coming from the doll room. Then I heard him up in one of the rooms on the third floor. And then . . . I know you told me not to go in but . . . I heard him calling me from inside the library."

Dax's smile fades from his face.

"I am really sorry. I was just convinced I knew where he was hiding. And you said no one was to go in . . ." My cheeks burn hot. I'm not going to mention the book I found nor what I suspect of his father. "When I walked into the library, he wasn't there. The room was empty. My friend thinks there's a ghost." I chuckle out loud.

Dax's face remains stern as he walks toward me. "There is no such thing as ghosts," he hisses.

My hands grab onto the cold hinges of the door as I back into a wall. My lower lip trembles. "Right, I know. Sorry. I shouldn't have gone into the library."

"It was probably just the neighbor's kid playing with the intercoms." He says, relaxing his shoulders.

Oh right, the intercoms. Now I feel stupid again. "I'll go call the alarm company for you," I say, gulping down on my own saliva. I move along the wall until I'm free from his icy stare. I look back at him and he remains staring at the wall. Holy shit! If he had been anyone other than my boss, I think I would have punched him in the face! And the way he was so dismissive, he has to be hiding something. I take a deep breath as I run down the stairs to call the alarm company. I am not going to take this personally; he's usually so caring and nice. Not everybody is the same person every day, I guess.

I google the number to the alarm company and make an appointment for someone to come in this afternoon. The Florida Keys isn't as busy as Miami, so it isn't odd that they would have time to come out the same day.

A few hours later, someone from the alarm company is at the door, looking up nervously at all the windows. He has on a red and blue jumpsuit and baseball cap, covering some white hair poking out from the sides. He walks right in as I open the door and shudders as he sets down his toolbox.

"Sorry, it's always so cold in here."

"Yep, I've been to this house before. Problem with the alarm?" He walks to the Venetian room and glances at the security box. "Looks alright to me, all the lights are lit up, which means the alarm is off. If you ever see one flashing red before you go, it's 'cause there's a door somewhere that hasn't been armed."

I nod. "Well, it's gone off for no reason twice in the past two days. Although, it could have been by accident; we just wanted to check and make sure."

The man chafes his chin with his hand. "Right, okay, were you out today?"

I explain to him what happened.

"Right then, no worries. Maybe I can help since I'm familiar with the house." He starts walking through the Venetian room. "Come over to this room full of dolls.

"See those marionettes up there? Sometimes the air conditioner pushes them, and they move, setting the alarm off. I would just take them down, to be honest. The alarm is functioning as it should."

I stare up at the three marionettes wearing elaborate Italian colors of red and gold. One stares down at me with his jester grin and I narrow my eyes at it. How does Dax not know about the marionettes possibly setting off the alarm?

If this technician knows this and he doesn't even live here . . . Something doesn't add up. I thank the technician and walk him to the door before rushing back to the doll room to take the marionettes down. Let's see if it happens again.

Despite the lights being on full power, the space remains dim. Pulling out an antique wooden chair, I slowly climb onto the seat and come face to face with a raccoon-masked, grinning marionette. The strange doll has on lavish clothes of satin in bright reds, blues, and greens adorned with feathers and gems. I take it down and set it on the shelf beside me, next to three musical marionettes. Their glassy, beady eyes stare directly at me. I swallow hard, fighting back images surfacing from my disturbing dream last night.

The next doll is wearing a black plague mask and is dressed in black and green velvet. The last one is a Victorian clown. I balance myself on the chair, reaching to the far right, careful not to fall or break anything.

My eyes dart to the ceiling as the lights flicker, and the slow sound of hinges twisting breaks the silence in the room. I look around, but the room is empty. My mind races as I stop to think about what could have opened, or . . . I swallow . . . moved. A door? A window? Maybe a doll?

I turn to face the enormous portrait of fifteen-year-old Dax Castillo. The dim lighting glows on his pale face against the painting's dark background. It gives the illusion he can walk out of the painting at any moment. His intense glare scans the room, his smile somewhat menacing. So creepy.

I lock eyes back at the clown, whose strings start to slowly swing back and forth, its beady eyes fixed on me. The hairs at the back of my neck spring up. I carefully reach for the clown, avoiding its jester smile and beady eyes as I pull it down from the ceiling. I sit it down on the table and pass my gaze to a familiar little monkey, from my nightmare, holding castanets. An uncomfortable turn in the pit of my stomach sends me running toward the door. I don't even remember ever seeing it! How did I dream it? Like, it's actually real. The door swings shut in front of me and I gasp. I grab onto the doorknob and twist. It's locked from the outside!

Seriously? I turn it again. It's definitely locked. I start banging on the door.

"Help! Dax! I'm locked in the doll room!" I start banging harder on the mahogany wood till my fists turn red. Sweat beads on my forehead. Who the hell shut the door? I slowly turn to face the room. Eyes are on me.

From every direction, there are dolls.

Their little faces twist just a smidge and glue their eyes on me. Out of the corner of my eye, I see the one doll with brown, wavy hair and honey-colored eyes. The one I thought felt familiar, the one that looks like me.

Her plastic neck squeaks as she too locks her gaze on me.

What . . . the . . . actual . . . fuck . . . I turn back around and start screaming louder. I yank on the door. And it finally swings open, sending me stumbling back. I race out of the room and don't look behind me until I reach the bedroom I'm staying in.

What the hell was that? I'm out of breath as I shut my door. Did that actually happen? No, I calm myself. No, it couldn't have. It was probably the air conditioning pushing the door . . . The heavy door? I open my bedroom door and nudge it closed. It moves only a smidge. Could the air conditioning have really forced the door open? I shake my head.

Listen to yourself! What am I thinking? Visuals of the creepy dolls twisting their heads to look at me makes me shudder. Okay, but that had to be my imagination. They didn't really turn their heads . . . did they?

I start pacing back and forth. And what about me getting lost today? Even though I know the way here, and especially when I didn't go far. It's not like I forgot. And my phone randomly loses reception . . . It's like something doesn't want me in this house.

I sit on my bed and close my eyes, taking deep breaths. I count to five. It was my imagination. That's that; I don't believe in the paranormal. I laugh out loud to myself. I check the time on my phone, it's six-thirty. I get up to go make Orlando his dinner.

Tonight, I just want to be alone. No kid playing games with me, no cordial conversations with anyone. I heat up the soup I made for Orlando and take it up to feed him and give him his medicine. I don't bother knocking on the door this time. He is obviously asleep.

"Orlando, it's time for your dinner."

No response. I turn the lights right on and set his soup down on the table. "Come on, Orlando, wake up. You have to eat some food." I purse my lips. "Dax is here."

"My boy?" He yawns and looks around.

My stomach tightens, and I soften my tone. "No, I'm sorry. But it is time for you to eat. You must be hungry. You haven't eaten anything all day," I say a bit cheerier, and I regret tricking him. That was mean of me; why did I do that? I hand him his pills this time and make sure to keep a close hand under his glass as he drinks his water. I do the same as he eats his soup. He is losing his dexterity. "Maybe tomorrow you'd like to come out for a walk?"

"Oh, maybe. We'll see." He takes another gulp of his soup.

"It might be good for you to do a little bit of exercise. You don't want to lose all your muscle tone, do you?" He smiles politely and finishes his soup.

"Come brush your teeth."

"Oh no, that's okay. I just want to go back to sleep."

"I promise you can as soon as you brush your teeth."

"No one is going to smell my breath."

I hold back a laugh. "True, but we don't want you to lose your teeth, do we?"

I finally convince him to walk over to the bathroom and I give him his privacy to complete his task. As expected, he goes right back to sleep when he is done.

I tuck him back into bed and he closes his eyes. "Your son is really nice. I can tell he cares a lot about you."

"Oh yes." He pulls the covers up to his face. "I just wish he'd cut his hair."

I walk out of the room feeling sorry for the old man. Dax has short hair. Orlando's completely confused about what day it is, or year, for that matter.

The house feels cold again. I put a sweater on and wash up the dishes in the kitchen. All I want to do is make myself some tea and relax before bed. Maybe I'll even get a chance to talk to Carl on the phone. I put the kettle on the stove and rummage through the cabinets for some tea bags.

"We have chamomile tea in the cabinet there."

I spin around. Dax stands at the entrance of the kitchen. "I'm sorry, I didn't mean to frighten you. Listen, I wanted to apologize for how I reacted today."

"Don't worry. I think we were both on edge." I move some tea boxes out of the way and find the chamomile tea. "Would you like some?"

"No thanks. I don't drink tea." He doesn't move from the entrance. He's wearing the same turtleneck sweater he had on when I met him. My shoulders tense as he watches me while I tidy up around the kitchen and wait for the water to boil. I glance at him and he flicks his gaze down to my herb scrapbook I brought out. He picks it up and starts flipping through the pages.

"That's an herb scrapbook I've started," I say.

"Oh, this is nice. My mother loved to garden. She would have liked this a lot."

"I've actually been meaning to ask you about that garden. It looks really overgrown and I—"

"Yes, no one's looked after it for years. I don't have much of a green thumb myself so . . . Hey, you can go out there whenever you like and grow stuff if it makes you happy."

"Really? I would love to! I've been living in an apartment with no room to grow anything. I always feel at peace in a garden."

"Then it's yours."

My eyes light up at him and I smile curtly. "That's very sweet of you."

"If you don't look after it, it's only going to get worse. Anyway, I must go. Enjoy your tea." He sets my notebook gently down and leaves me alone in the kitchen.

Back in my room, I change to get ready for bed. I pick up my phone to call Carl. I have twelve missed calls from him. Is he serious? He knows I've been at work. I start to text him, then stop myself. I'm not going to let myself get worked up about this, especially after today. I send him a quick text to let him know I'm getting ready for bed and I'll call him in a bit.

Oh crap, I left the lights on in the doll room downstairs. Oh well, I'm not going back there. Dax will probably turn them off. I pause at the foot of my bed. Or, he'll think I'm careless and irresponsible. What would I tell him? "Sorry Dax, I thought the room was haunted and the dolls were coming to life?" Yeah, I don't think so. Screw it, it was my imagination anyway.

I meander to the first floor and enter the lit doll room. I tuck the chair back under the table and move to turn off the light when something hanging from the ceiling catches me off guard from the corner of my eye. I freeze in place as I stare up at the corner of the room. "There's no way."

The three marionettes stare down at me. I gasp. Okay, there must be some explanation. Dax must have put them back. He didn't mention it though. Wouldn't he have also turned the light off and closed the door?

Icy clouds form out of my mouth as the temperature drops. "I hate this room." I shut the lights off and slam the door behind me.

WHAT ARE YOU DOING HERE?

ADDISON

Soft light bounces off the bedroom wall and I wrap the thick covers around my body, protecting myself from the freezing cold house. I plug in my phone and ring my boyfriend before he freaks out anymore. I should give him a break. We haven't spoken much since he told me he wanted to move in with me and he's probably thinking my silence means I want to break up. It's not that I'm purposely avoiding him, and even if I have, in my defense, I've been a bit distracted. The phone rings a few times before he answers.

"I've called you one hundred times. Come outside."

"What?"

"Come outside," he barks into the speaker.

I bolt out of bed and peer outside the balcony window. No way he came all the way over here.

"Addie?"

"Are you seriously outside right now?"

"Why don't you come find out?"

A smirk twitches the corners of my lips up at the seductive smile in his voice. "Where'd you park?"

"At the park outside the neighborhood. I wanted to surprise you but you were obviously ignoring my calls."

"Ignor—" I let out a controlled breath. "I was working." I open my door and run downstairs. Shit, Dax is going to hear me turn off the alarm. I tiptoe past the glass door that leads to the Venetian room. The lights are off.

"Are you coming?"

"Shh, I'm turning off the alarm," I whisper. Sucking in a breath, I hit the numbers slowly and grimace as each one makes a loud beep. I gaze in the direction of Dax's room and pause for a beat, trying to peer through the dark living space. There's no movement. Will he mind if my boyfriend comes over? Probably not, but he might find it unprofessional that I didn't tell him.

Then again, I didn't know. My cheeks burn as I open the door.

"Hey there, beautiful."

I stare at Carl's lean stature through the green iron gate and hit the buzzer. He opens it and saunters inside, his gaze fixed on me. "I can't believe you're here."

"I thought you'd be happy to see me."

"I am . . . but I would have at least liked to have asked my new boss first. How'd you even know where to go?"

He smirks. "Maybe he doesn't have to know. And come on, finding you was easy. You tell Ava everything."

Right. "Okay," I whisper. "Just be quiet, Dax is asleep."

He zips his lips and mimes throwing the key over his shoulder. I snicker and grab his hand, pulling him upstairs. The sooner we're back in my room, the safer we'll be and the less likely Dax is to wake up. Good thing this house is huge, and the walls are all thick mahogany.

Inside my room, I shut the door and dim the lights. Carl

drops his gaze to my lips and heat reaches my core. All at once, he grabs me by my waist and pulls me in. I arch my back, my lips meeting his. He was right. I was longing for him. For his touch.

His hands rise to my midriff and pushes me closer into him. My pace quickens as he kisses me furiously and I push him up against the vanity table, my fingers tracing his muscles under his shirt.

"Are you glad I came?" He asks.

"You haven't yet."

He sucks in a breath as a laugh escapes him.

"Shh."

"Sorry. Don't want your new keeper to wake up."

I stop kissing his stomach and glance up.

"Why'd you stop?"

"My new keeper? What's that supposed to mean?"

His face slackens. "I was only joking. You just seemed so uptight about not having me over. And you weren't even picking up your phone. It's just a job, Addie."

I stand upright. "It's not just a job, it's the start of my career."

"Right, okay, I'm sorry. But, you have been acting strange."

I pull my hair back from my face and straighten my PJs. "I've just been busy, is all."

"No, it's more than that. Ever since I asked you to move in with me, you've been distant."

"And you thought randomly showing up at my job would change something?" I squeeze my eyes shut the moment I say it.

"So, something has changed."

"No, it hasn't," my voice softens. "I just started this job, so

I haven't even figured out my living situation. I need more time, is all. What's the rush?"

He shrugs modestly. "No rush. Just want to know where we stand."

"Everything is fine, I promise."

"Then why ignore all my calls? I called like thirty times, for real."

I sigh. Do I tell him about the voices? And what I found in the library? I bite my upper lip.

"Addie?" He leans in closer. "What is it?"

"I may have had a few strange experiences while I've been here."

His brows furrow. "What kind of strange experiences?"

I shake my head and step back. "I don't know, it's dumb. I thought I heard someone calling my name. I thought it was a kid who visits but it turns out, it wasn't him. I think it was just the intercoms. Unfortunately, I followed the voice to the library, which I'm not allowed in and Dax found out."

"Found out?"

"Well, not exactly found out. I told him. But, he was pissed."

"Was he, now?" His voice raises an octave.

"It's no big deal. He's just a little intense. Anyway, my point is," I purposely leave out the doll room fiasco, "that's why I didn't pick up your calls. After that, I had to take care of Orlando and do my job."

"Why does he want you out of the library so badly?"

"You would never believe what's in there."

His brows arch up expectantly.

"Spell books," I whisper.

He stares blankly at me.

"Apparently, Orlando was into sorcery before his health went down."

"Right, okay, Addison. I've been patient but now I really don't feel comfortable with you staying here. I think you should quit and come back to Miami. We'll find you a new job."

"For what? A minor argument I had with my boss? Or because of a library full of *fiction?* This happens in all jobs."

"It's not the spell books. We don't know what these people are into. Why doesn't Dax just take his dad to a real hospital?"

"I don't know, because he doesn't want to move him? What's the big deal?"

"Why do you always have to argue with me?"

"I can handle myself."

He smiles and takes my hands in his. "I'm just worried about you."

Well, don't be. I made my decision to come down here and I'm not going to give up. And I don't believe in ghosts. I'm staying." I let go of his hands and cross my arms.

"Well, how about we stop talking about ghosts and do something else?" A seductive smirk spreads on his face and my heart skips a beat. He pushes himself off the vanity table and strides toward me. I take a few steps back, dipping my fingers into the seam of his pants, and lie down on the bed.

He tugs gently on my hair, arching my neck as he starts kissing under my chin.

I let out a soft moan which sends a flush to his cheeks. He pulls down my pajama pants and slides his tongue between my legs. My toes curl as I grab a handful of his hair and my eyes roll back. His tongue tickles me as it traces around my core, teasing me, making me want him.

I push up on my elbows and he gazes up at me, confusion flickering his face.

"I want you inside of me," I tell him. His eyes flush with

heat and he pulls himself over me. I grab onto the girth of his cock inside his pants as he struggles to take them off.

I suck in a breath as he drives his cock inside me. I squeeze the bed sheets and moan into his neck. I breathe heavily, trying not to make any noise.

His hips move rhythmically up and down. Up and down. My legs involuntarily wrap around him and squeeze, bringing him in deeper. I dig my fingers into his back as he fills me.

"Addison," he breathes. "This is what I want." he pulls out and thrusts hard into me again. I bite my bottom lip to keep from moaning loud, even though I want to. "For us to always be together."

"Mmm . . ."

He pistons in and out, faster and faster. "Don't you want that too?"

Seriously, how can he even think right now? "Mhmm . . ." I moan into him. "Don't—*stop,*" I plead.

"Giving you pleasure every night." He smiles down at me as he thrusts into me, thrust, after hard thrust.

"Yeah . . ."

He pulls out. "Let me hear you say it."

I blink. Why did he stop? "What?"

"Tell me, Addison. Tell me you want to be with me too. Always."

"I—" My chest rises and falls with each heavy breath. I don't know how to answer that. His eyes glint as he searches mine, I can tell this is important to him. I stroke his cheek with the back of my hand and give him a soft smile. He always knows what I want, and what to say. He drove all this way to see me just to make sure I'm okay. I'm an idiot for not wanting more of this. "I do," I tell him. "Always."

He marvels at me as I bring my hands down to his waist,

clutching him tight, encouraging him to keep going. He lifts my chin and kisses me deeply, as he strokes his cock deeper into my core.

I feel his cock thickening and my core clenches around him. Carl groans, the sound of it increasing my pleasure. His strokes deepen as he slams into me over and over, pulling into his climax. A moan escapes his lips and thank God this place is a mansion because I don't know if Dax could hear that and right now I don't care.

"No," he says. "Not yet."

He takes his fingers and thrums them over my clit.

"Oh . . .my . . .God." I don't think I can't take it. It's too much. "St--Sto—my God." He thrums me fast but sensually. I feel myself building. And building. And I bite my bottom lip to stop myself from crying out as my orgasm takes me, my back arching me into him as I'm momentarily blinded by pleasure.

His pace speeds up as he strokes me deeper and deeper, faster and faster. His eyebrows hike up and I feel him coming inside me. His pace slows and he brushes the top of my head with his hand, planting a kiss on my lips.

"Was that perfect?" He asks.

"Yes, it was."

He pushes off of me and lies his head down on the pillow. I quickly grab my pajamas off the floor and put them on.

"Why are you getting dressed?" He asks. "Come back here."

"In case I have to leave the room, this isn't my home, you know."

"Alright, alright."

I grab his boxers off the floor and fling them to him. He catches them and puts them on.

"Happy? Now come back to bed."

I nod and climb in under the covers.

"So, you do want more of this then?" "He whispers into my ear. "You'll move in with me?"

"I can get used to having a perfect boyfriend."

HOW CAN I BE DEAD?

ADDISON

My eyes flick open and it's pitch black. I try to sit up but I can't. I attempt to lift my head, but it's glued to my pillow.

What the hell is going on?

Why can't I move?

My pulse pounds in my ears as realization hits; I'm completely paralyzed. Am I dreaming? I try lifting myself up again, but this time, sharp pain sears through my neck and ears. Nope, I'm awake!

I scan the room for Carl but can't see him. Did he leave? Where the hell is he?

My breath catches in my throat as something rustles the covers at the far end of the bed, scratching at my feet. What the hell is down there? I strain my eyes but even if I could move my neck, it's too dark. Something starts crawling up my legs and I try to force myself to shake, but nothing happens. Pins and needles inch their way up my body, and I try to let out a shriek, but even my mouth is glued shut!

A heavy weight presses down on my chest and icy cold breath snarls close to my face.

My breathing stalls. My eyes are heavy, but I try to squint to make out the figure in the blackness. It is too dark. Whatever it is, it moves in closer to my head and sniffs my hair.

I shut my eyes again, as tightly as I can, holding my breath. My insides jolt as a sharp pain presses down on my stomach. What the hell is that? Knives? The feeling shifts swiftly, and I catch the sharp movement of claws and a tail by my feet. My heart skips a beat.

I try to move and scream again, but it is no use.

"*Carl!*" I yell inside my head.

The creature moves toward me again and clamps its large claws down on my neck. I scream silently, gasping for breath. My esophagus closes as the creature tightens its grip against my throat. My deepest fear of suffocation . . . It's finally happening. Tears form at the corners of my eyes. My mind grows hazy and my heartbeat slows.

Then something happens. The creature lets go of me, but I still cannot move. What's it doing?

A buzzing sound vibrates in my ears, growing louder and louder, nearly bursting my eardrums. The bedroom spins uncontrollably around me.

Suddenly, I'm hovering above my body. What the flying fuck is happening to me? Am I dying?

I try peering through the darkness for some sort of sign. The buzzing finally stops, and everything silences. I ascend completely above my body, but there is no bright light.

It is still dark, only now I can finally make out the details of the room. My room. I'm still here.

I can finally move again. I spin around, my arms wrapping around myself effortlessly. It's like I'm lighter than a feather. I spot the mirror in front of my bed and gasp. That's me, only, it doesn't look like me. The person in the mirror is smaller than expected, like a floating ghost. Despite my bodiless form, I shiver. I'm really dead, aren't I?

I hold my hands up to my eyes. They are tiny and blue and leave a trail that follows me as I move. My mouth drops open as I count only four fingers in each hand.

Glancing down at the bed, my eyes widen at the hand lying beside me. I jump, which almost sends me flying to the ceiling.

Who is that? I nudge the hand, but it barely moves. It is heavy, stiff and cold. I gasp at the strange sensation. The hand beside me is mine, belonging to my lifeless body lying on the bed, covered with scorpions. Those were the pins and needles I felt! I shudder at the strange sensation of touching my own dead body . . . Dead. How can I be dead?

It takes me a moment to process the situation. There was being choked . . . then there was the paralysis . . . Then the beast. I turn again, slowly.

And there it is, leering back at me with burning red eyes, filled with emptiness and wrath.

If I had seen this while in my body, I'd shit myself. The creature looks like some sort of hound, except it's ginormous! Its coat camouflages with the darkness of the room. If not for its eyes, I probably wouldn't see it. This is the thing that killed me? If I'm a ghost, can it still hurt me? Its chest is larger than my head. I start to back up, still not in full control of my weightless form. It opens its elongated jaw to show its sharp fangs, snarling at me. Too frightened to move, we stare each other down for a moment.

The creature backs itself into position, like a lion ready to pounce on its prey. That's when I jolt back. I fly up to the ceiling and the beast darts after me. I can fly? I'm flying! I fly through the door and out of the room. There's no way in hell I'm looking back. This thing wants to eat me! I spot an empty space under a table behind the family room couch and hide under there.

I close my eyes and try my hardest to keep still. If I had a pulse, it would be off the charts right now. Oddly enough, I can still feel my heart beating. The silence surrounding me is intense. The house feels completely lifeless. I open my eyes as if expecting the creature to have gone away. The room appears empty. Is it gone? Hot breath tickles my neck from behind.

I spin around slowly.

The creature licks its lips and leaps toward me. I let out a shrill scream that echoes throughout the house. My own voice, now unconfined to the parameters of a human body, resonates through my head. To my dismay, this only makes matters worse. The creature shakes itself furiously, as if trying to shake the noise away. Long drools of saliva slip from his jaw as it now prepares to eat my spirit whole.

"*Noooo.*" I shoot up through the table and gasp, coming face-to-face—not with the brawny beast chasing me—but with the evil garden gnome from my dream. What the hell is this doing here? I shake away the confusion. There is no time. The gnome squints its eyes as if furious I am standing in its way.

"Get *away.*" I dash toward the blazing fireplace. That wasn't lit before. The spirit of a lady flies in front of me. I follow her with my eyes and then catch a glimpse of another spirit form dancing in the middle of the room. When I spin around, there's more of them everywhere.

My gut sinks down to the floor, figuratively as I no longer have an actual gut. A sense of dread follows me; these spirits emanate fear, sadness, and anger. Overwhelming sadness pours in; the clay dolls overlook the room from the top windowsill. Their faceless heads weep in a sadness I have never before experienced. Even though they lack features, they screech with a sorrow that still sends shivers down my spineless back. In the dining room, a hauntingly beautiful violin tune resonates through the high ceiling as spirits dance in pairs, unaware of what's going on.

"Hey, you there. Can you hear me?" I call over to the spirits dancing away. Maybe they can help me. My voice echoes but they don't respond. They don't even stop to look at me. I glide over to them, but they continue their dance with blank stares on their faces. It's as if the world has stopped for them. I give up and float away from them. Where did this hound creature go? A figure moves into my peripheral vision and I dart my eyes toward it. It's making its way up the wall. As long as it's ignoring me, I'm good, but where is it going?

In the center of the chandelier, a woman hangs from a rope. I cover my mouth as I recognize the same shoulder length hair from the girl in the photo inside Dax's room. I grimace and shudder, turning away when I catch the beast reaching its long tongue and wrapping itself around the body. It pulls it to its mouth like a frog eating a fly.

I shut my eyes. It definitely eats spirits. Maybe now that it's occupied with its new meal, I have a chance to think. If only I had something to defend myself with. The swords in the doll room spring to mind. I can fly down there and try to grab one. But that seems too far to go and I might not even be able to grab anything; it'll catch up to me for sure. Not only that; do I really want to deal with creepy dolls right now?

The library? I can easily go through walls just as I did

getting out of my room. I fly out in front of the spirits and make a dash toward the mahogany doors. The giant beast turns its head and leaps right toward me, missing me by an inch as I fling myself into the dimly lit library.

I back up away from the door, waiting for the beast to follow me inside. Maybe this was a bad idea. I've trapped myself in a corner. A few seconds later, and nothing. Maybe this room is protected? I scan the library and notice inscriptions drawn on the walls I had never seen before. They light up bright as if ignited. Now that I'm in, what am I looking for? I search the room for anything helpful. I spot a small envelope cutter with a blue hilt inside one of the glass shelves. I reach for it, but my hand goes right through. Damnit! Now what? I turn to the old spellbook I found the other day. Could something be in there? I glide over to it and stare. What's the use? If I can't hold anything, how can I open the book? "I wish I had a sword."

Suddenly, a sword appears in my right hand. Woah! Where did this come from? Can I just wish things to me? This is awesome. Surprised at the grip I have on the hilt; I give it a swoosh. It slices through the air like I'm cutting a ripple in time. This is magnificent. Maybe being dead isn't so bad. With a new sense of courage, I dash back out into the family room, ready to face any demon that's lurking.

As if expecting me, the ugly gnome vibrates toward me at the same terrifying pace it did in my dream. I readily slash the sword toward it as it runs, but it gets intercepted by the beast. It slurps down the gnome with one gulp.

Well, now I know it'll eat anything.

The beast licks its lips and stares back at me, unfazed. "Oh, you're still hungry? That was just a snack for you?" I raise my new sword over my head and prepare for attack. It jumps right over me as I fling the sword to its belly with all the strength I can muster. The creature lands right behind me, completely unharmed.

"Oh great." I fly backward, holding the sword in front of me. "Nice giant pup, you don't really want to eat me, do you?" Now what do I do? The beast charges at me again. This time I am able to swing the sword hard enough to slash it. It skids off in surprise. The beast doesn't bleed. Instead, an orange light beams from the crooked slash on its side. He looks down at the wound as it seals itself and then up at me, snarling in anger. It leaps toward me, mouth agape. I duck over to my side, narrowly evading its teeth. Shit, that only pissed it off.

A noise creaks above us from the third floor. The beast looks up, distracted. I follow my eyes to the iron rail, right in front of Orlando's bedroom. Shrouded by a cloak of darkness is something leaning over the rail. I can't make out what it is, but my worst fears tremble through the depths of my soul because of it. I jump as it hops to the top of the rail, revealing a long, giant, scorpion-like pincer hanging over his head. His eyes glow a bright yellow but it's still too dark to see its face. My insides want to tear open as a long, narrow tongue rolls out of his mouth and hisses.

I can't move. Holy fuck, what is that? Orlando! Did that thing just come out of his bedroom?

The demon leaps down and lands right in front of me.

"You're mine." The beast whips its pincer and knocks the sword from my hand. Its voice screeches so loud I think my ears will bleed.

The demon claps its pincer and I fall to the ground, clinging to the floor as it begins to tilt, and the walls start closing in, as if I'm in a fun house from hell. I swallow hard as the demon's rancid breath flows toward me, blinding my sight.

His snake-like tongue flashes in front of me. I am paralyzed again. I wince as the grotesque tongue licks me slowly, from my neck up to the top of my head. A tear falls from my cheek. This is the end. But how? Aren't I already dead? Is there more? Can a demon eat a spirit? Stop consciousness altogether?

"MR. CROWLEY"

ADDISON

Wind gushes over me from the third floor, flinging my weightless form a few inches off the ground. I grasp at the air with my eight fingers, desperate to get out of the demon's reach.

"SCREECH!"

I duck my head under my opaque arms, able to move again.

Wait, I know that screech. I lift my head up, expecting to see the demon standing over me, keeping me from escaping, but it isn't anywhere. It's Crowley! Can he see me? How did he get in the house? He swoops down and grabs onto my spirit form, stretching my arms with his talons before carrying me back into my room.

"No, Crowley. Take me *away* from here." But the owl doesn't listen. He drops me down over my head and I fall.

I open my eyes to a soft light behind the curtain. I blink a few times and my vision comes into view. I'm . . . not dead? Was I dreaming this entire time? No, it was too real.

A tiny screech comes from the vanity table across the room. I rub my eyes and wince at the pain coming from my stomach and throat. I pull up my nightshirt and gasp at the red scratch marks embedded in my skin.

Holy shit, it *was* all real.

I stand up and walk over to the owl, who unexpectedly hops onto my arm. Less intimidated by his pointy beak and talons this time, I stroke his head feathers. "Am I imagining it, or are you enjoying this, Mr. Crowley? Thank you for saving me." I open the balcony door for him, and he looks back at me just once before taking off.

Okay, so I need to jot down the facts. I'm not dead. So, what was all that? I heard of astral projection before, from Ava during our late-night talks about her family's rituals and religious lore. Maybe I astral projected. Excitement and fear courses through my veins. I take a big deep breath. A breath I will never take for granted again. So, what now? Should I quit my job? This is way above my pay grade. Something very strange is happening in this house and there's no way in hell I want to be a part of it!

I grab my clothes from the closet and shove them into my bag. I bolt down the stairs and out of the house, fumbling for my keys in my purse until I find them.

I turn on the ignition and peel out of the driveway. Forget this place. I watch as the house grows smaller and smaller in my rear-view mirror. I come to a stop sign, and the cruel yellow eyes and long wet tongue of the demon guarding Orlando's bedroom shatter my thoughts. I envision the old man defenseless and sleeping in his room. If it wasn't a dream, which I definitely know it was not, then he is in danger, and so is Dax. Has this ever happened to him? I have to ask. I shake my head. "No, I'm leaving," I shout to myself. I hit the gas and then slam on the breaks. Luckily, it's a quiet neighborhood and I am the only one on the street.

Who am I kidding? I can't leave a poor old man defenseless to some demon. Even if it isn't my problem. Well, I guess it is now. Oh God, I can't believe I'm doing this. I make a U-turn and head back toward the house.

As I walk back inside, the cool air strikes my every pore. I had run outside in my pajamas.

"Addie?" Shock spreads on Carl's face as he stands at the top of the stairs in his boxers. "Where did you go?"

"Me? Where were you?" My voice is higher than I intended it to be but at this point I don't care if I wake Dax up.

"I went to the bathroom and when I got back you were gone."

"The bathroom?" My eyes move over to the open bathroom door next to my bedroom. Oh. Wait, all that happened while he was in the *bathroom?*

"Addie, what's wrong?"

Rubbing my arms, I climb the stairs to meet him. "Nothing. Never mind." I'm not telling him about the astral projection. He'll just tell me it was a dream or give me more reason to leave the house. "I had a strange dream."

"Well, it's still really early. Let's get back to bed."

"Actually Carl, I think you should go."

Disbelief crosses his face. "Now?"

"Yeah, while Dax is still asleep. I'm sorry, do you mind?"

He sighs and pinches the bridge of his nose. "Are you serious? It's literally the crack of dawn."

"Sorry. I don't want to have to explain to Dax that my boyfriend came over to surprise me and *spent the night.* It doesn't look professional."

"Fine, yeah sure. I'll get dressed."

"Thanks."

I change into a pair of my gray work scrubs with pink trimming and step out into the family room. Carl follows behind me. I half expect the fireplace to be lit again, with a creature lurking beside it, but the house is still.

We walk in silence down the steps and keep listening for anything out of the ordinary. No beasts or demons, or dancing spirits. Everything is just as it was before.

"I'd still like to meet this Dax guy," Carl says, breaking the silence as we step into the foyer.

"You will. Just now is not the best time."

"The best time for what?" Dax's voice makes the hairs in my arms stand on end. Carl looks past me and I quickly turn around. So much for him not finding out.

"Who are you?" Dax asks.

"Dax, hi." Oh God. "This is . . . my boyfriend, Carl. He came over to surprise me."

Dax searches my face, then looks at Carl. Carl stares right back at him, his gaze fierce, his posture rigid.

"He was just leaving . . ." I nudge Carl.

Dax sticks out his hand and smiles. "It's no problem at all. I'm Dax."

Carl stares at Dax's hand for an awkwardly long time and I want to die.

I clear my throat.

"Hi," Carl finally says, taking his hand.

Dax grips it tight. "Stop by anytime."

"I will, thanks."

Why is he acting *so freaking weird?*

Carl pulls his hand away from Dax's clutch and moves his eyes over to me. "I'll call you later."

"'Kay, bye."

He leaves and I quickly shut the door behind him, moving my attention to Dax. "I am so sorry. I didn't know he was coming. He just showed up, and it was late."

"That's okay, I don't mind."

"You don't?"

"No, you can have people over."

I relax my shoulders and he smiles. "Would you like coffee?"

"I'd love some." He nods and moves to fix us two cups.

"So, your boyfriend seems..."

I wait for him to finish his sentence, but he doesn't. "Seems?"

"Yes, hmm..."

I twist my lips. I mean, it was definitely an awkward moment between them.

I tie my hair back in a high ponytail and get on with Orlando's medicine. I'm in a rush to check on him, to make sure he is still okay. His steady snoring resonates throughout the empty house as I reach his bedroom. The old man is completely unbothered by the world around him. I give him his medicine, and like usual, he falls right back to sleep. I scan the room, searching for any hints of paranormal activity. I know it wasn't a dream. The scratches on my stomach are proof.

I know you're in here somewhere, you asshat, I'll figure out a way to kill you.

I spend the rest of the day glued to my phone, researching astral projection and demonology. I come across a website with tales of people claiming they had seen demons while under sleep paralysis. I read on while sipping my coffee by my favorite spot next to the piano. I think I'll avoid dark places in this house for as long as I can.

"What are you reading?" Dax's voice comes from behind

the door of the family room. Why was he always lurking in the shadows?

I scroll through my phone without looking up. "I'm doing a bit of research about something that happened to me last night." I change positions; my leg is starting to fall asleep.

"Did something happen to you last night? Do I need to call a medic for our nurse?" His voice sounds amused, but also sincere.

"Nothing like that," I hold myself back from bringing up anything about demons. I'm not sure how he'll handle it. Might think I'm crazy and fire me. The last time I mentioned a ghost he seemed very resistant, and I was only joking. Normally, I get along well with atheists, but after last night I'm in no mood. "I'm afraid you aren't going to believe me if I tell you."

"Why don't you come in here, so we can talk?" He hasn't moved from his spot.

My eyes narrow involuntarily at him. What's his deal? Why doesn't he want to come into this beautiful, sunny room? I keep my eyes glued to his as I get up and walk over to the family room, where I had had the most terrifying experience of my life.

"Do you have some sort of disease where you can't be in the sun?" I slam my hand over my mouth. What the hell is wrong with me? I can't talk to my boss like that! "Dax ... I ... am ... so sorry!" I wince as he arches an eyebrow impressively high and parts his lips. "That was so rude of me, I don't know what came over me. I–I didn't get enough sleep last night." Maybe insulting my boss is all I needed to leave the house permanently after all.

"Really, I'm sorry Dax. I'm just on edge and you only want to help."

His eyes relax and he lets out a chuckle. "Don't worry, let's just talk. What's the matter?"

"You mean I'm not fired?"

He laughs. "Fired? We all have bad days, Addison. Besides, I know you didn't sleep enough last night."

My cheeks flush. He means Carl coming over. God, so unprofessional.

"Nothing you can do will make me want to fire you."

Relief sweeps over me and I drop my shoulders. Wait, nothing? That's a little weird. What if I were to steal something? Not that I would, but it's an odd thing for a boss to tell one of his employees.

"Well? Are you going to tell me?"

I stammer a bit. Here goes nothing. "Have you ever heard of astral projection?" I wait for any hints of annoyance or hesitation in his face but if there are any, he is doing a good job of hiding it.

"Last night I was pulled out of my body"—I take a breath— "by some kind of demonic beast." I pause again, waiting for him to respond, but he doesn't. This time, he takes a deep breath, and I know he doesn't believe me. "Look, you asked me what the matter was and I'm telling you."

"I think you had a nightmare. An incredibly vivid nightmare. That's all."

My nails dig into my scrubs as my cheeks grow hot. "Listen to me, this was *not* a dream. This was as real as I am here talking to you now. You have to believe me, Dax. I never believed in this stuff before. But this really happened to me." I open the web browser on my phone to show it to him. "Look, I'm not the only one who has experienced paralysis and projection."

He leans in without taking my phone and looks at me

intently. "I promise you nothing is going on in this house, Addison." He stoops his posture a bit. "And I promise you are safe."

I shift my weight to one side, placing a hand on my hip. "Then how come none of this has ever happened to me before coming here?"

"Maybe because this is a creepy big house and you're just not used to living here yet."

My eyes don't move from his face as I resist the urge to roll them. Then, I remember the body of the girl hanging from the chandelier right before the beast swallowed her whole. Should I ask him about her? I struggle to round up the courage but what proof would I have?

He nods and I hold my breath for just a moment, trying to think of the right words. Here goes . . .

"Did a girl live in this house? Sort of shoulder length hair . . ." My words trail off as he winces, pain struck on his face. His eyes whip down on me.

"You've been in my room."

I gulp. Drats, the picture! "I mean, yes . . . but only because it was half open when I was looking for you . . . But what I mean is, I saw h—"

He turns his head away from me, wincing. "I'd rather not talk about it."

Okay, I definitely overstepped. I'm so stupid. The girl obviously killed herself, of course he doesn't want to talk about it. I can't just let him walk away. I take a deep breath. "Dax, you have to listen to me. Your father is in danger. I saw a demon in front of his bedroom last night," I blurt. My eyes begin to swell. I gasp and clutch my shirt. The claw mark! I can show him the claw marks! "Oh, it scratched me. Look." I move my hair away from my neck to show him, but his expression doesn't change. "*Look.*"

"I'm looking. I don't see anything."

"What?" I lift up my shirt, showing him my stomach. His cheeks flush and he momentarily averts his eyes. I gasp. It's just my bare skin, no scratch marks, no signs of attack. Nothing. "What the hell? They were here when I woke up."

"Addison . . ."

I run to the mirror in front of the stairwell leading to the first floor. I check my neck once again, but my skin is clear.

"Addison, it is only your mind playing tricks on you. It was a dream, nothing else." His calming voice reminds me of a psychiatrist, and I decide to stop while I'm ahead.

"Forget it. It was a dream, you're right." I spin around and walk down the stairs.

"Addison, don't be upset with me." He sounds concerned, but I ignore him. My cell phone vibrates. I glance at it. It's Carl. I put it on silent.

I walk outside to the back of the house and find a green wooden bench to sit by the water near a bougainvillea tree. It is my first time coming out here and the weather is perfect. Best of all, Dax won't follow me. I need some time to reflect on what happened, away from the house. I don't want to leave. I won't leave Orlando by himself, so I need to plot my next move. Should I try and leave my body again to try to kill those demons? Or should I try some other way? I hold my phone tightly while looking out to the waters of the Gulf. How did those marks go away so fast?

Sweat begins to drip from my brow. Autumn in South Florida still feels like summer. The sun kisses my honey-colored skin as I sit in contemplation. A swift breeze cools me down for a moment and I close my eyes, facing the sky. A warm smell of midnight jasmines suddenly fills my nostrils. The sweet scent of the flower brings with it a certain peace and familiarity.

I open my eyes to find a beautiful monarch butterfly has landed on my hand. Not wanting to startle it, I slowly lift my hand to admire it. Somehow the garden appears livelier and more beautiful, as if it blossomed overnight. The butterfly takes off and circles around me a few more times before disappearing into the mangroves. The smell of jasmines soon vanishes.

I revel in the calmness as it washes over me along with a sense of déjà vu. Being right here, near the water, in the garden, brings me closer to recalling a lingering memory. But that's silly. I've never been here before.

Suddenly, a tingling sensation on my feet and on my legs startles me. I scratch with one leg, and the feeling reaches my arms. I open my eyes and jump off the bench.

My skin is crawling with scorpions. Dozens of pincers dangle over their heads as their sickly, hairy legs carry them up my body.

"Oh!" My breath catches in my throat and I shake myself, trembling. Fucking scorpions! I'm about to jump into the canal when, suddenly, they're gone. I let out a cry. "I'm going *insane*." *Why* scorpions?

I bend down to pick up my phone. I click out of the ten missed calls from my boyfriend and dial a number. It rings a few times until somebody finally picks it up.

A groggy voice answers on the other end. "Hello?"

"Ava? I think I need your grandfather's help."

I open the glass back door of the bar area, and through the set of closed glass doors leading to the Venetian room, Dax stands there talking to two people in suits. Dax has his back facing me, with the two people in suits blocking his exit. I mentally prepare myself to politely interrupt what looks like a private meeting when Dax says, "I cannot come with you. You don't understand, I've finally found her."

I squint my eyes and silently close the door behind me, tiptoeing away from sight, just long enough to hear the context. Who's *her*? Is he talking about *me*?

"We understand that the circumstances are now sensitive, but we cannot wait much longer. You have to come with us, now." The woman talking shows no hint of courtesy in her voice. "There are rules, Dax, and every one of them has been broken."

I press my back against the bar, peeking in through the glass and accidentally knocking down a Red Solo cup. I wince as it bounces toward the inside of the bar. I see Dax chafing his chin and slightly turning toward my direction. "Give me some time, please. She's going to look after my dad once I'm gone," he whispers.

"Your time is soon to run out," the man with the chestnut hair says sharply. "And when it does, we *will* come for you."

No use in hiding now; he knows I'm here. I clear my throat, open the door, and walk in.

"Addison, these are my father's social workers." Dax turns toward me, gesturing to the man and the woman. I walk briskly and introduce myself.

The woman's posture is rigid, arms crossed in front of her black business jacket, odd as far as Florida attire goes. Her large green eyes scan me. My God she looks like a barbie doll—perfect in every way, with straight red hair and bangs that stay in place. Her skin is flawless and the rest of her—I take in a breath of air. I start to feel short and too shapely in comparison. There is a surreal essence about her.

Like she's no one to mess with. In fact, they both look like gods.

"My name is Deacon, and this is my"—Deacon clears her throat— "colleague, Ambrose." She turns to Ambrose whose eyes are furrowed.

"Nice to meet you, Addison." Ambrose's crystal blue eyes pierce through me, and my knees quiver. For a split second, I forget to breathe as my eyes lock with his. He's the man who saved me from that lowlife behind the gas station! Doesn't he recognize me? "W–we've met."

Dax raises an eyebrow so high it could fly off his head. "You have? How?"

"We had a run-in at the gas station," Ambrose says as we share a warm smile. My knees quiver and I reach up to twirl my hair but quickly force my hand down.

Dax clears his throat. "I was just telling them that having you here has made all the difference." He shifts uncomfortably as his eyes dart from me to Ambrose. "Addison, before you came along, it was only me, and I had no idea what I was doing. I might have to leave soon, and you will have to care for my father alone. At least for some time."

This snaps me out of my daze. "Wait, what? I don't understand. That doesn't seem right . . ."

Deacon straightens her jacket and leans toward the door. "He needs to come with us, Addison." Ambrose doesn't budge. He looks curious, like a toddler looking out into the ocean for the first time. He tilts his head toward Deacon but shifts his eyes toward Dax.

"Maybe, given the circumstances, we can allow Dax some more time."

Dax widens his eyes, looking hopeful.

My posture stiffens as I look back at Ambrose and

Deacon. "I still don't understand. Why would Dax have to go and not Orlando first?"

"Laws have been broken." Deacon's voice remains crisp. She turns sharply to Ambrose. "And this is not your call to make," she hisses.

Ambrose's facial features don't move a muscle as he calmly replies with an assertive, "It is, and I have."

I exchange glances with Dax, who looks uncomfortable at these two disagreeing with each other. I catch him staring at the door, as if looking for a way out.

"So where are the cops? Are they coming?" I tie my hair back and cross my arms.

"Cops?"

"You said laws have been broken. Where's the police then?"

"We thought it best for us to handle this situation. It is sensitive. No need to alert any authorities yet, as so far Dax has complied." Ambrose's voice has directness but is still far kinder than Deacon's.

"Complying?" I say, ignoring Ambrose's intense stare searing through me. Something about the way he looks at me and talks to me makes me want to rip off his clothes, even though we just met. Stop it Addison, you have a boyfriend! I look inquisitively at Dax. "What is this? Are you in trouble with the law, or not?"

Dax clears his throat. "Not exactly, Addison."

I scrunch up my face. I didn't see an ankle bracelet on him. What could he have done to have social workers involved? In fact, I know for certain that social workers are privatized and will only come if a doctor or the patient signs off for them to visit. They wouldn't just come unannounced . . . Something smells fishy.

"Fine then. We will not linger," Deacon says. "You can

have more time, but we will be keeping a close eye. Let's go, Ambrose."

Dax exhales in a long sigh of relief. "Addison, why don't you go up and check on my dad. I'll see them out the door."

I flutter my eyelashes. It's obvious I'm being dismissed, but I'll comply and give him some privacy to talk alone.

"If you do find yourself in any trouble Addison, we will be close," Ambrose says just as I take the first step toward the stairs. I glance back at him and smile sweetly as I catch those piercing blue eyes looking back at me again. He gives me the most innocent smile a man could possess. "Thanks, I'll keep that in mind," is all I muster. The more his words ring through my brain, I think it's kind of an odd thing to say. They'll be close by? Like watching us? Most people will offer a card or a number. Does that offer come with a ghost-buster? I hold out my hand and he stares at it.

Okay, maybe he's just a pretty face. "Never mind then. Goodbye, Ambrose." I at least like him better than Deacon.

I reach the top of the stairs and walk into my room. I really don't want to be watching over Orlando by myself. Besides, the reason they want to take him away isn't really any of my business, but this isn't what I signed up for. So, what? I'd live in this big house that's full of demons and shit by myself? I sigh and drop to the bed. I did however decide to stay for a while, at least until I get to the bottom of what is happening in the house. For Orlando's sake.

I bring my phone up to my face. Meeting Ambrose awoke certain unexpected feelings inside of me, which shouldn't have happened, because I have a boyfriend. I click open a text message from Carl.

Carl: Hey pretty, I was thinking, why don't you ask Dax if I could stay with you for a little bit? At least until I know you're safe, and you're used to being there.

Maybe that's not such a bad idea. Especially now.

Me: I'll see what I can do.

At night, I'm afraid to fall asleep, so I sit in the living room, the TV keeping me company when a beautiful sound comes from the living room. I turn off the TV and walk over to find Dax sitting on the couch playing his guitar.

"I knew you could play the guitar. We have something in common then."

His eyes flick up at me and he grins. He continues playing the tune from "Stairway to Heaven" by Led Zeppelin. Despite the argument we had earlier, he nudges his chin for me to sit by his side. I do so and reach over to one of the pillows on the corner of the couch and make myself comfortable.

"You know, even though the house kind of freaks me out sometimes, it does look very beautiful at night."

"My mother used to decorate the entire house for the holidays." He quickly glances over to me, not taking his hand off the chords.

"It must have looked wonderful." I yawn.

"Addison? You never mention your parents."

I pause for a moment and hug my pillow. I don't want to react like I did the last time he asked. "They died when I was young. I don't remember them." I better keep it simple. There's no reason to tell him about any underlying trauma that may have caused me to block out my childhood.

Dax softens his squinting eyes at me. "Hmm, I am sorry to hear that." He continues to play for a few more seconds until he stops and turns to me. "There's something I wanted to ask you."

"Oh?"

"It's about your boyfriend."

"Oh, I wanted to ask you something too."

"You first."

"No, you go ahead," I urge.

He takes a deep breath and strokes the chords a few times before asking, "so, where did you two meet?"

I laugh. "That's what you wanted to ask me?" Why is he so serious about it? "We met one night when I was coming home from the university library."

"How long ago was that?" His voice sounds like he's forcing himself to be chipper. I narrow my eyes.

"I don't know, like four months ago. Why?"

"That's not a very long time."

"I haven't really thought about it, it feels longer."

"I bet it does." He looks back down at his guitar and keeps playing.

"You bet it does?"

He glances at me and shakes his head with a smile. "You know, he just seemed really into you, is all. Since he drove all this way to surprise you. Apologies, I'm just being curious. What were you going to ask me?"

"Oh, I was wondering if you'd mind him staying with me here? Just for a few nights?"

Dax stays quiet for a lot longer than expected. Right when I'm about to take it back, he finally speaks.

"You really like this guy, huh?"

"I um . . ." I don't want to tell him I don't want to be alone to watch over his dad. "I do, yes." I mean, not enough to move in with him.

He sets his guitar to the side. "What do you like about him?"

Wow, he's really pressing this. "Well, he's very caring, and sweet. He's pretty perfect."

"Perfect? Yeah, he seems it. I did notice that about him."

Wait—what? "What's that supposed to mean?"

He gives me a disbelieving stare with a thin smile. "Perfect hair, perfect smile, perfect clothes . . . Pretty perfect."

"Is it bad that a guy likes to take care of himself?"

"Perfect muscles."

"I get it. Not to be rude Dax, but if you don't like him, you can just tell me. He doesn't need to stay over."

"I just feel like he's . . . too perfect."

"Now you lost me. What's *that* supposed to mean?"

"No one is perfect, Addie. I would never trust a guy that seemed *too* perfect."

I blink. He's never called me by my nickname before, but I ignore it.

"Addison." He corrects. "Sorry"

"That's fine, I prefer Addie."

"I'm just saying, if anyone seemed so perfect, I'd be looking a little deeper."

I search his features as he grabs his guitar back up and continues playing. Whatever. What does he know?

"But you know what?" he says. "I can understand why you'd want him over."

"You do?"

"Sure, it's a lonely house. Tell him yes."

Relief overwhelms me as I take out my phone to tell him. "Thank you so much, Dax."

We spend the rest of the night in silence, simply enjoying each other's company. I don't even remember falling asleep on the couch.

"CAN'T GET ENOUGH"

AMBROSE

The raucous and repetitive music vibrates through my skeletal form, making me shift back to my human appearance. Still nerve-racking, but at least less shattering to my bones.

Invisible to humans, I stand with Deacon just behind me, waiting for the next person to meet their untimely death. Although, with the cloud of cigarette smoke around us, I hardly think we even need our invisibility cloak on.

"Loud music I can usually bear, but this would even wake the dead," Deacon states.

I give her a sideways glance and nod. "I'll take this one, if it bothers you that much."

"Go on then."

My scythe gives off a single glow and a sea of people unknowingly make way for me to walk through. I stop at a beat-up, dust-ridden couch and gaze down to a young lady with closed eyes and a defeated expression on her face. Her hand opens, dropping a spoon and lighter that clangs when it hits the ground. A few coughs escape her lungs, getting progressively worse.

Twenty-two years old. A year younger than Addison. She almost has the same brown hair color, except Addison has highlights that almost look honey colored in the light, which complements her light amber eyes. So fragile, life.

My mind drifts to when I saw Addison back at the mansion. So strong tempered. The way her hair fell on her face when she questioned us with such authority. A smile creases my face and I feel a pulse in my loins. My eyes flick down to the floor. Why did that just happen?

"Ambrose, she's choking. Are you going to take her or not?"

I straighten myself up and gasp at the girl suffocating in the vomit gouging out from her mouth.

I grip my scythe and, with one glow, I reap her soul.

The girl gasps beside me. "Holy shit, I thought I was dying," she says.

I turn to look at her; vomit still covers her face and chest, as she doesn't know what happened yet.

"I was high out of my mind and then . . . I knew something was wrong. I couldn't breathe . . ." Her eyes fall on her body and her lower lip trembles. Before I can tell her what happened, Deacon speaks for me.

"Yes Shawna, you overdosed. It is time to come with us." Deacon opens a portal and I follow them out. The girl glances back at her body, mouth agape; her vomit disappears. Deacon leads her to the left and then turns to look at me on the bridge.

"What happened back there?"

"I . . . got distracted."

She purses her lips. "Distracted? By what?"

"I—Something about her made me think of the mansion." I'm careful with my wording so as to not raise suspicion from Deacon. That would be the last thing I need from her right now. Not even I can explain what happened to me back there. Why did I have that . . . reaction when I thought of Addison? Why is she even in my mind?

Something about her incites something in me . . . something I don't understand. I must find out. I tilt my head back as Deacon opens the next portal.

"I think we should check on Dax."

"What for? We were just there."

"Just to see how the process is going. You do want to go home soon, don't you?"

Deacon relaxes her shoulders. "Very well, I suppose we should. Otherwise, who knows how long we'll be here for."

"If you're opposed to going, we can split up. I'll meet you at the following appointment when I leave there."

"Right then, try to make it snappy."

I watch as she steps through her portal before I open one to a hidden nook in the mansion's garden.

As I approach the house, I hope I will see her again. There is so much in this world I do not understand, and something about that day, about meeting Addison, makes me all the more curious.

Unseen by any passerby, I step out and ring the doorbell.

A few minutes later, the door unlocks and opens to Addison, holding a towel in her hand as she pats her hair dry.

"Oh, hi!" Her brown eyes gleam from inside and I have to steady my nerves. "I hope you weren't waiting long. I was getting ready to head out." An eyebrow raises and I can tell she's wondering what I'm doing back here. If I'm honest, I'm wondering the exact same thing.

"I'm sorry for interrupting you then. I was just making rounds." Now I'm lying? Reapers don't lie. What am I doing? "Is Dax home?" I already know the answer, yet I dart my eyes past her, as if looking for him.

She widens the door, stepping to the side to let me in. Her curves showcase as the sunlight hits her from an angle. I suppress my urge to admire them as I walk into the foyer and dart my eyes in the direction of Dax's room. I hide a smirk and flick my eyes back to her. Maybe this was a mistake.

"In that case, I can go. I can come back later."

"No," she says, twirling her hair. "W–would you um . . . like to wait for him?"

The way she told me no makes me peer into her eyes. Trying to read them without wanting to ask her . . . I don't even know what I would ask her if I knew how to put it into words. I lock eyes with her for just a second until she lowers her gaze to the side. "Yes, if you don't mind," I quickly say.

She gives me a warm smile and my breath catches.

"Come on upstairs. I was about to prepare Orlando's food and medicine before I left. Would you like anything to drink?"

I follow her up to the second floor. "No, thank you." The sweet scent of vanilla reaches my nose as we reach the kitchen.

"What's that smell?" I ask.

"What smell?" she says, her hair whipping around her as she turns to face me.

"It smells . . . nice . . . sweet." I wrinkle my nose.

She mimics me. "Oh. It's probably from my shampoo. I just washed my hair," she says, giggling. "I thought you meant something smelled bad."

"No, not at all. I just didn't know what it was. I like it," I say as I follow her with my eyes as she walks around the kitchen. I smile at her, and she blushes before reaching into a cabinet for a bowl.

I watch her a bit longer as she reaches for what I presume to be Orlando's medicine bottles. I think back at how I felt earlier when I thought about her. Although I'm much more controlled now, I must admit, her presence puts me . . . strangely at ease, but also, I do not want to leave. I'm conflicted on if I should be feeling anything, but also too curious to suppress them and turn around and leave. Although, I probably should. It's not like I could act on anything. I wouldn't even know how. And what would the council say? My brows furrow as I watch her face drop.

Am I being too quiet? Perhaps my being here has made her feel awkward. "I apologize if my standing here is making you uncomfortable."

Her eyes flick up at me. "Oh no, not at all. It's not that." She sets something down inside the refrigerator and stands by me at the entrance of the kitchen.

"Is everything alright?" I ask, furrowing my brows.

Her eyes widen and she lets out a nervous laugh. "Oh, you'd never believe me if I told you."

I raise an eyebrow. "Is it a lie?"

Addison narrows her eyes at me. Did I say something wrong?

"A lie?" She laughs. "No, it's just kind of . . . unbelievable. Not sure I believe it all myself."

"Oh, I think I understand. Well, why don't you tell me anyway? And then we'll see if I *believe* you." I lend her a warm smile in hopes of making her feel at ease.

Addison opens her mouth to speak, leaning her head

back a bit. She squints for a split second, visibly trying to assess me. "Really?" she finally says.

She was a lot more assertive when we first met. Given the circumstances of the house, something definitely has her shaken up. My lips part and I lower my head a little toward her. "Did something happen?"

"I'm scared you'll think I'm crazy."

"I doubt it."

She takes a deep breath and walks briskly to the window by the piano in the other room. "Do you . . . believe in the paranormal?" she asks, taking a seat.

"What do you mean by paranormal?" I ask, sitting next to her.

"You know, things that go bump in the night. Ghosts, maybe? Demons? That sort of thing."

I frown. Deacon is right about one thing: The situation here needs to move along before someone else gets hurt. I fear that will be Addison.

"Never mind. I should never . . ."

I smile at her and interrupt. "There are things in this world that most hu—people do not admit exist."

This makes her eyes light up and she twirls her hair between her fingers. She catches me observing her doing that and she flings her hair behind her shoulder. "Well, Dax doesn't believe anything. He just . . . makes me so angry sometimes. And I know he's only my boss and I shouldn't care but . . . I'm living here now, you know? I don't like the feeling of somebody thinking I'm silly, or stupid."

My mouth parts slightly as I look at her. "Addison, you are not stupid. And from what I know about Dax, although as brief as our encounter was, I know he doesn't think you are stupid, or silly. In fact, he believes you are the only person on this planet capable of being trusted with his father."

Addison drops her shoulders and lowers her gaze to her hands. "I know . . . but what if that has changed?"

I lean in a little closer and lift up her chin. "What happened last night?"

She sucks in a breath and I quickly realize I just touched her. My gaze falls to her lips and I bring my hand back. I'm at odds with myself. This kind of impropriety isn't like me at all.

She takes in a deep breath and starts to tell me everything. Did she ignore my sudden touch of her skin? Should I interrupt her to apologize? No. Just listen.

She tells me about her waking up in paralysis, all the way to the moment the owl dropped her back inside her body. She pauses in between, making sure I'm still listening to her. When she finishes, she drops her shoulders and takes a deep breath.

I've been reaping long enough to know by the expressions I'm given in my skeletal form that humans are by no means used to seeing behind the veil. This is going to be tricky. She's stuck in a position where she's going to need to learn about this soon if she's going to be able to protect herself and Orlando. But I can't reveal anything to her. The shock will halt her progress. She's going to have to learn this the hard way. "I don't think you're crazy, Addison," I say, softening my eyes at her. "I wish I had some way to help, but I hope just talking will help ease things for you."

"Thank you . . . I can't imagine how you could possibly help." She giggles. "But it does feel good to get that off my chest. You're easy to talk to, Ambrose."

I smile back at her. "I enjoyed our conversation." I remember the little device Deacon handed me that I still don't understand. She said something about it being a way people here communicate. I reach for it in my coat pocket. "If you ever feel like talking, you can always give me a call."

Addison smirks and takes the phone out of my hand. She dials a few things in it and then presses a button. Her phone vibrates in her pocket.

"There. Now we have each other's number."

I take the phone back and feel my cheeks burning.

"Well, I better go. My friend is expecting me." Her cheeks are flushed as she stands up. "Are you going to stay and wait for Dax?"

"No, I better go," I say as I get up to follow her out. We walk silently down the stairs and I get a whiff of her shampoo. I don't understand why that makes me yearn for her touch. I came here to see if I could understand why my body reacted the way it did at the thought of her before. But after talking with her just now, I'm more confused than ever. I don't feel any different. I enjoy her company, but this is so far-fetched for a reaper, I don't think I can handle it.

We get to the bottom of the stairs and Addison turns to face me. My breath catches in my chest and I struggle to steady my breathing. Her honey-colored eyes light up this dark foyer and I wish I didn't have to leave. Before I can say anything, she wraps her arms around me and gives me a tight squeeze. "Thanks again," she says.

I stammer something back as she lets go of me.

I close my lips as her eyes widen. "I'm sorry, was that okay?" she asks. "I hug everyone! I'm so sorry!"

"N–no, that was p–perfectly fine," I say, clearing my throat at the end. My cheeks burn as a smile slides on her face and she opens the door. I follow her outside, keen on getting back to work. I need something to get my mind off Addison.

"See you around, Ambrose," she says, just before getting in her car.

I can still feel the impression of her warm embrace around my body. "Goodbye." I wave her off. *Reapers aren't to have relations with humans. But . . . is it possible? And if I am falling for a human . . . it could indeed lead to my death.*

"FOLLOW THE BUTTERFLIES"

ADDISON

"Just in time," Ava says as I park my car on her grandfather's circular driveway. "I got here a minute ago."

I lend her a half smile as I take my key out of the ignition and roll up the window.

"Aww, don't look so gutted. It'll be fine."

"My mind is just so clouded right now, you know? You should have seen it, it was grotesque. And then telling Dax about it, and Carl . . ." I let my words trail off as I pull my hair back in a tight ponytail.

"Woah, slow down. You told your boss this stuff?"

I sigh, pinching the top of my nose. "I sure did."

Ava's eyebrows reach the center of her forehead as she smiles at me.

I shrug. "It's okay. I'm glad to be here with you now. Thanks for asking your grandad if he could help." Sweat forms in the back of my neck as the heat from the sun intensifies. Ava knocks on the door. Chatter and drumming sound from behind the walls.

A lady wearing a white headdress and beads opens the

door to greet us. "You came on a good night. The ritual is about to start." Sophia, Ava's godmother, holds a dove in her hand as she beckons for us to stand at the entrance. "Quickly now, stand right there. No one comes into this house today without me cleansing them of their"—she clears her throat and gives me a sassy look— "impurities."

Sophia raises a frightened dove over my head, and I shut my eyes tightly, my muscles tensing, as she starts to gently tap it all over my body. I hold my breath to keep from breathing in the tiny loose feathers being dropped. "Oh, girl, especially you. You are *full* of negative energy. Where have you been?" she asks.

When she finishes, I raise an eyebrow at Ava. A blank, dull look washes over her face. She is obviously used to the custom.

"Now then, all finished. Your clothes won't do though. Ava, you know better than that. Only white clothes are permitted on ritual days."

I look down at my black tank top and blue jean shorts.

"I didn't realize there would be a ritual today, *madrina*." Ava arches her eyebrows at her godmother. The sounds of the drums bang rhythmically from the backyard. The strong smell of sage and tobacco surround us as we are led by Sophia into one of the bedrooms. More people dressed in white pass us on their way to the yard.

"Here, quickly, change into these and Marcelo will see you soon." She hands us both long white skirts with white blouses. We change our clothes and meet Ava's godmother and grandfather down the hall. Drumming and laughter continue out in the yard by a big bonfire. Sophia closes the door, so we won't be interrupted by anyone preparing for the ritual outside. Marcelo had agreed to squeeze in a private reading for me, since I'm his granddaughter's friend.

"Those aren't just dolls," Ava whispers as we wait for her grandfather to finish preparing himself for the reading. "They are empty shells for the saints." My hand squeezes the handle of my coffee mug tighter as my eyes wander around the living room. Great. Just when I thought I had enough experiences with dolls to last a lifetime.

My eyes grow hazy as I fixate on the wall. The dolls' shadows come to life as the candle flames dance violently before them.

The fumes of coffee, sage, and tobacco fester in the room, making my head foggy. I lower my head into my hand as my eyes fall on a tall, black doll wearing a bright yellow dress. The doll's glassy eyes stare back at me. Maybe it's a trick of the light, but I swear the doll's face turns toward me. I squint and the doll curls her lips at me.

I almost drop my coffee cup.

"Don't mind her, my dear. That's Ochún. She loves to come *alive,* that one." Sophia mimics the doll's smile as she takes my coffee cup. Her bangles clanging as she walks. My back stiffens as chills run down my spine.

"*Ahora, vamos a empezar.*" Marcelo clears his throat as he shakes his cigar over the ashtray, careful not to get any ashes on his white suit. "Now, we begin." Ava and I both lean in as we watch him scatter shells onto the table in front of him. His eyebrows furrow as he pays close attention to the positioning of the *Odu.* The room grows quiet as he sits motionless in concentration.

The flames flicker, drawing me in deeper into the ambiance of the room.

Marcelo erupts into laughter and I jump. As if I hadn't already been on edge.

My eyes widen and a huge sigh escapes my chest. Is he trying to give me a heart attack?

"I know who you are," he says. I scrunch my face in confusion.

"You don't know who you are." His cackling rings in my ears, as if he had just heard a funny joke. "But *I* do."

"Huh?" I say. "Of course, I know who I am."

Ava wipes her face with her hand. "Ay, Abuelo, cut her a break, please."

"I am laughing because your true self is hidden, and only you can discover it."

I rub my eyes. What does he mean he knows who I am? The sudden urge to leave grips me, but I don't, because that would be rude. He tilts his ear to his left as if listening to someone. I lean toward him.

He bellows with laughter, nearly causing me to jump out of my skin. His eyes glisten, and he takes my hand. "Addison, you are special, but the situation you have found yourself in is serious. And that is all I shall say."

"What do you mean, serious? Please. Tell me."

"This reading. It comes with *osorbo,* meaning much misfortune and death. You have had a curse placed on you, my child." I inhale deeply and fight the urge to roll my eyes.

"Your Egun speaks to me. A woman. She is keeping you safe."

"What does that mean?"

"Your ancestors. They tell me you are living with *un demonio.* Somebody very bad. And you have already met him." This time, I lean in and listen.

"Yes; the other night, I think I was taken out of my body. I believe I astral projected and I saw them. It's more than one."

"One of them is a hellhound, and of those, there are plenty. You have to be very careful, Addison."

"How do I get rid of that creature?" I sit back in my chair.

Ava has been sitting quietly at the far end of the table, her eyes wide open.

His white teeth contrast with his dark skin as he opens his mouth to laugh once again. It takes everything in me to hold my composure. His excitement is beginning to strike a nerve. No offense to Ava's grandpa or anything, but I'm pretty sure he's enjoying himself at my expense.

"Let me tell you a secret first." He looks to his left and then to his right, and then leans in closer. I catch a glimpse of Ava shaking her head.

"*Más sabe el diablo por viejo que por diablo.*" He leans back in his chair. "Do you know what that means?"

I shake my head. Even though I know the literal translation, I don't know what this Spanish idiom has to do with anything.

"The devil knows more because he's old, not because he's the devil." Marcelo gives me another broad smile and nods his head. "I am not trying to discourage you. I am trying to *help* you."

My stomach churns. He's talking about me thinking he's nuts. I smile sheepishly.

Taking another puff of his cigar, he blows the smoke down on his shells. "If in this world—" He pauses and points down hard on the table. "*If* in this world there was never any evil, then we would know no good." He opens his eyes wide and claps his hands together once, his voice rising as he speaks.

"And, if in this world no good ever existed, then we would know no bad." He smiles again. "What do you think of that?" I pause to think, but he speaks again before I can form a reply. "Yes, this path is a strange one you're on, but . . . it is yours. I cannot tell you how to solve it, but I can show you how to protect yourself."

I'm all ears now.

"From now on, you must only wear white. That is the first rule you must follow. Then, the most important rule: you must learn who you are. You are powerful. Learn to understand and harness that power."

"How am I supposed to do that?"

"Find it. That is all I will tell you." He reaches for a small block of white chalk nearby and puts it in my hand. "Take this cascarilla. It is yours. Draw a cross on the door where you sleep and draw another cross on your forehead. It will keep you from being pulled out of your body. Do that no more while the *demonio* is there. You understand?" I nod quickly and stick it in my pocket. It's not like I had been *trying* to astral project.

"I do have one question though: Why white?"

"Black attracts *muertos*, which for you is very bad right now. If you must wear other colors, do so, but stay away from black."

The drums begin to form a song as someone in the background starts singing in a language I have never heard of. Sophia peeks her head in the door. "Marcelo, they are ready to begin playing *el toque*. We are waiting for you."

"Okay, let's go! Are you staying for the ritual?" He looks at me and then at his granddaughter.

"No, Abuelo. She has a long drive back to the Keys."

"Well, you better go then. Be safe." He kisses us both on our foreheads and then turns back to me. "Tonight, pay attention to your dreams, my child. Many truths can be revealed if you pay attention."

Sophia walks us to the front door. "You better hurry. Once the ritual starts you won't be able to leave." Sophia opens the front door and as the sounds of the drums become louder and louder, I want to stay. Sophia glares at me for a split second. "You best listen to Marcelo. I can tell you have a little bit of a witch in you." A dimple pops on her cheek as she grabs the doorknob.

"Why won't we be able to leave once it starts?" I say, taking a step down on the doorstep.

"Because once we start, the Orichás visit. And if you leave, you'll die."

The door closes, and we turn to leave.

"I'm sorry, my grandfather can be so cryptic." Ava plays with her car keys. "And dramatic, but believe me, he's very respected in this community. He is very wise and is a *Babalawo*, and a *padrino*, godfather, to many people in Santeria."

I let out a long sigh. "I know he's just trying to help. I didn't want to seem so skeptical, especially after everything I've seen. I can tell he is very wise though. What did Sophia mean by dying if we left during the ritual?"

"The Orichás are spirits that come down and possess people for the benefit of the community while they dance. It's incredible to watch, really. But if the door opens and somebody steps out, all the bad energy being expelled during the ritual goes into that person and they will meet their death."

My head starts to throb from so much talk about demons and spirit possessions. "I'm so ready for all this to be over."

That night, I dreamt I was a little girl, alone in the garden. I was wearing a floral summer dress tied around the waist with a yellow ribbon. I was by myself, playing and spinning around in circles and chasing the butterflies deep into the bushes.

I chase the butterflies down one of the garden paths. The warm summer sun kisses my face; it feels so real. I follow the butterflies to where a woman is sitting in front of a white gazebo. Her hands are covered in dirt and she is holding a gardening trowel in one hand and pink peonies in the other.

"Addison, you're going to get your dress all dirty." She isn't mad; in fact, she has a huge smile on her face. "*Venga para qa*. Come here." I do as I'm told and run over to her.

"Mama?" Love and happiness wash over me as I run toward my mother at full speed. But the more I run, the farther away my mother becomes. Even in the dream, anticipation grows into desperation.

"*Ma*."

Finally, I reach her and hug her tightly, never wanting to let go. I look up, expecting my mother to be smiling, but her face transforms into a disfigured skull.

Her jaw stretches, her bones clanking as they become displaced, and she lets out a horrific scream. Quickly, I let go and everything around me starts to die. The butterflies catch fire and the garden starts to rot, maggots appearing on top of the grass. I hold my little hands up to my eyes and scream.

I wake up in a cold sweat as early morning sets in. "That's *enough*." I pull the covers away from me and set out to the forbidden library to find something I can use.

I flip through the pages of a recipe book, looking for a soup I can make for Orlando's dinner. I'm rushing—set on sneaking into the library before Dax pops up and strikes a conversation. Getting my hands on those books is the only game plan I have left. I try to concentrate on a zucchini soup but Marcelo's voice haunts my thoughts.

You must learn who you are. You are powerful, Addison. Learn that and learn your power.

What was he on about? Crazy old man. I curl the corner of a page with my fingertips. Then his voice echoes in my mind again. Something about having to protect myself.

I grab the sides of my scrubs; they are dark gray with a pink trim. Well, at least they aren't black this time. Oh, who am I kidding? What does it matter what color clothes I'm wearing? One thing is for sure though, I need to get my hands on those books. I have to find out what's going on in this house. At least before Dax has to leave.

I stand by the chimney, trying to listen for any sign of Dax. I need a better plan. I could just walk in and close the doors. No, the lights will clearly show through the stained-glass windows from the family room next door. What if I use a flashlight? Then again, what if Dax comes looking for me? I can leave him a note saying I went out to the store to get a few things for dinner . . .

"What are you doing?"

I jump nearly a foot in the air and spin around. It's only the kid.

"I think the real question is, what are you doing here?" I lower my arms to my waist.

"I'm pretending to hunt ghosts."

My face grows pale. "What? Why? What do you know?"

The boy takes a step back. "Because it's fun."

"Hey kid, do you know something about this house?" I say, towering over him.

"You're scaring me." The boy fidgets with the bottom of his T-shirt, attempting to avoid my gaze.

I sigh to myself. Of course, he doesn't know anything. It's a creepy old house and he's just a kid. "I'm sorry. I got a little carried away. Now, beat it. I'm trying to work."

"But I like hanging out with you." His voice cracks.

My eyelids drop as his face reddens. Who knows what this kid's situation is? I offer him a sluggish smile; maybe I can keep him occupied just for a little while. "Tell you what. Come into the kitchen with me while I get Orlando's food ready and I can give you some ice cream. Then you can talk to me all you want. How's that sound?"

The boy's eyes brighten, and he nods his head. I skip over to the kitchen and have him follow me. "I hope you like chocolate ice cream because that's all I have here." As soon as I step into the kitchen, his footsteps become quiet. I turn and he's no longer trotting behind me. Maybe he has changed his mind and gone away. I spin around, glance right, then left, but there is no sign of the boy anywhere.

I poke my head around the corner, expecting him to be hiding. "Hey, kid? Don't you want ice cream? Where'd you go?" He couldn't have left that fast. "I thought you liked hanging out with me?" I wait outside the kitchen, listening for him, but after a few moments I give up. Screw it, he's probably hiding again. Any other explanation would bring up unsettling feelings and at this moment I have more pressing things on my mind.

I go back to preparing Orlando's food for the day, in silence, and collect his medicine and water. I no longer attempt to push conversations with him. He isn't interested, and to be honest, it might be safer for him to stay in this room. I listen for Dax, and for the boy. The house is as silent as a graveyard at sunrise. I really hope the boy just went off to play and wasn't abducted by any demons.

I push the thought from my head. Time to complete my mission.

I tiptoe down the terra-cotta staircase, looking around for any signs of movement. The coast is clear.

I make my way to the library doors and reach for the key, hidden in the same place I had found it before. As I do, something makes the hairs on my arms stand straight. I clench my eyes tight, afraid to turn around. "Dax?"

I wait for him to say something, but nothing happens.

Icy clouds start coming from my mouth. I turn around slowly, and there it is.

A large, black mass of energy. Its cloud-like form lurks before me, formless and floating.

I stare at the iridescent black form as it moves closer. I have never seen anything like this before. I have heard of spirits being white or opaque, shining even. But black? What if it's the demon trying to cast itself into the physical world? What should I do? No weapons nearby. Think.

The mass of energy is moving quicker now. I spot a slim walking cane resting itself on the border of the door. I grab it and swing. My jaw drops as half of the cane disappears into the black cloud. I let go and it falls to the ground. So much for being inconspicuous.

"What do you want?" My fingers tremble. The dark mass, now inches from my face, is a solid black void when I peer into it. No eyes, no nose, nor a mouth that I can tell. Any closer and I'll be able to inhale the darkness.

Inching over to my right, I make a dash for the key and grab it. The black orb starts to lengthen itself. I turn the lock as fast as I can. The doors are heavy, but I manage to push them open enough to squeeze through.

Once in, my back slides against the closed doors and I take a deep breath.

That was a close one. What was that thing? It seemed like a black, endless void. Whatever it was, it certainly didn't give off any positive vibes. Then it dawns on me. If the walking cane went right into it, it could go through the wall.

Goosebumps ripple over my body as I go for the light switch.

The lights come on and I stare at the door for a few seconds. Whatever it is, it doesn't seem to follow me into the library. At least, not yet. I wrap my arms around myself, still freezing from the temperature drop.

I dim the lights but can still make out the room. The shelves are covered in dust. My eyes skim the titles before reaching the Goetia in case anything else appears of use. *The Secret Book of Artephius*. I keep skimming. I've never heard of most of these titles. A variety of manuscripts from Roger Bacon, Nicholas Flamel, John Reid, and Andrew Chumbley. I need to hurry up—who am I kidding? I wouldn't recognize any of these books as helpful if they turned into a snake and bit me in the ass.

I walk straight to the Goetia and open the book, a cloud of dust poofs into my face. Not knowing what I am looking for exactly, I skip the introductory pages and mentions of ceremonial magick.

"The Book of Evil Spirits" I read carefully through the page. My arms get itchy, and despite the coldness of the room, I start to sweat. Time is not on my side, and the book, although written in English, is hard to understand. I can't find anything about how to get rid of a demon. I continue to flip through until I reach a list of names, pages and pages long, of what appears to be a hierarchy of demons. BAEL, AGARES, VASSAGO; AZAZEL, I briefly skim through their descriptions in hopes of finding something about how to get rid of them, but to no avail; it only describes who they are.

I don't know what to call this creature. As per their descriptions, elaborate seals belonging to each one of the names are drawn along the sides of the pages. I look over my shoulder to make sure nothing is coming through the walls. Still nothing.

I am about to give up when a thin crimson bookmark holding the place of one of the pages close to the beginning pops out at me. I had somehow skipped it. (9) PAIMON, my eyes skim his description.

"A great king, obedient unto LUCIFER." Chills suddenly run down my spine. What was Orlando researching? I read further: "This spirit can teach secrets of the arts and sciences." I raise my eyebrows. "He giveth good familiars and can reanimate the dead." What does all this mean? Why is this page marked?

A buzzing comes from my pocket and it makes me jump. It's Carl. He is going to have to wait. I put my phone on silent and grab for the book. Maybe I can take it with me, so I could study it a bit more without having to sneak into the library. Dax never goes in anyway, he won't notice. I try lifting it with both hands, but the book won't budge. I try to lift it carefully. No use. It appears to be stuck to the podium. I run my fingers along the back of the book, searching for a clasp or release button. In doing so, I move all the pages to the other side and reveal a little switch popping out from the back cover. I check over my shoulder one more time to make sure I'm still alone. Knowing I might not get another chance, I flip the switch and close my eyes, not expecting what it will do. The switch makes a soft clicking noise and then . . . nothing.

I open my eyes and listen. Nothing happens.

Well, this was a big waste of time. Now what? How do I get rid of the demon? I turn around to leave and air catches in my chest. Just when I had started to forget about it, the black mass of energy materializes in the center of the room. This time, it is larger and darker, blocking my way out. I shuffle slowly past the podium, pressing my back against the bookshelf. The darkness is making its way closer and closer to me. What the fuck do I do? The book wasn't any help. My eyes widen in fear.

I lean back further, my hand pressing against one of the shelves. It moves behind me. What's this? I push back harder. A secret passageway? The switch must have opened something after all.

I disappear into the unknown and push the shelves back in place. When I turn, I find myself in complete darkness. There is a cool mist in the air, and my body shivers uncontrollably. I wave my hands around in hopes of finding a wall with a light switch somewhere. Afraid to trip, I take small steps before deciding I'm in an open space.

Deafening silence brings a ringing in my ears. My heart beats against my ribs as I feel my way back to the library door. After a few minutes of walking, my pulse starts to race. What's happening? It is as if the door has disappeared completely. Am I even walking in the right direction? Demon in the library or not, I have to get back to Orlando. It is only a matter of time before Dax gets back and finds I was not there—or worse, that someone has been in the library. He would never trust me again. I swallow hard. I have to get back.

Oh, damn this dark room. Think Addison, think. Remembering the buzzing nuisance before, I reach for my phone in my pocket. No signal, but I can still use the flashlight app. I shine the light around but I still can't make out any walls. My stomach turns. Something tells me I'm no longer in the house. Did I somehow fall over and get knocked out? I walk on a bit further.

Out in the distance, a soft glow appears. Anticipation sends me forward and as I move closer, a patch of green is visible in the distance; mangroves. Nearing the area, the trees grow bigger. It looks like the dock at the back of the house. I slowly set foot on top of the green mahogany floorboards. How the hell did I end up here? I dart my eyes behind me and suddenly I'm outside completely. The darkness is gone, and it is as if I had never been coming out of the library at all.

I rub my forehead. None of this makes any sense. I spin on my heel back toward the water, and that's when I spot him. Orlando is sitting on the edge, with his feet hanging out. I almost don't notice the temperature hasn't changed one bit since I stepped out of the darkness. It is freezing cold in the Florida Keys, when it should be a humid autumn. A foggy mist covers the ground. The skies are a purplish-gray, casting no shadows.

"Orlando. What are you doing out here?" Not that he is discouraged to leave his room, but it is completely out of the norm. I run over to him and put my hand on his shoulder. He doesn't react. "Orlando?" I call out a little louder, remembering he is hard of hearing. "Hey." I kneel next to him and stare into his face. "Orlando, are you alright? Come on, let's get you back inside." His eyes are glossed over, and he seems to be completely incoherent, as if he is under a spell. I wave my hand out in front of him. No reaction.

I stand up and run my fingers through my hair. What is the purpose of a secret passageway that leads you back outside? Is it an escape exit? Am I even still at the mansion? And how the hell did it get so cold? I flick my gaze back down at Orlando and furrow my eyebrows. He moved positions, pointing to something on his left.

I follow where he's pointing with my eyes. A chest covered in seaweed and chains is on top of the dock. "What's in there?" Orlando doesn't respond, he just sits there, eyes glazed over, pointing.

I walk over to it. The chest is wet and full of muck, and my hand slips as I try pulling it open. I grab a thick branch and use it to pry the rusty lock away from the latch. Inside, is a leather-bound book. I quickly wipe my hands on my scrubs and pick it up. The book has gold trimmings, and the cover has a family crest embellished with leaves and a tiny seahorse on the bottom. I open it to the first page, which reads *Book of Shadows*.

I glare at Orlando, whose arm is back down to his side. I flip the page, squinting my eyes, trying to make out the handwritten text. The gray skies above start to darken. It was only early afternoon when I snuck into the library, now it looks like it's nearly night. Maybe this book is what I need.

I keep flipping through the book, reading the titles. I pass a chapter called "How to Create Servitors and How to Banish Them"—the instructions follow for some pages. How to Banish Egregores, more words I don't understand. I stop skimming when I come to two different titles. One says, "How to Banish Demons or Unwanted Foes," and the other reads "How to Get Rid of Evil Spirits." Hoping to find an answer, I read on.

"SCREECH."

Looking up, I spot Crowley flying in a circle overhead. "Crowley. What are you doing here?" At this point, I'm convinced I somehow entered another world. There is no other way to explain Orlando's glossy eyes, the chest, and the biting cold. Denial isn't going to help me anymore.

"SCREECH."

Lightning flashes through the clouds and wind starts to pick up. Orlando is still sitting on the dock, completely oblivious to his surroundings. Should I try to get him inside? I take another glance at the pages of the book. The wind flips a few pages and I narrow my eyes to a familiar name written on it. Paimon. I recognize the name from the Goetia. Reading a little further, it seems Orlando was using a few pages near the end as a journal. I struggle to read his scribblings; it's some sort of plan. Some sort of ritual.

Crowley swoops down and grabs ahold of the *Book of Shadows* with his sharp talons.

"Hey, stop it. No, Crowley." I fight with the bird, gripping on tightly to the book. "Bad bird, Crowley. NO. Give that back." I don't understand. He's helped me before. Why is he trying to take the book away? It's too late; the owl snaps its beak and I let go of the book.

My heart begins to race. The black energy manifests itself again. Not this again! Now what? My eyes grow wide as Crowley follows the darkness. "No Crowley, stop." I watch as he circles, moving closer to the blackness before disappearing into the dark hole.

What?

Crowley's head pops back out and he screeches once more. It's not a demon, it's a portal! He wants me to follow him! I slowly inch my way toward the form, and it lengthens itself, as it had earlier. I step through and seconds later find myself back in the library. Did I just go through all of that for no reason?

I brush myself off and walk toward the doors, careful not to knock anything over in the dark. I slide them open and to my utter disappointment, an angry Dax stands in the doorway, arms folded with his fists clenched in place. I was so close to getting away with this. So close.

"HEARTLESS"

AMBROSE

I take a sip of my black coffee and swoosh it around in my mouth. I have never tasted the black liquid humans find pleasurable. I inhale. "Somewhat . . . tasteless, and yet, bitter." I tilt my head up, trying to decide on whether I'll keep drinking. "I have no use for this beverage, regardless of its effect," I say, placing the mug down on the table.

"Try it with some sugar and milk," Deacon says while opening up the tenth bag of sugar and pouring it into her cup.

I follow her lead and take a long sip. "Hmm. This is a lot more to my liking."

"Yes, I thought you might agree." Deacon hints at a rare smile.

A waitress with straight gray hair pulled back in a ponytail appears holding a tray full of IHOP's finest cuisine. "Here ya are, sweet pea. Two full stacks o' pancakes topped with fruits and whipped cream, with a side o' eggs, bacon, and sausages for the both o' ya. Can I get you anything else, sugar?"

"We already have a lot of sugar on the table, thank you," I say. The waitress looks bemused and I furrow my eyebrows.

"That'll be all, Sherry, thank you," Deacon finishes the formality with the waitress. "The word 'sugar' is sometimes used as a term to call others when they want to appear kind or sweet." She points to my plate. "Try the food."

I stare at my silverware.

"Ambrose, how long are we expecting to wait for collection?"

"As long as it takes." I cut down into the pancakes with my knife, mimicking Deacon. Despite spending time on Earth observing human interaction, I never cared to take part in any of these rituals. Deacon, on the other hand, ironically despising humans, finds food and beverage to be the only thing worth coming here for.

"Here, use your fork as well. Like this," she says, picking up her utensils to show me. "Oh, and you'll want to pour one of these syrups on it."

I look at the selection of syrups to my right, reading each one carefully.

"As much as I do enjoy my Earthly visits, we don't want to be obliterated, do we?" she says.

"It shouldn't take long. I trust the girl is catching on."

"We are falling behind on our collections; this is messing up the order—"

"You go on your collections. I will watch the house." I select the glass jar with the red lid, labelled *strawberry syrup*, and pour it on a small bite and stick it in my mouth. My eyes widen, and I pour a handsome amount on the rest of my pancakes.

"I hardly think splitting up is a good idea."

"We cannot just collect the soul in that house by force, and while they breathe."

Deacon sits back in her chair.

"I am enjoying myself for the time being. Understand, this is a unique case and we need to tread with caution." I glance at a man and woman at the table diagonally from us. The man has his arm wrapped around the woman as she caresses his knee. I stare at them for a minute longer, imagining what it's like to be human and to have someone who cares about you. And vice versa. Deacon turns her head to see where I'm looking and scoffs.

"I saw the way you two were looking at each other," she snaps, bringing my attention back to her. "Reapers are not to have relations with humans." Deacon stares at me disapprovingly. "In fact, we don't have relations—period. You know the rules. I shouldn't have to remind you."

"Having a relationship with a human is the furthest thing from my mind. I am only curious about all of my new surroundings." I stand up from the table and start heading out the door. I pass the waitress on my way out. "Thank you for a lovely meal. Deacon has the currency to pay you."

"Oh, it is my pleasure. I'll be here all week, you come back now."

I shift toward her with a blank stare. "Regrettably, no you won't. You will be deceased before the week is finished." I turn my back and walk out the door, leaving a confused and insulted Sherry to her work.

I stroll toward the mansion, enjoying the hot air against my skin. I stop a few times to listen to the birds singing and enjoy the laughter and chatter of passersby. To the left of the sidewalk, a small park filled with children playing and joggers going on their daily exercise routines makes me stop to observe human activity. A couple sitting under a tree are intimately embraced. I watch as the man moves his hand up the young woman's arm. She tilts her head up and kisses him on the lips. Is this what people do when they're in love?

The fast passing of the cars distract me as a traffic light turns green and the flow of traffic continues, spinning me around to watch as they disappear into the road. It still amazes me how they claim to value their lives but put themselves in dangerous situations every day. I don't always know when someone is going to die. Life holds many different opportunities, and one opportunity could lead to several different paths. Only when their death is close can I hear their time clocks ticking.

I glance back at the bench but the couple is walking away.

My mind drifts to the other day when I met Addison, and the way her wavy brown hair falls over her tanned face.

I approach the gate and come to an abrupt stop. In broad daylight stands a prying creature with long sharp claws and pointy ears. Saliva falls from its jaws as it watches Addison open the front door. I ignore all of my Judge's commands about not interfering with human affairs. I have to protect Addison.

I step through the gate and take out a sharp, curved blade I have hidden inside my jacket. A smaller scythe, akin to the one Deacon and I have on our suits, is engraved on the blade.

I grip my weapon and move swiftly forward.

"THE TRUTH WILL SET YOU FREE"

ADDISON

I stand at the entrance of the library with my cheeks flushed red. I've been caught.

"I can explain." I twirl my hair in between my fingers and try to calm down my racing heart. He stays silent, waiting for me to finish fumbling with my words. "You know what? I can't explain anything to you because you don't believe anything I've been telling you anyway. And you know what else? I would walk away from all this. Anyone in their right mind would just quit and leave here forever after seeing everything I have seen and been through in this house. But I won't, because I care about your father and what's going to happen after you leave." My voice rises, but I don't care.

Dax widens his eyes and takes a gentle step toward me.

"And I'm glad I went in there today. I learned a lot and saw . . . probably more than I should have."

"Okay Addison, I'm not mad. Let's just both calm down—"

"I won't calm down because I know you think I'm crazy.

Go ahead, call the loony bin if you like. If you want me to go, I'll just go."

"I won't do that, Addison. Just calm down, please."

I squint my eyes at him. He must know something then. He's hiding something. "Your dad was some kind of sorcerer, wasn't he?"

Dax relaxes his face and sighs. "He was an occultist, yes. Don't meddle in things you don't understand. He ended up this way because magick drove him crazy. Yes, he was very good at what he did when in his prime. But his mind was failing. All of these books . . ."—Dax gestures to the spellbooks and bottles on the shelves— "they affected him."

I understand what he's telling me, but something still doesn't add up. "You say you don't believe in what I've been seeing in this house. Then how did you know what I was doing?"

He narrows his eyes at me. "I don't understand what you're implying."

"You knew I was in here. You were ready to barge in here to yell at me. You do know something is wrong."

"No. I *heard* you in here. I simply don't want you messing with his stuff."

"I call bullshit. You specifically said you didn't want me meddling with things I don't understand. But you *do* understand something, don't you? And what's with those social workers, huh? Are they even that?" I shut my mouth at my own mention of the words "social workers." Ambrose had just been here. Despite me not believing he is a social worker, I still felt safe around him. Most importantly, he doesn't think I'm crazy and I felt like I could talk to him. I swallow as my eyes bore into Dax. I really want to believe Ambrose is what he says he is.

Dax takes a deep breath and relaxes his jaw. "I believe all

of this got to his head, Addison. The same could happen to you if you're not careful. That's all. I understand something is driving your curiosity and I should not have put such restrictions on this room. I think it only made things worse. I'll leave you to get back to work now." He turns on his heel and leaves me to my frustration.

He has to be hiding something. I know better. I have seen those creatures. None of this is my imagination. And he didn't answer my question about the social workers! This might be a good thing though . . .

Either way, it doesn't matter because I have a boyfriend, as I keep telling myself.

My phone buzzes again from inside of my pocket. Twenty missed calls from Carl. Jeez. I need to get some air anyway. I go for a drink of water in the kitchen and then head outside to call my boyfriend and to hopefully clear my mind.

The day is a steaming eighty-four degrees and the sun immediately makes me regret not putting on sunscreen. In the near distance, someone is walking in through the gate. I squint and recognize Carl's buff posture.

Took him long enough.

"Sorry I'm late. I called you but you didn't pick up." He walks toward the house and I start moving to meet him. I stop as something moves from behind him. Who is that? I squint and realize the only man who would be wearing a black suit through the unbearable heat is the social worker Ambrose from the other day. What does he want now? My heart flutters a little, but I fight it back.

Ambrose takes out something shiny. It looks like a blade. What is he doing? My eyes widen as he pulls his arm back. What the fuck? It takes me a moment to process what is going on before I can yell. "Carl, behind you!" Carl's eyes grow big as Ambrose moves swiftly around him, blocking his way. A different kind of flutter hits me in the chest. I think my heart actually did skip a beat.

Ambrose jabs Carl in the chest and pulls his scythe out in one clean blow.

Carl's mouth hangs open as his body writhes. For a moment, he looks as if he has been suspended in time. I'm frozen to the ground as he gives one last gasp of air, and then lets out a shriek as he reaches for me.

I still can't bring myself to budge. My eyes swell up and my sight blurs as I witness blood seeping out from my boyfriend's gaping lips.

His body falls to the ground with a loud thud, his face pressed hard against the brick pavement.

I gasp. "What did you do?" I finally move my legs and sprint toward Carl. Ambrose stands next to his body, bloody knife in hand and with a confused look on his face.

"I killed a monster." His voice is uncomfortably calm. I gape at him as I lift Carl's head into my lap. My blood boils as Ambrose looks like someone who just watched a boring movie for the hundredth time.

"You killed my boyfriend," I roar, my voice rasping at the last word.

"Boyfriend?" His eyes peer deeply into mine. "Addison, this was no boy, and it most certainly was not a friend."

With tears heavy in my eyes, I look down at Carl's lifeless body and I quickly hover over him, hugging him. "W–why did you st–stab him?" My voice trembles and my stomach knots. How could I ever have been thinking about Ambrose as anything other than a friend? Except now, he's a murderer.

He takes out a handkerchief and wipes down his blade. "Addison, would you kindly let go of that body?"

"No. I'm calling the police." I reach for my phone in my pocket and unlock the screen, my fingers shaking as I do so.

"Addison, you will want to step away from the creature's body now," he says with his voice sounding too bemused for my liking.

Did he just call my boyfriend a creature? "What the hell are you talking about? Are you crazy?" Tears roll off my cheeks and fall on Carl's. I move to wipe them away, but jump back, dropping his head to the ground. Air catches in my chest, followed by a sharp pain. Carl's body morphs into a grotesque creature. Its long, narrow tongue seeps out of its contorted face. I scurry back and scream. A sticky black substance is all over my hands. What the fuck is this? Tears seep down my face as black blood pools out from his chest wound. My lips tremble as I try to speak. I try standing up. Then, everything goes black and I fall.

My vision is blurry as I blink myself awake. Indistinct chatter comes from somewhere around the bar. The red and gold embellishments of the Venetian room's wallpaper come into focus. I reach for my throbbing head. What happened?

From the other room, Dax whispers, "I need to tell her, but how?"

"It seems the situation is far worse than you anticipated."

"I noticed he was strange when I met him, but I didn't know how to tell Addie. She asked if he could stay and I thought by keeping him close, I could keep an eye on him. I should have warned you. Now, what am I supposed to do?"

"Tell her the truth."

My memories flood in all at once. I jump off the couch and run to the bar area. "Tell me the truth."

Dax's eyebrows arch on his forehead.

"Addison . . . I—"

"Ahem," Ambrose's throat clears from behind me, color flushes out of my face and I spin on my heel.

"Murderer," I say with a raspy voice. I point to him. "Why is he still here? He killed Carl." My hands and knees shake, and the world turns red; all feelings I may have had about him fleeing my bones. I grab my chest as another shock of pain hits me.

Ambrose takes one step back, his face solemn, paler than usual.

"Addison, calm down. There are things you don't understand," Dax says.

I turn my neck over to Dax. "Oh, now, there are things I don't understand?" I say, accusingly. "Well then, explain them, because I would love to know why this murderer is not being arrested."

Ambrose and Dax look at each other.

Ambrose breaks the silence. "What do you remember after I told you to look down at the creature?" I forgot that part. My mind must have blocked it out. Because it—it's just not possible. I thought I was hallucinating.

"That was real?"

"Yes, it was real."

My heart starts picking up speed again and I stumble back. My eyes wander down to the floor as I try to make sense of everything.

"He turned, didn't he?" Ambrose says softly. I look up at him, tears forming in my eyes again. "What was that thing? What is happening?"

"He was a demon posing as your boyfriend to keep you in the dark about the house."

Keep me in the dark? What the hell is that supposed to mean? "Wait, he was just posing as my boyfriend? So, the real Carl is still at home?" My eyes flick up at him.

"I'm afraid not, Addison. The Carl you knew never existed. He was specifically crafted and sent here to distract you."

"How do you know this? Who are you? You're not social services, are you?"

"In a way, yes. But no, you are right, my job is much more than that."

Dax coughs and exchanges a glance with Ambrose. My blood boils. I knew Dax had been keeping secrets.

Ambrose continues. "I think, for now, we should stick to one explanation at a time."

He's covering for Dax! "So, the demon is real! You lied to me," I say, turning to Dax. "This whole time." I don't know what I think I can do to a six-foot-two, muscular man, but I lunge at him.

"I was only trying to protect you." He calmly grabs me and moves me over to the side, completely unphased by my being aggressive.

My head pounds and I grab at my temple.

"You have to understand; this wasn't information I could just tell my hired nurse." Dax throws his arms down. "But now that you know . . . I can be honest with you. I think a demon is keeping my dad in his current state."

"Is he dying?" I ask somberly.

Dax shrugs. "Whatever is happening, I think the longer the demon keeps him alive, the stronger it gets . . . until he doesn't need him anymore."

"It appears your demon boyfriend was intended to keep you from discovering the truth," Ambrose explains.

I shoot him an irritated glance. "What are you still doing here?"

Ambrose tightens his face, struggling to hide his perplexity. I clench my fists.

"It is clear my presence here upsets you." He turns to Dax. "I'll wait for you in the kitchen; we still have things we need to discuss."

Dax waits for him to climb the stairs. "That wasn't your boyfriend," he says, turning back to me. "And, if I had known about him, I would have checked him out sooner."

My vision swims. "That doesn't change the fact that our relationship was a lie. I saw someone I thought I knew murdered right in front of me. By that man up there!" I bury my head in my hands. "None of this makes any sense. Why would the demon that has your dad have sent me a distraction months ago?"

"It knew I had been looking to hire you."

"You had been looking to hire me months before I applied?" I squint at him. This is starting to sound too creepy, and like way more than I bargained for.

Dax falls short. "No, but it knows things sooner than we do. A lot sooner."

My lips start to tremble. "Dax," I start. "I have to go home. I can't keep working here."

Dax's eyes widen. "Addison, you don't understand. You can't leave."

My mouth drops and I start to back up. "What d–do you mean I can't leave? A demon was pretending to be a person —my boyfriend. Since I got here, I've been haunted, taken out of my body, almost eaten by a hellhound, and nearly killed by a demon. I think I should call it quits and go home."

"What I mean is, you're a part of this. If you leave, another demon will follow you to keep tabs on you. Despite what's going on in this house, the only way you'll be safe is by being here with me."

I shake my head. "None of this shit makes any sense. Why are demons keeping tabs on me?"

"I know it's a lot to take in, but I promise you, we will get to the bottom of it. And ease up on Ambrose a little, will you? I know it doesn't seem like it, but he actually saved your life. Will you trust me?"

My eyes graze over him. Can I trust him? After he kept everything a secret from me and made me think I was crazy? "No, but I guess I have to," I say, before leaving to check on Orlando. Famous last words.

"DON'T CALL ME 'SPOCK'"

AMBROSE

I stand in the kitchen, with my hands folded in front of me, trying to think of a way I could have handled it all differently. I killed a demon. And in doing so, I turned an innocent human's world upside down. And the way she looked at me . . . She most certainly hates me now.

"Let's talk." Dax enters the kitchen, interrupting my train of thought.

"Well, stabbing her boyfriend definitely introduced a subtle way for me to break the truth to her," he says.

"I'd say it did the exact opposite."

Dax slaps himself in the face. "Next time there's a demon hanging around in disguise, try to be more discreet."

"We don't see their disguises, only their true form. And now that she knows part of the truth, why is killing these creatures with discretion necessary?"

Dax walks over to the kitchen table and takes a seat, putting his legs up on the chair next to him and clasping his hands. "This may be true, but while you're here, you need to act human. You can't have people, especially Addison, finding out what you really are. It will not go well."

"Oh?" I smirk.

"People don't generally like the idea of death itself, let alone an angel of death," Dax says, keeping his voice low, I presume so Addison won't hear. He tilts his head back and rubs his face. "Why did you guys have to say you were social workers?" he mumbles between his fingers.

"Reaper. I merely do my job. I'm not an angel. And perhaps Deacon underestimated Addison's knowledge of social workers . . ."

"She's a nurse!"

"There's no point in hiding the truth from her now, Dax."

"Whatever. Be it as it may, just follow my lead."

"Your lead?"

"Yes."

"You want me to follow *your* lead?" I look idly at him.

"Did I stutter?"

"A ghost is going to teach *me* how to act human?" I attempt a smile.

Dax sighs deeply.

"Alright then, if I am to stay and help, I will follow your lead. On a more important note, be careful not to tell her everything all at once. These things take time to unfold. You need to be clever in finding out how to break the spell. You're being spied on, but you must hurry up. I cannot stall the reaping for too much longer and Deacon is becoming impatient. We must be moving on soon and we can't until we are finished here."

"Why are you being so helpful? What is your interest in Addison?"

"I am only being sensitive, as this is a most interesting case. If I take what I've come for, then a demon that should not be thriving on Earth will remain. And we cannot have that either."

Dax nods, but keeps his eyes narrowed. "You make sure you keep your reaper claws off of her," he hisses.

I arch an eyebrow. "Are you threatening me, Dax? Bear in mind that despite any rules we reapers follow, and no matter what I have Deacon believing I will do, I *can* just take you away and reap you out of here. And the hell with your father, and any demon." I pause to let my words sink in, despite me knowing perfectly well we can't just reap or kill anyone who stands. But he doesn't know that. "And I don't have claws . . ." I say, looking down at my hands.

Dax scoffs, trying to hide his fear.

"Can I come in?" Addison stumbles into the kitchen without waiting for a reply. She rubs her bloodshot eyes. "Orlando is fine. I need some coffee. Does anyone want a cup?"

"I would love some coffee actually." My eyes follow her, trying to catch her gaze, hoping for any hint of redemption, but when she doesn't react it's obvious to me that she's avoiding looking in my direction. My gut sinks.

"Dax?"

"No thank you," Dax responds without moving his glance away from me.

Addison fumbles to get the moka pot open, cleaning it quickly, and looking seemingly deep in thought, until she breaks the silence—drawing my attention away from Dax. "About earlier," she clears her throat. "I was really rude. Sorry. Dax says you saved my life. It's just hard for me to understand." She peers at me from the corner of her eye as she sets the moka pot down and resumes preparing the coffee. I release a slow breath. At least she's talking to me.

I watch in silence as she moves around the kitchen. I

enjoy paying attention to details, specifically when they involve everyday rituals people take for granted. "I don't require an apology."

Addison finishes adding the sugar to her mixer and stands, waiting for the coffee to rise. "Yeah well, it just happened so . . . I didn't understand what was going on. But after I learned about everything, I shouldn't have treated you that way. I was in shock."

"In shock?" I ask. Of course I know what shock means, but I don't know how long it takes for a human to get out of shock.

Addison flicks her eyes up at me. "Look, nothing like this has ever happened to me and I'm still shaking." The water starts to boil, and the smell of coffee lifts in the air. She moves swiftly to collect the first drops and sets it back down on the stove, lowering the temperature.

A smile quirks on my face as I admire how she moves, trying to remember if I have ever felt the sort of shock she describes. Her shirt moves snugly, hugging the lining of her breasts as she sets the moka pot down with one hand, and I dart my eyes away.

"The way you reacted was perfectly natural for someone of your nature, and I would have expected nothing less. Like I said before, you don't need to waste your breath apologizing."

Addison beats the sugar with her spoon. "Thanks, I guess I'm just reflecting—hang on. Someone of my nature? What do you mean?" She flicks her eyes back up at me. "You'd expect nothing less from someone of my nature?" She starts to beat the sugar even faster.

I glance at Dax, who lets out a chuckle. "Alright Spock, how are you getting yourself outta this one?"

Who is Spock? Why does Dax keep insinuating odd lies?

"I meant a, um, a person who had just undergone the traumatic experience of losing what they thought was a loved one. And then, of course, realizing the entire time spent with him was a manipulation. A lie. Deceptive—"

"Okay, I get it." She sets down two espresso cups and starts to pour.

"Smooth," Dax mutters.

"Do you have . . . sugar?" I ask, taking the cup from the table.

"Oh, this already has a lot of sugar."

I take my first sip and close my eyes, savoring the taste. "This is very good. It truly is delicious. Do you have more sugar?"

Addison screws up her face and a laugh comes from Dax. "You want more sugar? Seriously?"

I look into her eyes and notice a twinkle. If I had a heart, it would be melting. Her lips curl into a smile as she hands me the sugar jar. "You know, Cubans take a lot of pride in their coffee. Not sure how I feel about you adding more sugar to my art."

I take the teaspoon and add another spoonful of sugar to my coffee. I close my eyes and drink the rest.

"Sweet tooth much?"

I open my mouth to respond and catch a glimpse of Dax's jester grin in the background. I close my mouth, unsure how to respond to her. I presume having a sweet tooth does not actually imply my tooth tastes sweet. I wonder if there is a guidebook for these sorts of things. I don't respond and smile back at her, setting down my cup on the kitchen island and straightening my back.

"More sugar?" she chides.

"No thanks."

"Where are you from, Ambrose?" she asks, sipping her coffee.

I squint, ignoring Dax's death glare behind her. "I'm from out of town."

"You're not going to tell me where?"

"I'm from out of town," I repeat.

"Right, okay, more secrets. Guess I should just get used to it," she says. "So, what do we do from here?"

Dax brings his legs down from the table and stands up. "We work together."

"Fine by me," Addison says. "But do you mind if we start tomorrow? This is all too much for one day. I need a break." I soften my eyes at her and grin, showing my teeth. Her cheeks redden as my laugh catches her attention.

Dax's eyes burn into me as I say, "I'll be looking forward to it."

"BACK AGAIN"

ADDISON

I startle awake. My heart thuds as I sit up in bed, darting my eyes from side to side. The smell of bacon and pancakes fills the air. It takes me a few moments to remember where I am. For a split second, I think I'm back at my apartment and Ava is making breakfast in the kitchen. Just a few days ago, my life seemed normal. I had a roommate, I was looking for a job to start off my career, I lived a completely normal and stressful Miami life. Now, the stress is higher, but circumstances have completely changed—for the worse. It all seems so surreal.

I let out a deep breath and fall back onto my pillow. My eyes well up as my reality catches up to me.

Carl is dead.

And . . . he wasn't *real*? My throat clogs up and I press my eyes shut as tears start to well. I clutch my stomach with my hand.

My life with Carl was an illusion. All to keep me in the dark about Orlando? And the house? But why? Why me? Something doesn't add up. Even though I now know Carl wasn't a real person, which I am still having a hard time believing, the feeling of loss in the pit of my stomach refuses to go away. I bite my lip and wrap the covers over my head. I hesitated to answer him when he asked me to move in. Maybe deep down, I didn't love him because it all felt fake. Or maybe I just didn't feel anything deep for him because he lacked true substance. I probably only wanted it to work because it all seemed perfect. Too perfect, like Dax said. He was so right.

I'm so stupid. Dax noticed it was weird, how come I didn't?

I shake my head. I couldn't have known. He seemed normal, talked normal, related to me. Wow, he was good. Despite him trying to control my job choices, that is. Although, he should have known the more he argued with me, the more I would want to stay. What secret was he trying to keep me away from?

Oh my god, I've been having sex with a demon.

I can't believe it took me a whole day to realize it but I have been having sex with a real freaking demon. I think I'm gonna be sick. I sprint out of bed and book it to the toilet and vomit my guts out.

I climb back into bed and give myself another cry. *I had agreed to move in with him.*

And it was all a lie. All of it. The pretty words he spoke while he was in this bed. None of it was sincere.

The smell of breakfast and coffee festers, which makes my stomach grumble. Breakfast is probably Dax forcing me to not think of Carl. Damn him.

The idea of coffee right now brings my mind to Ambrose's eyes when he asked me for more sugar. A smile creeps on my lips and I kick my legs under the covers. The vision of Ambrose's cute dimples surfaces in my memory. The way he sips his coffee, the way he looks at me . . . so intrigued by my movement. I turn on my stomach, pressing my groin into the bed as I imagine him taking off his shirt . . .

Guilt rises up. I probably shouldn't be thinking of another man when my boyfriend was just killed. By him. Even though Carl wasn't a real person.

This is so confusing. Why should I feel guilty? Complicated is what this is. Ambrose is a blunt man, no arguing there, but something about him makes me feel safe. Could be the fact that he saw danger and went for it, and absolutely unapologetic about it. Dax is right though; he did save me. How did Ambrose know Carl was a demon though? Some social worker. Yeah right.

Raindrops hit the balcony windows as the soft morning sun shines through the mauve curtains and into the pink room. The touch of the heavy embroidered sheets brings me back to the present. I don't even remember falling back asleep, but I don't want to leave the warm bed. Heavy-hearted, I pick myself up and get myself ready. If anything, I'm hungry.

"You alright? Thought you were going to sleep all morning." Dax greets me in the kitchen with a full breakfast of scrambled eggs, bacon, and pancakes. "I hope you're hungry. Made some coffee for you too."

I take a few slow, incredulous steps into the kitchen. "Yeah, I kind of wanted to sleep all morning," I say sheepishly. "Between the stupendous amounts of Cuban coffee I consumed yesterday, and, well . . . you know." Dax seems a lot chirpier than usual, not to mention more relaxed. "I didn't know you could cook," I say.

He hides a smile. "I can cook. Come, take a seat."

I make my way to the chair and he scoots it in for me as I sit down.

"I just thought, well, with all that's been going on and how hard you've been working and looking after my dad, I would make you breakfast." He turns to bring me my plate.

"This is sweet of you. You didn't have to, but thanks." I take a bite of my eggs. "Mmm, this is great."

Dax hands me a mug of coffee. "Well, it's the least I could do."

I glance around the table and realize I'm the only one eating. The table is set for one despite there being two people in the room. "Sorry again if I kept you waiting, did you already eat?"

"Oh, I had coffee earlier. I'm not much of a breakfast person. You enjoy."

Not a breakfast person? Dax looks like he could put down two of these plates, but okay.

"So anyway, I thought maybe today, now that we are, well, better situated with the situation—" he stops himself.

I laugh. "Uh-huh, go on."

"Right. I thought we could maybe do some research in the library. Together."

I pour maple syrup over my pancakes and refrain from smirking. "Oh, you want to do research in the library *together*, do you?"

Dax sighs. "Addison, I am sorry about before. I should not have kept so many secrets from you. And I should not have gotten so mad at you."

That's what I wanted to hear. "No, it's okay. I understand.

Yes, of course, I think that's where we should start." I take a sip of my coffee. "Yum."

A grin spreads across Dax's face.

A tapping noise on the balcony windows makes me do a double take as Crowley, seeking shelter from the rain, is intent on breaking through the glass. Dax opens the balcony door.

"Are you going to let him in?"

"He comes in whenever he feels the need." The owl flies up to his shoulder, giving him a tiny screech.

"I still can't get over how he flies around in broad daylight," I say as I stick another piece of pancake in my mouth.

"Eastern screech owls are nocturnal, but Crowley is special indeed. He just does what he wants." Dax softly strokes the owl's feathers. Crowley rotates his head as he fixes his eyes on me. Rain trickles down from the leaves outside. The humid rain smell comes into the house and mixes with Dax's tobacco aroma and the smell of coffee. For a moment, I feel right at home.

We walk up to check on Orlando together and to give him his medicine before we set off on our research.

Dax takes a seat at the corner of his father's bed while I check his vitals. Orlando's breathing is steady and even. I glance over at Dax and give him a nod to let him know all is good with his father's health, so far. I'm taken aback at the way Dax's eyes are glossy, as if he's about to become teary-eyed staring at his dad. "Dax? You okay?"

"Addison, I–I wish I hadn't yelled at you yesterday. I

really am very sorry. I guess I just became overwhelmed with so much at stake and I thought by keeping you in the dark about who my father is, it would keep you here to care for him. And I thought I could keep you safe. But I was so wrong."

I walk over and place a hand on his shoulder. "It's okay, Dax. I get why you didn't tell me. I guess whatever your dad accidentally summoned here has Ambrose all worked up. At least he's around, right?"

Dax widens his eyes at me.

"With whatever he actually does for a living."

Dax chuckles. "Yeah, I guess I am kind of glad Ambrose is stalking the house, even though he is annoying as hell."

Annoying? More like hot.

Dax looks down at his dad, his eyes wet with remorse. "Jeez Pop, what did you do?" He sighs. "I can't bear to see him like this. Asleep all the time, incoherent, and loopy when he is awake. Nearly completely wiped of his memory.

"It seems like only yesterday that I was a small boy, bothering him while he was in his study, drawing out plans for another castle he wanted to build someday. Don't worry, Pop. I'm not leaving till you're fully recovered," he says.

My heart sinks to the pit of my stomach. "Shall we go?"

"Okay, so first things first. What are we looking for, exactly?" I reach over and turn on the lights inside the library.

"Clues about how to defeat a demon." Dax walks straight over to his dad's podium where the Goetia is.

"I didn't manage to find anything in that book, although I was skimming fast."

"Trying not to get caught?" Dax chuckles.

I ignore him. Does he know about the button in the book that opens the secret portal? "There's something I have to tell you. When I snuck in here, I found a secret portal."

"What do you mean? Like, to another dimension?"

"I don't know. It didn't start out like that. I thought I was going down some secret passageway, but then on the way back, I came back through some sort of portal."

"That makes no sense."

"I know. Which is why I wasn't even sure how to tell you. I didn't know how to put it into words. Crowley was there."

"Crowley?"

"Yeah, he brought me back through the portal. I thought it was some sort of demon, and Crowley had chased me into it, but I ended up right back here. It was strange, and icy cold, but I was still here. At the house, I mean. Like, outside on the dock."

"So, what, like a parallel universe?" Dax is still hovered over the book but looking right at me.

"I don't think so. Wouldn't Crowley have been a different Crowley? He recognized me and wanted me to come back. Oh, and your dad was there."

"My dad?"

I nod. "He was sitting with his legs hanging off the dock, and he was staring at the water till I approached him. It hadn't hit me yet that the place wasn't real. Or real, but different? I can't describe it properly."

"Sounds real. What did my dad do?"

"He pointed to a chest that had appeared. There was a book inside. This is where it gets even more interesting. I skimmed through the pages. There was a chapter about banishing demons and unwanted foes or something. And another one about getting rid of evil spirits. I think what we're looking for has to be in that book."

"You couldn't bring it with you?"

"Crowley got a hold of it and flew back into the portal. Maybe it's here somewhere. But where?" I scan the room.

Dax stands up. "Why would Crowley take the book?" We both move around the library, not knowing where the owl could have hidden it from us.

"When I got back, I was the only one in the room. Crowley wasn't here."

"I thought you said he came back with you?" Dax says as he takes books down from the shelves.

"Well, I don't exactly know how it works," I say. "He came through the black portal, but maybe he went a different direction?"

"So . . . the book could be anywhere."

I let out a loud sigh. "What's that bird done with it?"

"Wait a minute." Dax rubs his chin. "How did you come across this portal?"

I reach over to the Goetia and flip the pages to one side, revealing the switch at the end. "I flipped this switch, wondering what it would do. Then the door opened, and I walked through."

Dax stares blankly at the bookcase. He flips the switch.

"You didn't know it was there?" I ask him.

"I didn't. My dad designed this house with many trap doors and tricks. He kept his magick very secret though. Even from me."

A clicking noise sounds.

"Well? Shall we go in?" he urges.

I hesitate. "What if we can't get back? Last time that portal had shown up out of nowhere before I even went through the door."

"Maybe we can just walk back the way we came." He opens the bookcase wider, revealing the dark, cold room I had found myself roaming alone the day before. At least I won't be alone this time. I quickly hurry behind him.

"It's just completely dark. How did you get there from here?" Dax asks.

"To be honest, I was completely disoriented at first. I thought I was lost but I just kept walking and finally found myself outside. Or, the other outside . . ."

"But how do we know which way to walk? It's too dark."

"I really don't know. We should stay close."

"We should have grabbed a flashlight."

"It won't do any good here. I tried it last time. It just shined through endless darkness. I don't understand how all this is possible."

"Anything is possible, Addison."

We continue walking, striding carefully and close to each other through the pitch-black path. After a few moments, Dax breaks the silence again. "Addison?"

"I'm still here."

"You know your journal with your gardening notes on it?" His voice sounds far away.

"Hey, where are you going? I'm trying to catch up."

"I'm right here, Addison. It's okay."

"Yeah of course. What about the journal?"

"Well, I noticed different handwriting on the pages. Did you work on it with someone, or did it belong to someone before you?"

"That is random! Yes, I . . . it was left to me by some-one," I say, remembering a recent dream I had. "My mother, I think. But I wouldn't know because, well, I told you. I never met her. I've just always had it, I . . . Dax?" I spin around. "Dax." I squint into the darkness. What's going on? We had just been talking! "Dax? Where are you?" I shout.

A cool breeze blows through my hair and I'm tempted to walk further into the mist rising from the ground. I must be getting closer. Trying to force my eyes to focus, I miss my footing and trip over a ledge, falling to my knees with a hard thump.

I dust myself off and look behind me. I fell off a steep step leading into the backyard of the house. At least I can see again.

The sky is pink. The familiar haziness of the place tells me I'm no longer in my own dimension. The air is different here. Thinner. Lighter. I look around, trying to find my boss. Where did he go? Dax was right next to me a moment ago, or at least, I thought he was. How could he just disappear?

Something rattles the branches of the bushes just behind me. I spin around and catch a glimpse of a pair of shoes running on the garden trail. "Hey." I take a few steps toward them, then stop. Whatever it is, it disappears into the bushes.

Suddenly, a child zooms past me. "Hey, stop! Come back here."

Laughter erupts from behind the bushes. I stride over and jump into the bushes as I catch a glimpse of a kid wearing khaki shorts and tennis shoes. "Come back here." But the child disappears into the leaves. I shuffle around but find nothing.

"Addison."

"Dax? Is that you?" Wait no, that sounds more like Orlando. But . . . that can't be.

I run out of the bushes and stare in the direction the voice is coming from. "Hello?" It sounds like it is coming from behind the house, but there is no one in sight.

"Addison."

I creep to the side of the house and try peering through the ivy-covered windows but can't see a thing. I walk to the front and try opening the gate. Maybe Orlando is calling me from inside. The gate is locked. I turn around to go back. A child's laughter peels through the air, making my skin crawl.

"Argh, why must you do that?" I look behind me and gasp. It's the boy from the house. "You. How did you get in here? Why were you scaring me before?"

The kid looks up at me with a confused look on his face. Wait, he's wearing blue jeans. Not khaki shorts. "Is there another kid in here with you?" Of course he knows about this place. It's probably how he's always sneaking into the house! "Okay mister, you're coming with me." I reach for his hand. His skin is ice cold. "How long have you been here? You're freezing to death."

The boy shrugs.

"Alright, well, where's your friend? I'm taking you both back now." I skim the grounds with my eyes but can't see any sign of the other kid.

"Listen," I say. "I really need to find Orlando and Dax, so follow me, okay?" I peer down at the kid, but he is gone. I spin around quickly and look for him everywhere. "Kid, where did you go now?"

"Addison, where are you?" the voice asks.

I run closer to the sound and the silhouette of a man appears by the last steps near the dock. It is Orlando. I was right, that was Orlando's voice. But he sounds so . . . coherent. It can't be him. Can it?

"Orlando? Is that you?" I approach him slowly, trying not to scare him. The last time I was here he was sitting on the dock, dazed, staring out into the mangroves.

"Addison, don't run from me," Orlando's voice trills as if he's singing.

"I'm not. Orlando, I'm here." I reach him and stand right in front of him. "Orlando, I'm right here. Let me get you back, okay?"

His smile widens, and his eyes glaze over.

"Addison, why are you running?" He hovers a little, not looking directly at me, as if he is speaking to a small child.

". . . Orlando?"

His smile remains fixed as he talks. "Come on, it's time to come inside," he says.

Shivers run down my spine, and I take a few steps back. His gaze remains in the same direction even though I have moved away. I don't think this is Orlando. I make a dash for the back door. Maybe I can go back into the portal through the library in this dimension. I dart right past Orlando and try for the door.

"Oh, please be open, please be open." I twist the doorknob, but it is locked. "No." I spin around, hoping for the black portal to reappear. "Where is that owl when I need him?" I turn back to the door and shout, "Why can't you be open?"

As if hearing my command, the door opens on its own. I stare at it in hesitation. Why did it open like that? Should I really leave Orlando? What if it is him, and he's just stuck in some sort of loop? I look back at the old man—he hasn't moved a muscle. Suddenly, his head turns but his body stays still and blood oozes from his misty gaze.

"Addison where are you going?" he wails.

Shit. Definitely not Orlando. I bolt through the door like a bat out of hell. "Dax! Dax, are you here? Damnit, where the hell are you?" Up the stairs, snoring comes from Orlando's room. I stand at the steps and look up. Is it him this time? Things are so different in this world. Voices from the kitchen distract me. It sounds like women speaking in Spanish.

"*Y que vamos hacer, entonces?*"

"*No se, que problema tenemos.*"

I peek around the wall of the kitchen. An old lady wearing a long black dress with white polka dots stirs a big saucepan over the stove. She is speaking to a middle-aged woman with blonde hair who is sitting at the table.

"Excuse me?"

The ladies ignore me and keep chatting.

"*Permisso?*" I try again in Spanish, but nothing. I walk in and stand right in front of them. "Can't you see me?" They stare through me as if I'm not even here.

Screw it, it's no use. I better try finding Dax.

Growling comes from outside the kitchen. I creep to the edge of the hallway, and there, lurking in the shadows, is a large black hound with red eyes. Saliva drips from its sharp teeth as it snarls at me. It's a hellhound. Like the ones Marcelo talked about.

Before I can scream, it leaps toward me. I shut my eyes and throw a punch. Surprised at myself, I look down at my hand and then back at the hellhound.

Unphased, the dog jumps past me and into the kitchen where the two ladies are talking. It opens its long jaws and leaps onto the one standing over the stove, swallowing her in one mouthful.

My jaw drops as the beast devours the old lady. The hellhound licks its mouth and turns its gaze toward the middle-aged woman, who hasn't moved. I take a few steps closer and attempt to grab the woman, but she vanishes.

The beast turns its attention to me, lowering its head, preparing to pounce. I raise my hands in front of me and a hot burst of energy shoots from my palms, sending the hell-hound flying back into the shadows. It yelps and lands on its back, its legs flailing in the air, trying to regain control.

I hold out my palms. Well, this is new. I search the room for the hellhound but it seems to have disappeared.

"BACK OFF 'CUJO'"

ADDISON

The snoring continues.

Dancing flames burn bright in the fireplace beside me. I stand right where I had when the scorpion-like demon licked my face. There's no time to reminisce though. I need answers.

Holding my breath, I push the heavy sliding doors to the side and enter the library. I'm not quite ready to go back yet, but I wonder if this is where Crowley hid the book.

The Goetia is flipped open to a page with strange symbols. Next to one of the symbols, the name Paimon is highlighted. I remember reading about him before—he was a king. I run my fingers down the page and read on . . . "He giveth a good familiar, and can teach all arts and sciences, knows secrets of the universe." I keep reading and my eyes widen. If he is summoned, a great sacrifice would be made.

The book closes by itself and I gasp. A gust of wind blows in my face. Is this the demon we're dealing with? This is wrong. This king is all-knowing and powerful. Surely, a great demon wouldn't need to feed off an old man. Would it?

A low growl comes from right behind me. I turn to face

the hellhound that has reappeared. "Ready when you are, Cujo," I say.

The beast takes an unexpected turn and darts out of the room. I bolt out of the library doors after it.

In the far-right corner, a ghost is climbing up the stairs. The hellhound leaps into the air, mouth gaping open, and swallows it whole.

As it faces me again, a child's laughter comes from another room. The hellhound turns on its heel, twisting its ear toward the sound.

The kid comes running out of the family room behind the chimney but comes to a full stop upon sighting the hound. The hellhound licks his lips and lowers itself to the floor.

"Oh no, you don't!" I thrust my hands toward the hellhound, and a white light shoots from my palms. The hellhound leaps to the side, avoiding the beam of light.

When I turn around, the boy is gone. "What's going on?" I look back, and the hellhound is gone too. Did I scare it off?

I turn toward the stairs to go and check on Orlando. Another hellhound appears and heads for the bedrooms.

"You leave Orlando alone." I race up the stairs after it. When I reach the bedroom door, the hellhound is sitting calmly.

"What's wrong? Decide you're full?"

The snoring has come to an abrupt stop.

I furrow my eyebrows and inch the door open. Orlando isn't in bed. I open it wider and step inside. To my surprise, he was up and standing next to his bed, with his back facing me.

"Orlando? Is it really you?"

His head spins, a full one-eighty degrees. "Addison, you've come back." Nope! Not the real Orlando. I take a few steps forward. His lips spread out in a menacing grin and his chin dislocates, falling down toward his neck. I back up as darkness fills his eyes.

A large pincer protrudes from Orlando's back, attached to an arm and dripping a black liquid as it hovers over his head. His body contorts. Orlando's eyes bulge and his tongue hangs out of his mouth, lengthening in size like a snake's. It's aimed at me. His skin starts to crack, revealing red scar tissue underneath.

I try to will the power into my hands, but nothing happens. The demon reaches over and grabs me, squeezing tightly. Its nostrils flare as he inhales my essence. I scream, squiggling to get free.

How did I release that power before? I was afraid, and it just happened. Well, I'm scared shitless now and it still ain't happening! What do I do? Black droplets of goo drip on my head, falling down my brow. My vision becomes hazy.

I'm falling. I no longer know where I am, or who I am. A child's laughter echoes in my memories and an image of a man pops in my mind. Dax.

A warm feeling comes over my hands. I open my eyes and a blast of energy separates me from the demon; the entire room is filled with a blinding white light.

I blink my eyes open and Dax's stern, brooding face comes into view. "Ow." I rub my head.

"Hey, you," he says.

I slowly sit up; my eyes fixed on the bookcase. How did I get back to the library?

His eyes light up. "You're okay. You must have hit your

head hard. I carried you back as soon as I saw you on the ground in the hidden tunnel."

I blink my eyes a few times, adjusting to the light. "How long have I been out?"

"Not sure; I carried you back a few minutes ago I think."

"Wait, a few minutes? You carried me back from where? I've been gone for hours."

"Hours? Are you sure?"

"I'm sure of it. A lot has happened. I was practically stuck there . . . you have no idea—the things I saw," I say. I rub my cheeks with my palms. "Wait a minute, where did you go? We were walking together and talking . . . you had asked me about my herb notes, and then you were just . . . gone. I called out your name, I looked everywhere for you."

"The same happened to me, Addison. Your voice trailed off and then I couldn't find you. I called your name too, over and over again, but you were nowhere. So, I kept on walking, hoping we would meet but then I just ended up back where I started. Then I looked back and you were suddenly lying there on the floor, unconscious. I picked you up and brought you back here. It must have only been a few minutes from when I got back and saw you though. I wasn't even walking for that long. I just figured it was a giant loop."

I inch away from Dax as my head starts throbbing harder. I must have hit the floor hard. Dax's usual tobacco smell is a bit unwelcome at this point. "Time must work differently there."

"Where did you go?"

"I went back to where I was last time. It was here, or the back of the house but on the other side."

"I suppose the question, then, is where is the other side?"

"I think it's actually the astral plane, except we can go there physically through the portal."

"Well, maybe you can. I was led right back here."

"Yeah, that is strange. I wonder if maybe the portal is conscious, and chooses who can go through? Anyway, it was a trap."

Dax's eyes squint. "How do you mean?"

I take a deep breath. "The demon was disguised as your dad," I say, as I prop myself up. "It had led me to believe Orlando was in trouble. When I got to his room, your father transformed into a hideous creature. And it grabbed me. I felt myself falling. And then . . . something brought me back, but I can't make sense out of it . . ." I lower my eyes to the floor. How did a memory of Dax make me cast out that energy? I shrug. I guess it was a reminder I needed to get back.

"Holy shit."

"Yeah, it was an intense experience, to say the least. Oh, there's something else: I know it's the same demon I saw before because a scorpion pincer hangs over its head."

"A scorpion demon?"

My eyes flick upward. "Have you ever heard of that? A black liquid was dripping from the pincer."

"No, but scorpions have venom, so maybe that's what's keeping my dad in his state?"

"That would make sense." I smacked my face and Dax stares at me, eyes narrowed. Gross. The goo dripped on my face. I gasp. Would it have taken my memories too? Something about Dax seems . . . off. But also . . . comforting. Familiar. It's like . . . I knew him from before all this.

But that can't be. Right?

"What else happened?" he asks, bringing my attention back.

"There were gigantic hounds running around eating ghosts."

"What?"

"Yes. I'm talking, huge, muscular, Doberman Pinscher type dogs but with glowing red eyes, and sharper teeth. And, they fucking fly! Devouring ghosts all over the house."

"Hellhounds," Dax says, his face turning even paler. "This day can't get any stranger."

"I think I deserve a pay raise," I say jokingly.

We both laugh.

"Glad you can keep a cool sense of humor. I don't think anyone else would have lasted this long."

Oh shit, the kid! "Dax. You know that boy? The one that comes around here to play on the dock?"

"Yeah, what about him?"

"Have you seen him? I saw him out there with another kid, a girl. I tried to save his friend, but I think a hellhound might have got him."

Dax's face falls. "Are you sure?"

"No . . . I found out something else while I was there. This is going to sound crazy but, well, it's the astral plane, right? And after everything, what the heck? I could somehow shoot energy out of my hands. I managed to do it to save him, but . . . I think I might have missed. I didn't actually see the boy get eaten, but when I looked neither the kid nor the beast was there."

Dax twists his face, but I continue before he can speak.

"Something else I noticed though. The first ghost I saw it eat . . . it didn't see me. There were these two ladies, an old one and a middle-aged one. I think they were mother and daughter. I tried to talk to them, but they didn't even look at me. I tried to warn them, but they couldn't hear me. And then a hellhound came out of nowhere and swallowed the older one whole. The younger woman disappeared into thin air." My eyes trail off to the side, trying to remember. "See, the difference is, the boy did see me. He communicated."

"So, you think maybe those other ghosts were reenactments or something?"

"Like trapped energy? Or real ghosts stuck in a loop?" I hadn't thought of that, but it makes sense for spirits who died traumatically to reenact the way they died over and over, like people who have PTSD often do in their mind . . . I wipe my face with my hand.

Dax relaxes his shoulders. "I think he might have run away somehow. I'm glad you're okay."

"I don't know if he ran away . . . I can't shake the feeling he's a ghost because he kept disappearing, but how would he be so physical in this world? Oh, maybe he has a twin!" Goosebumps ripple over my flesh, sending a shiver slithering down my spine. "Maybe that's who the kid is playing with all the time! His twin brother? And there was another kid there with him!"

Dax nods in agreement. "Yeah sure, that makes sense. So how exactly did you get away from the demon?"

"I managed to calm myself down and try to focus on getting out of there. It somehow worked. Not sure how, but I'm glad it did. Light shot out of my hands and blinded my vision. I think I actually might have killed it."

"Really?" Dax raises a brow and scrunches his face.

"Well, I couldn't find much about the demon. I can't find that book anywhere. However, the Goetia," I point to the book on the podium behind me, "was flipped open to a name I forgot to tell you I had seen before."

"Oh?"

I nod. "Paimon, but I don't know why because it seems far unlike the one I dealt with—the one feeding off your dad. We should go check on him. Maybe he's back to normal."

"Do you remember what page it was flipped to?" Dax says as he stands up and walks over to the Goetia.

"No, but I remember Paimon is number nine."

He starts flipping through the pages.

"It says he's some sort of king with many legions and is a grand teacher. Doesn't seem like this snarling creature at all," I say.

Dax closes the book. "No, it doesn't. I have another suspicion. Let's go check on my dad first."

We leave the library, but when we approach the hallway, snoring resonates through the open space.

"Maybe he just hasn't woken up yet? I mean, if I killed the demon, wouldn't he wake up?"

"I don't know." Dax opens the door and I follow closely behind him. The room is a few degrees colder in temperature than the rest of the house, as usual. I grip my arms.

"Pop?"

"Orlando?"

The snoring continues. He looks comfortable with his blanket up to his nose.

"It's almost time for his medicine," I say.

"Pop," Dax calls out his name a bit louder and Orlando shifts. He slowly opens his eyes.

"What? What happened?"

"Dad? Are you okay?" A hint of hope glistens in the corner of Dax's eye.

"Oh yeah, I'm fine. I was just dreaming . . . of you when you were a little kid." He yawns and rubs his eyes. "Oh, look who it is. Addison, how are you, *mi cielo*, my heaven?"

Dax beams with excitement. "Addison, you did it." He turns and shakes my shoulders and I laugh.

"Do you think you can get me some coconut water?" Orlando asks while fumbling with his collar.

We both laugh. "Sure, of course, I'll go out and get you some. Hey, that's an improvement, right?" I say, turning to Dax.

Orlando turns his back over and yawns. "Thank you, that's nice. I'm going back to sleep. I'm so tired."

What? But he's been asleep for weeks! I open my mouth to speak but Dax beats me to the punch. "You're going back to sleep, Pop? Haven't you slept enough?" Orlando is already getting himself comfortable inside his sheets.

"Dad," Dax's voice shakes.

If he could just stand up and stretch his legs ...

"What happened?" Orlando opens his eyes again. "Oh hello. And who is this?" His eyes falling back onto me.

This time, actual tears started to form at the corner of my eyes. "Addison . . ." I shift uncomfortably and clear my throat, shaking the sadness away. I reach for Dax's arm. "Come on, let him rest. We'll figure it out." Dax slowly moves out of the room.

"Goodnight Pop, I love you."

We walk out of the room and close the door behind us.

"I guess I didn't kill the demon. I'm sorry."

"As you said, we will figure this out." Dax has that brooding look on his face, like he is contemplating something.

Maybe I'm not strong enough to kill the demon with my power. Perhaps I need to practice a little more in order to hit the right spot next time. "What was your theory you wanted to tell me?"

Dax pauses for a moment, leaving me in suspense. We walk all the way down to the first floor, and just as I grab my keys to go out to buy Orlando some coconut water, he finally speaks.

"You know the Goetia in the library?"

"Yeah."

"From flipping through my dad's grimoire, I think he did conjure a demon, but the wrong one came through."

"20 QUESTIONS"

ADDISON

I nearly rake the curb as I pull into the Ol Mangrove shopping center parking lot. Having been so preoccupied with the events happening at the house, I almost forgot I'm driving. Full-blown automatic pilot. I quickly pull into one of the unshaded parking spots at the further end of the lot. I don't feel like circling around to find the perfect shaded, and closest to the entrance, spot.

The wind carries the fallen leaves through the parking lot, burned from the hot Florida sun. Autumn in Florida means the leaves will fall, but the only color they change to is a tawny burned shade. Because, you know, they're burnt to death by the sun.

Cold air blows on my face as I step inside of a freezing cold Winn Dixie. As hot as Florida is, one would find themselves freezing inside of any given facility due to the extreme air conditioning. Why am I here again? Oh yeah, coconut water.

Minutes later, I leave with a bottle of coconut water, an Almond Joy, and a Coke. My skin defrosts as I walk out into the parking lot and grab my bottle of soda. As I twist the cap, something shiny catches my eye. Over to the left is a trendy coffee shop, and inside sit two familiar suits with shiny pins on their collars. I guess this is where they hang out to keep tabs on the house. I catch a glimpse at Ambrose's profile and butterflies start stirring in my stomach. Then the reflection of the sun catches on Deacon's red hair. I ignore the butterflies and head toward my blue bug. My phone vibrates.

Ambrose is calling.

Holy shit, did he see me looking at him? It's either a butterfly still trapped in my stomach or the gas from the Coke, but I can't resist a smile when I answer my phone.

"Care for a coffee?"

I pause. What do I say? Should I follow my butterflies and go to him? As much as I want to spend time with him, I should be getting back to Dax and Orlando. Joining him with Deacon there might be awkward. That woman hates me. "I wouldn't want to interrupt," I say. Ugh, now I sound like I'm fishing for him to insist.

"You're not interrupting. Deacon is just leaving."

My stomach flips. Maybe for a few minutes . . . "Why not?" I dump my Coke in the nearest trash can and head into Tiny Turtle's Tea Room. It's decorated with fake autumn leaves on the windowsills with two funny-looking jack o' lanterns that stay lit up until closing. The bells above the door sound off as I push it open and pass two young ladies who looked like they have swum their way from the bridge, conversing between themselves.

Being a small town so close to the beaches, dress codes aren't always enforced. In some establishments across the nation, one has to wear closed shoes and a shirt. Here in

Tavernier Key, anyone wearing flip flops and a bikini top or trunks can walk into a restaurant and be served crab legs with a side of fries.

I get caught behind a group of people waiting to be served, and I spot Ambrose sitting across from Deacon sitting at a table in the second row to the window. Too bad they don't know that in about thirty minutes, the lunch crew will leave this place barren for the rest of the day, just like every food joint in the Keys. Despite the chatter, I catch snippets of their conversation. Deacon fidgets with her jacket, draping it over the back of the chair.

"Take your coat off. You look ridiculous," Deacon says, tucking herself into her chair.

"I highly doubt anyone will suspect us of being who we are, Deacon. I hardly see the point of blending in."

"You're still drawing attention to us. Locals don't wear jackets in Florida."

"Hey look, it's the grim reaper dancing with a flamingo!" A fat kid at the far end of the cafe points to an overhead poster. He and his friends laugh at the image of a skeleton wearing a grim reaper outfit and sunglasses, grinning as he embraces a dancing flamingo.

I smile as I maneuver through the crowd and eye Ambrose raising an eyebrow at the poster. I approach the table and stop just as Deacon asks, "Are they making any progress in the house?"

"Slightly." Ambrose averts his attention from Deacon. My gaze locks with his piercing blue eyes.

Deacon turns her attention to me and purses her lips before standing up. "Heed my warning, Ambrose. I'm tired of this dump. Good day, Addison." She grabs her black suit coat and pushes past me.

"Hi," I say, feeling awkward to have stepped into their conversation. "Sorry, I didn't mean to interrupt."

"No, not at all. My cohort is never really satisfied, don't take it personally. Please, take a seat." Ambrose points to where Deacon had been sitting.

I take my seat and nervously pick up the menu. "I've never been here before. What's good?"

"Neither had I; I figured I'd try some more of the local coffee and, well, this place was in the vicinity." He curls his lip, lending me a boyish smirk I haven't seen on him before. I breathe in as he looks at me. For a moment time stops.

Boisterous laughter erupts from the kids near the poster and I snap myself out of it.

"You really like coffee huh?"

"Recently, yes. I had never had it before. It introduced some excitement."

"Excitement? Yeah, caffeine will do that to ya."

A lady with dyed red hair pulled back in a high ponytail approaches our table. A few loose strands of hair overlap her name tag, which reads "Cheyanne." A "Happy Halloween" pin is clipped onto her apron. "Hi, hun, can I get ya anythin'?"

I hand her the menu. "I'd love a vanilla latte and a slice of key lime pie please."

"Coming right up." She smiles before turning on her heels and walks toward the kitchen.

Ambrose's eyebrows crease upon his normally stoic face. "Key lime pie?"

I blush. "Oh, that's right, you're not from around here! The Florida Keys are famous for their key lime pies, you gotta try some."

"Sounds delightful."

I hide my urge to giggle and wander my eyes toward the poster.

"Listen, I wanted to tell you. Recently, it has been brought to my attention that I appear heartless and unsympathetic. I wanted to try and express to you how sorry I am about killing your boyfriend."

And just like that, I'm brought back to Earth. My eyes bulge as I dart my gaze around the restaurant to make sure no one can hear him. "Can we please not talk about Carl?"

Ambrose either doesn't hear me or ignores my plea. "I understand now that even though he wasn't truly your boyfriend, you had already formed an emotional connection—something which I am now beginning to understand exists."

"You don't have to keep apologiz—what do you mean 'beginning to understand'?"

The doorbell jingles as it opens, letting some people out.

Ambrose takes off his jacket and hangs it on his chair behind him, showcasing his arm and back muscles as he moves.

"And why do you wear a coat in South Florida?"

"Where I come from it is a requirement for the job, despite the temperature of whatever location I'm needed. And yes—also where I come from, emotions are taken out of the equation lest they create a conflict of interest."

"Sounds strict. Where are you from, exactly?"

Ambrose shrinks his head in his collar at the question. "I am not from this place."

"Okay, enough with the bullshit. You're a bad liar. Can we try the truth, please?"

Ambrose sits upright in his chair and squints at me. Across the room, laughter breaks out as people get up to leave. "Addison, I admit I have been lying to you. It is not a practice I am accustomed to. Where I come from—"

"What? Oh, come on, now you're going to tell me people don't lie where you come from?" I lend him a sly smile but his expression remains straight.

"It is not a practice known to our operatives."

I shake my head. "You just keep getting weirder and weirder." Cute, but weird.

"Have I said something wrong?"

"Lying is not a practice known to operatives? You sound as if your job is where you're from, or who you are."

"Well, it is."

"No, it isn't."

Ambrose curls one side of his lips up into a half smile. "Okay, Addison. Now I'm intrigued. Why is what I do not who I am?"

"Because what you do for a living is separate from who you are as a person."

"As a person?"

"Yes, as a person. Take our waitress for example." I point to behind me with my thumb. "She works here, serving people cakes and coffees, but when she goes home, she might be a painter, or singer, or be going to school to be a doctor, and she might have a cat."

"She can be all those things, huh?" he says, leaning into the table.

"Well, maybe she's going to school to be an astronaut."

Ambrose smiles. "Is that so?"

"Are you messing with me?"

He laughs. "I believe I do understand what you mean, Addison, but it is different for people like me and Deacon."

"Why?"

"Because we were created for the sole purpose of doing our jobs."

I stare into his crystal blue eyes, noting hints of silver specs in them.

The waitress comes back around with her hands full. "One latte and a key lime pie. And a top off for your coffee, sir?"

"Please."

I wait for the waitress to leave and push my key lime pie forward, offering it to Ambrose.

"I don't understand. What kind of social worker are you? Were you trained by the CIA for supernatural events or something?

"No, none of those things," he mumbles as he takes a bite of the pie from his spoon and scrunches his lips.

"Oh, I should have warned you. Key lime pie can be rather tart; some places make it a little sweeter, though."

He pushes my plate back to me and smiles. "Thank you. That was delightful."

I chuckle.

"Addison, I would love to tell you the truth of where I come from, but it's forbidden, a secret, and quite frankly," he smirks, "you wouldn't believe me."

"Try me. I promise I won't tell anyone."

Ambrose takes a sip of his coffee. "What I can tell you is, I might be able to help you defeat this demon."

I sigh. "Okay. Well, the more people to help the merrier I guess." I sip my latte and smirk. "You're FBI, aren't you?"

"No."

The ticking sound coming from the cuckoo clock above the chimney echoes in the main living room while I leave Orlando's' bedroom and wait for Dax. The sun is beginning to set, and he's disappeared again, as usual.

Where does he go? The last time I thought he left the house, he was hidden away in his room. I close Orlando's door behind me, carrying a tray in my hands. After all that, he didn't even remember asking me for coconut water. Didn't even look at it. After my whole mission on the other side, he hasn't even changed a bit, apart from those few seconds.

Think, think, think. If I wasn't strong enough to kill it, then what had made Orlando so alert? Maybe I had only knocked him out long enough to give Orlando a bit of his memory back, but not enough to restore him. Yeah, sounds about right.

I need to get stronger, but how? I don't know how to leave my body. And it's too dangerous to keep going through this portal. I don't even know how any of it works. Could there be a way to get myself stronger from out here? I reach the foot of the stairs and set the tray down on a table by the couch. I find one of Dax's lighters on the table and walk up to the chimney mantle, lighting the candles. No use in waiting for Dax to come back, I'll just have to do some research on my own. With a library full of magickal books, there's bound to be something in there to help me learn the basics.

My phone buzzes in my pocket. It's Ava.

"Girl, you won't even believe me when I tell you all the things that have happened since last I saw you," I say.

"And you're gonna have to save it for later. My grandfather called me on some urgent business saying you're in 'grave danger,' as he put it. You have to leave the house now," Ava says.

I clutch the phone as I skim through the books on the bookshelf. "Look, I can't leave. Too much is at stake here. I'm staying to help."

"Addison, you don't understand." Ava sounds erratic. "My grandfather . . . he had a vision; bad things are about to happen. You can't stay there, chica."

"Tell your grandfather thank you for worrying about me, but I won't abandon my friends. I have to go."

"IT'S BEEN NICE KNOWING YOU"

AMBROSE

The cool breeze coming from the portal closing behind me ruffles the back of my hair just as I step behind Deacon on the bridge. My insides are still radiating with electricity from having shared some time with Addison at the cafe. I know I shouldn't be feeling this way, but I can't suppress the permanent grin forcing itself on my face.

"I'm sorry I'm late," I say, not bothering to change back to skeletal form despite Deacon's resentment of it.

She cranes her neck over her shoulder. "Have fun on your little date?"

I quirk a brow and force a frown. "Date? What makes you say that?" I say, trying my best to sound neutral.

"Don't be coy with me, Ambrose," she spits. "I do not approve of you having had whatever that was with Addison over at the cafe. I am starting to believe you want to stay here because of her. Which, I do not have to remind you, is *against* the rules. The Judge gave us three days—it has been weeks! We're lucky the Judge hasn't come down to incinerate us already," she rambles while pacing back and forth on the bridge. "How are you developing feelings, anyway?" I pause to think for a second and she gapes. "You are, aren't you?"

I scrunch my facial muscles and sigh into my hand. "No, you don't understand. When I went to check on how things were progressing, she was going through . . . a difficult time processing some things that happened to her. She saw the demon."

Deacon spins around completely, now looking at me with her wide, hollowed eyes. "So, there is progress? Why haven't you told me?"

"I didn't think it was necessary; she is still coming into it. Soon, all will be revealed to her. I am certain her memories will come back and she can be left alone, and *safe*."

"Safe? I thought this was about collection. I knew it," she hisses. "You are after the demon."

"Knew it? First you accuse me of having feelings for Addison, now I'm just after the demon? Which is it, Deacon?"

"You could be after both."

I sigh again, louder this time. "Deacon, after all of our time working together, why do you still think I want to defy orders? Haven't you noticed the demon *is* still here? *It* has caused this mess. And the Judge has done nothing to take care of it. Have you ever once stopped to think why the Judge is the one in charge? Why he is in charge of cleaning up a demon's mess, yet none of us can get involved?"

"We have our roles; he takes care of the rest."

"So, where is he then? This isn't a matter of developing empathy, Deacon. Perhaps someone should take initiative when they can, like he once did."

Deacon scowls. "And what about Addison? Look me in the eye and tell me you were only finding out about her progress back there."

Now it's my turn to hesitate. I don't want to lie to her. But if I confess my love for Addison, it will kill me.

"I knew it," she hisses.

A blinding whitish blue light flashes in front of us and the Judge appears. His shadow towers over us as he steps onto the bridge.

"Knew what, Deacon?" he says as he closes up in front of her.

Deacon and I exchange glances. He must be furious to have teleported. Even though he's the only one with that power, he doesn't always use it. He was surely watching us through his scrying bowl and has come because we've taken longer than promised to collect the problem soul. That's enough reason to off us both. Let him find out about my feelings for Addison and . . .

"Nothing, Your Honor, I was simply telling Ambrose that *I knew* we were close to finishing this up. I know we have taken far longer than intended. I do apologize."

"Far longer you say. I gave you three days." The Judge's scythe gives off a bright glow as he aims it toward us. "I warned you both to be quick about this. I can't have any reapers going rogue." Pointing his scythe at Deacon, he pauses to look at her. "I had hoped you wouldn't disappoint me."

My legs quiver as Deacon bows her head, waiting for the Judge to incinerate her. I almost can't believe it. I knew he didn't hold an ounce of empathy in his bones, but why spend so much time training Deacon if he won't give her the time of day to explain herself? A storm of confliction brews in my core as I battle the purpose of reapers having no mercy. I need to stop him. But I can't imagine going up against the Judge. The synapses in my brain quicken as the gold from the scythe lets out a flash of light. It's now or never. "Wait!" I shout.

Both Deacon and the Judge stare back at me. The light from his scythe dims and I stammer.

"You better make this quick," the Judge spits. I've never seen him so angry.

"You can't obliterate Deacon. Won't you just settle for me? You've trained her for so long, it would be a waste to have to start all over, wouldn't it?"

"Save your manipulation, Ambrose. You are far more deranged than I anticipated. You both have spent enough time on Earth; it has started to change the both of you. Unfortunately, I cannot take any chances, for the sake of the other reapers."

I chuckle. "Please, it's not like we're contagious."

"That very same wit from you, Ambrose, proves my point. The order of the universe, with reapers alike, is out of bounds. I must fix this before it is irreparable.

"How about starting with that demon that escaped?" I say.

"Ambrose!" Deacon hisses. The Judge twists his face and he closes in on me.

"There are things at work here you are not comprehending. Let me make it clear to you. You have interfered *enough*. You have gotten in my way *enough*. And by you constantly taking it upon yourself to fix things, the demon Abyzou, whom you were meant to ignore, was used as a catalyst to transfer your scythe key to unlock the cage of an even bigger monster. The little demon haunting Paradise House is the least of our worries." He darts his eyes toward Deacon, whose mouth hangs open. "Get in and get out is what you both were meant to do."

"So the rumors are true . . ." Deacon's voice trails off.

The Judge slams the bottom of his scythe on the bridge and leans on it.

"Your Honor, if I may . . ."

The Judge's gaze falls to the ground, but he doesn't interrupt me.

"If this is truly all my fault, let me correct it. I will capture the demon and retrieve the soul. But please let Deacon go."

Dead silence fills the air and neither one of us moves a muscle while the Judge contemplates, staring out over the bridge, into the abyss of lost souls. "Ambrose, this is your only chance. If you correct this, you will have my mercy. But if you do not . . . both you and Deacon will not get a chance to speak the next time I see you." He turns his head to each of us and we both agree. His cloak flows behind him as a portal opens up to the swing of his scythe. Before leaving, he turns his attention back to us. "Never say a reaper shows no mercy after this." And he leaves.

We wait until he's fully gone and the portal closes behind him to relax our muscles.

"I truly thought we were both about to die," I flick my eyes to Deacon. She is panting, staring down at the gray stones of the bridge. "Are you alright?"

When she doesn't say anything, I move forward.

"Stay away from me," she spits.

"He gave us another chance, Deacon. What's the matter?" I've never seen her like this. She looks like she's just seen . . . Ah. I think I know. She looks like the way I felt when the Judge had threatened my existence back at the High Court. Before that, I had never thought about what it would be like to never exist. Like a human does. "Deacon, it's okay," I start. "I won't let him kill you."

"Shut up, Ambrose. I'm fine." She straightens herself up but struggles to hide the stricken expression on her face. "No more fooling around with Addison, do you hear me? In and out, you heard the Judge. Let's get a move on!"

"ESCAPING DEMONS"

ADDISON

First off, why the hell would anyone in their right mind want to conjure a demon? *My dad conjured a demon, but the wrong one came through.* I mean, seriously? If Dax is right, and that's really what happened, then we're fucked. Completely and utterly fucked. Where would we even start to send that thing back?

I keep myself busy by cleaning up the kitchen and putting away the plates and tray from Orlando's dinner. A set of heavy boots against the tile floor comes from behind me and I think it's Dax. "Finally," I say, spinning around. "Where have you been? I thought we were going to do research together." I pause at the pair of fierce eyes staring back at me. "Oh, uh . . . hello. I didn't realize you had a key."

Deacon's facial expression doesn't twitch as she slowly walks toward me, pushing me into a corner.

"It seems you and I have similar interests, and it is becoming a problem for me."

"Umm . . . similar interests? I don't understand what—"

"Don't interrupt. I have grown tired of waiting. Look into my eyes. They're tired of—"

"I can pour you a cup of coffee—"

"Shut up." Deacon takes out a scythe from her coat pocket and holds it up to my neck.

"Woah, back off!" This bitch is crazy! I move my arms up but Deacon pushes them down with unexpected strength. I hold my breath, trying to push back tears involuntarily forming at the corners of my eyes as she pushes the cold blade against my skin. My back presses against the wall. "What the fuck are you doing?" I say, clenching my stomach muscles, trying to remain strong.

"Listen closely, human. I need you out of my way. I want to go home and you're keeping me here."

I cock my head back, trying to lean away from the scythe. I relax my muscles and lift my hand up to the curved blade.

"That's all? You want to go home? You mean, you're not talking about Ambrose?"

"Yes, I *am* talking about Ambrose." Deacon inches down her scythe and my eyes follow. "He's my ticket out of here. He holds the key to get us both home. Whoever holds the key for the job calls the shots, and right now, that's Ambrose."

A sigh of relief escapes my lungs. I thought this was a jealousy thing.

"Okay . . . Can you put that thing away now?" A ball forms in my throat as I muster up the will to say the next lines. "There's nothing going on between me and Ambrose . . . he's just been helping Dax with Orlando. But you can both go home. Besides, why not just make a copy of the key?"

"It's not that kind of key." Deacon squints her eyes at me as she tucks her scythe inside her jacket and takes a few steps back. "Whatever is going on between you two needs to stop; it is unnatural. Consider this visit a warning."

"Nothing is happening between me and your boyfriend. You're lucky I'm not reaching to call the police."

I jerk my head back at her laughing at my mention of calling the police.

"I could disappear and leave you here looking like a crazed mental patient to be locked away, and then finally I'd be able to go home. I would welcome that phone call," Deacon says crisply. "And we don't have relationships. He is not my boyfriend."

My stomach drops. "You don't have relationships?" So, are they polyamorous? I try my best to keep a straight face. "Well, it doesn't matter anyway, because nothing is going on," I say, after clearing my throat.

Both our heads turn at the sound of heavy footsteps approaching the kitchen. My eyes light up as Ambrose barges in and I move to the side, away from Deacon.

"Deacon? Leave, *now*."

"I just swung by to have a little chat with Addison here."

"Conversation's over. Leave."

Deacon takes one long look at me and gives me a sly smile. "We were finished anyway." She makes her way slowly out of the kitchen, passing Ambrose. "Remember what I told you. Hurry it up."

Ambrose takes a menacing step closer to Deacon. "I said, leave."

"I want to go home," Deacon whispers, "and I will tell Headquarters about everything you're doing here." Ambrose visibly shuts his lips tight, holding back any last retorts.

"Time is ticking." Deacon spins on her heel and leaves the house.

"Did she hurt you?" he says, walking up to me. His eyes soften as he approaches, and I wish he would hug me. But I know that would be awkward and inappropriate.

Instead, I stretch my neck. "No, but she threatened me with a scythe. A *scythe*. Dramatic much? Who uses scythes, besides the grim reaper? Or a farmer?" Ambrose remains quiet. "Which reminds me. What's with the little scythe pins you both wear on your collars, huh?"

Ambrose lowers his head and scratches at his hair. "Addison, I—"

My heart flutters, sending a little bit of pain up my chest, causing me to rub it. This doesn't go unnoticed.

Ambrose takes a step forward, his icy blue eyes peering deep into mine. "Is there a problem with your chest, Addison?" My knees quiver at his gaze and I bring my arm down.

"No, I'm fine. It's probably just from the excitement." I ignore the fact that this has been happening a lot recently. "And fine, you want to keep hiding the truth, that's fine. You don't owe me anything. It doesn't really matter anyway. I have bigger issues than dealing with you and your girl-friend's secrets."

"Girlfriend?"

"Or ex-girlfriend, since you guys don't have relationships."

Ambrose sighs deeply. He looks as if he wants to tell me something. I don't know if I want to hear it. "Addison, there's —" The doorbell rings, saving him.

"Great, more visitors," I grunt. "Maybe this time it'll be someone wearing an hourglass, or a big fat man in a red suit."

Ambrose follows me down to the front door, silent until he finally asks: "Were you not expecting any visitors?"

"Nope. I only work here. I wouldn't be expecting anyone.

Maybe Dax is, but how would I know? He hasn't been home since yesterday."

"He is here, Addison."

"Who? Dax? No, he isn't."

"I am sure of it."

I eye him dubiously before looking out through the peephole of the front door. "Oh my God." Padrino! Crap— he came all this way because I wouldn't listen to Ava? I don't have time for pleasantries right now!

"Who is it?" Ambrose says.

I quickly hit the buzzer to open the gate. "My best friend's grandfather. He called her and said he was worried about me, but I told them not to fret." I unlock the front door and open it to let in an elderly man dressed from head to toe in white. "Padrino Marcelo, I'm so surprised to see you. Please, come in . . ."

Despite the grave message he left with Ava, Marcelo seems as cheerful as ever. "Ahhh, Padrino is fine *mi niña*. I couldn't stay away from someone who needs my help." He takes a long look at Ambrose. "It seems things here are much more serious than I thought."

"Well, let's go up and I can make you some coffee. I have to tell you though, my boss doesn't know—"

"Addison was expecting a visitor." Dax finishes my sentence from the entrance of the foyer.

I spin around in shock. "Where have you been?"

"I've been reflecting, in my room."

"Well, I could have used you earlier. And I stayed up reading . . . something I thought we were going to do together."

Dax frowns at me. "I'm sorry, Addison, I'll explain later."

Ambrose stands awkward and unmoving from the stairway. "Marcelo, is it? We have everything under control. It is in your best interest that you turn around and leave."

My mouth drops. "Ambrose!" I say. I know he is usually fairly blunt, but damn!

"Ambrose, it's okay, he has been worried about me missing in action back home. But not to worry, Marcelo," I say, turning toward him, "I live here and look after Orlando. Please, stay for coffee. Right, Dax?"

"Eh . . . right. Please stay for a coffee and you can see there's nothing to fear."

Marcelo's eyes are fixed on Ambrose, who stares right back at him.

Silence fills the foyer and my voice becomes shrill. "Right then, coffee!" I reach for Ambrose's arm and pull him up the stairs.

At the bottom step, I catch a glimpse of Marcelo leaning in close to Dax with his knowing smile and whispering, "I know who you are, but what are you doing *here*?"

I don't know whether to laugh or to roll my eyes. Does he do that to everyone?

But the look of shock on Dax's face catches me off guard.

"How—" Dax says, as I slowly take the next step.

"The question is, how will you make it right?" Marcelo interrupts him.

Dax stammers. "Believe me, I've been trying."

"I know, my friend, I know. That is why I am here. To try and help."

Ambrose is close behind me and it urges me to keep going. I wonder what that was about all the way to the kitchen.

I clean out the moka pot to make a fresh brew, while keeping my ears peeled at them talking at the table.

Ambrose opens his mouth and I cringe. A man like him should come with a warning.

"I heard you like to ask people what they're doing here," Ambrose starts. "But I'd like to turn the question over on you. What do you think you are doing here?"

I flick my gaze over my shoulder. Marcelo smiles at him. "I have given my life to helping others find their way."

"Is that so?" says Ambrose.

"Yes."

"So, do you find it rewarding to meddle with the natural cycle of life? Isn't that tampering with fate?" Ambrose asks him.

"No, I do not meddle with their choices, I only help them to realize they do have a choice."

"So, then what are you doing here?"

"*Ambrose*." I say, turning off the faucet. "What is up with you? Why can't you just accept that he's checking up on me? He's a very caring person."

At this, Marcelo responds to me with his usual cheerful laughter. "It is quite alright, Addison. I love to converse. I am not offended, do not worry about me."

I smile back and turn toward the stove to continue making the coffee, now with the table to the left of my peripherals. I can sense Dax is also growing impatient by the way he shifts in his chair and taps his foot.

Marcelo sits back and faces Ambrose with authority of his own. "When I see things becoming too risky in the unnatural, I intervene to make sure nobody living gets hurt. And while we are on the topic of intervening, why are you here?" He gives Ambrose one of his warm smiles, but in his case, I believe it is meant to taunt him.

"The same as you."

Marcelo scoffs.

Ambrose lowers his voice. "Forgive me for saying this, but some circumstances can't be helped, and you are power-less against them. This is why you must go."

"I will die trying. Like I said, I have given my life to helping others find their way." He glances over at Dax, who is now sitting with his legs crossed, unsure of what to say.

I set down four cups on the table and take a seat. "Your father is still sleeping. I gave him his medication, but nothing has changed," I say, changing the subject.

"Thank you, Addison, you're a great help." Dax turns to Marcelo, who is sipping his Cuban coffee.

"Oh Addison, this is perfection. *Gracias*. Nothing like a little *colada* after a long drive."

"So, how exactly do you plan on helping us?" Dax stares at his cup and raises it to his nose to smell the coffee.

"Yes, exactly how are you going to help? I have to get you up to speed. So much has happened since I last spoke to you," I say.

Dax shoots me a hard stare and Ambrose raises his brows. Shit, Dax is probably pissed off because I told people about what's going on in his house. But, I mean, he wasn't listening to me. What else was I supposed to do? I needed to get help. Besides, it's obvious just by looking at Marcello, all dressed in white with his Santeria beads, that he has way more experience with this stuff than I ever will. "Now I get why you're here," Dax adds, facing Marcelo.

I begin to spit out days of information while Marcelo listens intently. He nods, and when I'm finished, he leans in.

"First, I will rest. The drive made me very tired, despite this delicious *cafecito*. Then in a few hours I will begin my *ceremonia* to call down the powers of my *muertos* to help fight this demon." Marcelo turns to Dax. "And only then, after the demon is defeated, will your father be himself again, and everything will fall back into place."

I smirk at Ambrose rolling his eyes. It's the first time he ever does something actually normal.

Marcelo shoots him a stern stare. "And then *you* can go home."

"I urge you again to please turn back, now."

My hopes are smashed by Ambrose's obscure negativity. "I thought you wanted to help, Ambrose?"

"Addison, there's something I've been needing to tell you."

Dax bolts upright in his chair. "Addison, why don't you help Marcelo to a room where he can rest? Ambrose and I have some catching up to do." I do as he says and show Marcelo to the library.

As I walk out of the kitchen, I listen for their murmuring, knowing Dax rushed us out on purpose.

"Do you often eavesdrop?" Marcelo asks me with an open grin. I can't help but laugh at his question.

"Not usually, but lately I—"

"Find yourself wondering who to trust?" Marcelo's question hits the spot and I frown. I can still hear them chattering in the kitchen but can't make out everything they're saying.

Marcelo places his hand on my arm and urges me forward.

"You better be right about this," Ambrose says.

"After all, he sees right through you. How terrible of a magickian can he be?"

"I don't understand your implication."

Dax scoffs.

I hide a smile at Ambrose's inability to understand sarcasm, but wish I could have heard the rest of what they had said. "You can rest in the library. There's tons of spellbooks in here, but Dax knows you know this stuff. Otherwise, there are two extra bedrooms on the third floor, but that might be too much of a stretch for you."

"This is fine, I won't be here long," he says, plopping himself down on one of the library couches.

After the sun sets, Marcelo takes up the living room, in front of the chimney, preparing for the ceremony. Crowley perches himself on a house plant on the third floor —the door had been left open for him. I wave up at him as I walk in all dressed in white, as requested. I wonder if he senses what is about to happen.

"Dax, you are much too close to this situation. It is probably best you wait in another room." Marcelo says, giving him a wink. "Ambrose, if I fail, can you manage?"

Ambrose sighs deeply. "Yes."

That spins me around. "How can Ambrose manage?"

"Oh, never mind. Come here, girl. Dax, now you will go." Marcelo waves Dax away.

The three of us sit silently while Dax waits in his father's bedroom. Marcelo lights his cigar and inhales. He closes his eyes and begins chanting verses in another language. I try to relax as he does this and observe. His eyes roll to the back of his head and gray clouds fill the remaining whiteness. The lights flicker. I look over at Ambrose. He's sitting next to me, face serious.

"Don't worry," I whisper. "I've seen him do this before."

"This isn't what worries me. Stay alert."

The moment he says this, the lights go out and darkness engulfs the house.

"Marcelo? What's going on?" An impulse in me makes me want to grab hold of Ambrose. I fight it off for just a second, but then do it anyway. I reach for Ambrose's hand. His hand twitches as I catch him off guard. Uh oh . . . I shouldn't have. I start to pull my hand back, but he touches it and holds it instead. My breathing grows shallow as I feel his cold hand in mine, and for a second I'm glad the lights are out to hide my smile.

My eyes slowly adjust to the darkness of the room and Marcelo's eyes and features pop into view. Soft crackling noises come from Marcelo's throat. This snaps me back to reality and I tighten my grip on Ambrose's hand. "Oh my god, Marcelo . . . ?"

"I see him," Marcelo says. "He is here." The gray clouds in his eyes get darker as he opens his mouth to speak.

"Demon, answer me now. What do you want? Why have you come?"

I lean in, waiting for a response, but Ambrose nudges me to stay back.

"I want what everyone wants." His voice turns into a deep and unsettling echo; something is speaking through him.

"And what is that?" Marcelo asks.

At first there is silence. Marcelo's head snaps back and his face faces the ceiling, his body remaining in place.

"TO LIVE."

Marcelo handles the channeling well and speaks calmly. "You are causing much pain; you cannot live here. I ask you kindly to go."

"PAIN AND SUFFERING FUEL ME AND WHEN I AM FINISHED WITH ONE, I WILL EAT THE PAINS OF ANOTHER."

"The pains of another? It eats pain? That's what it's

doing to poor Orlando? And what it wanted to do to me?" I say. Marcelo holds his hand up to shut me up.

"Who are you? I demand to know your name."

"You do not demand me," it hisses.

"Tell me now, what is your name, demon?" Padrino tries again.

"I AM . . . OZO, and only my King commands me."

"Who is your King?" Padrino persists.

All the candles burst into flames. Marcelo is staring right at me. I pull away from Ambrose in shock.

"YOU INSUFFERABLE MORTAL. YOU WILL NOT DEFEAT ME. I WILL KILL YOU." Marcelo's face turns to peer into Ambrose's eyes. "AND YOU," he hisses, "REAPER OF THE NIGHT. YOU ARE POWERLESS AGAINST ME."

Marcelo's body collapses and he screams, his body twitching uncontrollably.

"Marcelo! Marcelo!" I turn to Ambrose, who is looking off to the distance, instead of Marcelo. "What do we do?" My stomach churns as the stench of rotting flesh fills my nostrils. I cup my nose and mouth with my hands and fight down my urge to gag.

"Ambrose, I need help." I dart my eyes over at the wall where Ambrose is staring at. Faceless demons, camouflaged by the wallpaper, emerge from the walls. And we're surrounded.

Dax dashes out of his father's room to see what is happening. He races down the stairs, but he suddenly stops in his tracks.

"Dax?" I yell.

Dax twists himself uncontrollably, but he doesn't lift a foot. I don't think he can move. He looks at me and opens his mouth, but no words come out. I start to move back into a wall as his eyes glaze over and his head becomes fixed in place.

The creatures continue to pour in from all sides of the living room. Crowley swoops down, talons forward, ready to attack.

"Crowley, *no,*" I scream, fearing for the bird's life.

Ambrose draws out his scythe. A powerful stream of energy flows through his hands and into the blade, turning it a bright blue color. He swings wildly as the creatures attempt to swarm him.

What the fucking shit! He has *powers*? Are you freaking kidding me? I stumble back, not knowing what to do. Ozo called him a reaper . . . but how is that possible?

I try to ignore what I just saw and bring my focus to my own powers. There will be time for him to explain later. Right now, I can't be powerless. I suppress my fear and try to focus my concentration on summoning my inner strength. If these creatures can inhabit the physical world, then hopefully so can my powers. I imagine power coursing through my body, just like it did on the other side. I force it to flow into my arms and through my fingertips as I thrust my arms forward.

Nothing happens.

I face my palms toward the creatures again. Some of them turn their bald, faceless heads to me, inching themselves closer. My pulse quickens and I lose sight of Ambrose. Spinning myself around looking for him, I find them coming from behind me as well. The demon's words repeat themselves in my mind: *I WILL KILL YOU.*

This is it.

In the distance, one of the creatures stretches out an arm and it transforms into a claw-like hand. It grabs Crowley as he attempts to swoop again, squeezing the owl tightly before throwing him hard against the bookcase. Tears roll down my face as I witness the lifeless bird fall to the ground. My eyes flick over to Dax, who is still immobilized at the front step. Pressure seizes me as I think about Orlando. Has the demon reached his room? Have the creatures gotten to him?

I try once more to summon my power, but nothing happens. I close my eyes and try again when one of them grabs me. I jolt upward, spinning myself around, trying to get away. I take one good look at the faceless thing; a seam splits at its center, showing rows of sharp teeth. I scream.

A bright blue glow blinds me as Ambrose swings through the creatures. I freeze as my demon's head comes straight off, the body dropping dryly on the floor. Ambrose is already moving on, cutting them down until the remaining few fear for their lives and retreat to the darkness, leaving me shaking with my arms at my sides and my heart pounding in my chest.

I run to Marcelo, who lies lifeless on the floor. "Oh no . . . I think he's . . ."

"Addison, step away from him now."

"What?"

"Step away from his body *now*," Ambrose demands while looking toward the ceiling.

The smell of rotting flesh fills the room again. I look up. A hideous, scorpion-like creature hangs from the ceiling. Pointed arms cover its body. I recognize his yellow eyes and pincer. He leaps down and clings on to the wall of the second floor.

Ambrose inches toward me, waving at me to get close to him.

Ozo twists his head toward me and leaps.

"MAGIC WITH A 'K'"

ADDISON

As I lunge to the right, Ambrose grabs me, pulling me into him and escaping the demon's clutches by a hair. "What do we do, Ambrose? Why does it want me dead?"

"Worry about that later. Addison, you are more powerful than you know. When he comes toward you, allow your fear to surface, and then focus your energy."

"I tried that already, it didn't work!" I say, panic rising in my voice. I walk backward, eyeing the demon. His claws scratch the surface of the wall and he glares at us, his long tongue dangling out.

"Yes, you do. You've done it before."

"That was *different.*"

My chest is about to burst. This is what I get for trying to be a hero. Why didn't I leave when I had the chance?

Ozo licks his lips. Before we can run, he leaps into the air. Ambrose, scythe in hand, is ready when he lands. He lifts the blade and with one single blow slices at the demon's hanging tongue. Ozo shrieks in laughter as black blood drips from the wound.

I gape as the blood dries and the tongue begins to reform in Ozo's mouth.

His head snaps toward Ambrose, yellow eyes narrowing. Ambrose moves back and lengthens his arm, swiping at the demon again. Ozo dodges and whips at the blade with his pincer, sending it flying across the room before lunging toward me.

This time, I give in to my fear, letting it freeze me in place. Ozo lands and pins me to the ground, saliva flowing from his mouth. I close my eyes and focus on moving the energy through my arms. My hands warm and soft, yellow lights flow from my palms. Yes! It's happening! I'm doing it. My lip trembles as the light dies and my breath catches in my throat.

Ambrose calls my name, but his voice becomes distant. The demon closes its large pincer around my neck, his venom dripping over my scrub shirt. I kick furiously. He is far too strong. The demon moves closer; his hot, rancid breath fills my nostrils and blurs my vision.

Darkness clouds my peripherals and I'm falling. My breath becomes shallow. I'm too weak to fight. The venom drips down my head and my insides seize with electricity. Pain overtakes me, and I let the darkness consume me.

When I open my eyes, all I see is a bright blue light. My lungs open as Ambrose leaps over to where his scythe had fallen, Ozo watching him every step of the way. The power I had summoned minutes before courses through my palms, releasing a blinding white light, sending Ozo flying from the room. I gasp for air.

Ambrose kneels beside me.

"Where did he go?" I ask. "I can't see where he landed!"

Dax, finally able to move again, collapses to the floor. "You blew him right out of the physical plane, Addison."

My heart skips a beat and I rub my chest, still feeling the remnants from the electric shocks. I dash over to Marcelo's side and press my ear to his chest, putting two fingers on his neck. "Oh no . . ." Tears roll down my face.

"He's alive." Ambrose walks toward me.

I wipe my face, trying to keep my voice from cracking. "He has no pulse. He's gone."

"No, believe me, Addison. It's the demon's venom." Ambrose bends down and lifts him up, carrying him like a baby. "This is why I told you to leave, you old fool." He walks toward my bedroom. "Is it okay if I put him in here for now?"

"Go ahead," I say, relieved he's not actually dead. Probably better for him to lie down on an actual bed than on a couch with a portal in the same room.

Ambrose sets him down comfortably on the bed and closes the door behind him.

All the candles go out all at once.

"Maybe this means the power is back on?" I hit one of the light switches, but nothing happens.

"Oh shit, Crowley!" I stammer, looking for the owl, but Dax's eyes already tell me he's found him. I walk over by the side of the spiral staircase and pick up the mass of feathers lying still on the ground. "Oh Dax, I'm so sorry . . . He was such a brave bird."

Dax's face drops and his cheeks redden. "Yes, he's been a good friend to me."

"You mean he *is* a brave bird," Ambrose says as he approaches us.

I furrow my eyebrows. "What do you mean?"

"Birds, I can help with." Ambrose takes out his scythe and moves the blade toward Crowley.

"No, what are you doing!" I reach out to stop him, but Dax interrupts me.

"It's okay, just watch."

The scythe glows blue and a once lifeless Crowley shakes his feathers and stands up before hopping onto Dax's arm.

I stare at Ambrose through the glowing curved blade. "Who *are* you?"

Ambrose curls his lips and winks. "Later. First, let's get out of here."

Ambrose leads the way down the stairs, using his scythe as a flashlight. When we get to the foot of the stairs, Dax tries the front door, but it doesn't budge. He tries to pry it open, using all his force, but it's stuck. "That's not good."

"I'll try the back door," I suggest, jogging over to the bar. I unlock the door and twist the doorknob. A shock of electricity snaps my fingers. Ouch; son of a bitch! I speed walk back to the foyer, shaking my hand. "The back door is locked too. We can try the doors leading out from the second floor. There's a staircase leading outside."

"Can you give it a go?" Dax says, turning to Ambrose.

Ambrose raises an eyebrow. "I'm afraid it won't work." He scans the walls with his eyes. "There are sigils everywhere made to keep me trapped." He grabs onto the door handle and it glows with an Enochian symbol.

"It'll be no use," Dax says, turning to me. "Demon's got us trapped."

"Yeah, I kind of figured," I say, shaking the electric shock from my hand. "So, now what?"

We walk over to the Venetian room in silence and sit on the couches, the soft glow from the moonlight through the clouds offers dim lighting, enough for us to see each other.

Dax sighs. "I suppose for now, at least until daylight, we

keep a close eye on my dad and Marcelo. Make sure their vitals are okay and nothing happens to them."

"True, we can keep watch in case that thing comes back. But how are we going to stop him?" I check my phone. I should tell Ava what happened. No signal. I set it on airplane mode to preserve the battery.

I glance at Ambrose, who is up and pacing around the room, staring at the walls.

There is definitely more than meets the eye about him. Magickal scythe, he can see Enochian sigils. Not to mention, dreamy.

Thunder roars from the outside.

"That's right, it's meant to storm tonight, isn't it?" Well, we can't just wait around down here all night. I stand up and Dax stares at me. "Right then, shall we go upstairs, light some candles in the library. and find out what we can do?"

Dax stands up. "I think you're onto something, Addison. It's time for you to learn some skills."

The cold air from the library makes my arms and legs shiver as I make my way around the room lighting the candles. Ambrose's eyes are on me. When I light the last candle, I turn to him. "I know you don't want to answer my questions but—"

"It's okay, we should talk." he says. From the corner of my eye, Dax shifts his head over from his armchair.

"For starters, who are you, really?"

"I am a reaper. I collect souls, but sometimes they are less than willing." He smirks at Dax, who purses his lips tightly.

His eyes fix on mine as the lights from the candles reflect on his face.

Air catches in my throat. A reaper? I mean . . . I guess that explains the scythe. And why he used it to kill . . . Carl. Who I now know was not a real human, and who I am trying to forget. I close my mouth, realizing I had it wide open.

"Addison? Are you alright?"

I struggle to find my words but nod a few times. "Mm hmm," I let out a cough. "Just trying to wrap my head around everything. But, after everything I've seen, I guess it only makes sense for reapers to be real too." I pause for a few moments, my eyes falling to the floor, and then look back up at him. "Are you here for Orlando?"

Ambrose pauses before answering. "Inevitably."

"Well, I guess we're stuck working together then."

A smile creeps on his face and he holds eye contact with me for a little longer. "Yes, well, our circumstances do bring us together."

I blush and lower my eyes, only to bring them back up again. "What about Deacon? Where does she fit into the situation?"

"Deacon is also a reaper. We normally work alone, but certain"—he pauses as if searching for the right words —"circumstances brought us to work together. Without my saying so, she cannot go back home. The longer we stay here, the more humanized we become, and she has strong aversions toward . . ."

"Humans?"

"I was going to say toward losing a part of herself."

"Oh."

"She feels my work has been unsatisfactory and I have become too close to my clients."

I eye him but remain silent. What does that mean? How close? And with all of his clients?

"Dax has asked that I give his father a chance at survival." He flicks his gaze over at Dax. "If we can save him, then I leave without taking him; if he dies, then he comes with me. Deacon feels I shouldn't care and should just close the case. But I refuse. At first, it was so I could spend time here and learn about . . . humanity . . . enjoy my time on Earth . . . but now it has become more than that."

I lean to my side. "How so?"

Ambrose flips up his hands. "Well, I've tried food, Cuban coffee, sugar, and met wonderful people." I feel myself reddening.

I pass my hand through my hair, suppressing a giggle, when Dax interrupts. "Addison, remember when you kept finding the name Paimon everywhere? In the Goetia and in the other spellbook you found in the other realm?"

I squint my eyes. "Are you thinking this is the demon we're dealing with?"

"Not exactly. What if my dad had tried to summon Paimon, but failed because another demon intervened?"

"Could that happen? I remember you mentioning another demon possibly getting through."

"Only to inexperienced sorcerers, which my dad is not. Unless . . ."

I walk over to the couch and take a seat, facing Dax's armchair. "Unless what?"

"Unless it happened because he was weak."

"Or the other demon was stronger," Ambrose suggests.

I tilt my head up at him. "This Paimon demon appears to be a king though. Surely that makes him more powerful, right? Ozo is strong, but . . . stronger than a demon king?"

"Ozo mentioned something about only his king commanding him. Do you remember?"

I gasp. "Shit, with everything that happened, I guess I must have blocked that out. You're right! He must be here following someone else's orders." I flick my gaze back at Dax. "Maybe Paimon wasn't as helpful as your father had hoped. Maybe he sent Ozo to attack him instead."

Dax broods. "No, something about that doesn't add up. Why would an all-powerful king send a scorpion demon here to feed off of Orlando when he can just take what he wants himself?"

The room quiets. I somehow allowed myself to get involved with all this, but I still want to save Orlando. I just need to shut my brain off about wanting to learn more about Ambrose.

Dax stands up and scans through pages of the Goetia again.

"But who is he?" Dax closes the book and rests his head in his hand.

"Paimon?" Ambrose enquires. "He's a king of the lower half of the astral plane. He's like a god to his legion. The demon outside is not he."

"No, but what's he got to do with my father is the question."

"Well, assuming he was actually conjured by Orlando, Paimon holds great knowledge of the universe and is able to teach the most forbidden of sorcery, that which defies nature." Ambrose paused for a moment in epiphany. "Dax, if someone wanted to bring back the dead, Paimon would be the one to conjure."

Dax falls silent.

I raise my eyebrows. "Holy shit, do you mean Orlando was trying to bring back the dead?" My eyes dart from

Ambrose to Dax, and back. "Who was he trying to bring back?" Ambrose's expression doesn't change as his eyes fall to Dax, who was holding his breath.

Then it hits me, and I gasp. "His wife!" That's so sweet! In a weird, necromantic way . . .

"That's my dad . . . the helpless romantic."

I sit back in my chair. I guess when you have that much power, what's to stop you from attempting the impossible?

Ambrose leans forward. "I think we now know what we have to do."

Dax holds out the Goetia. "Addison, how would you like to learn how to open portals?"

I narrow my eyes at them. "Are you crazy? What if something else comes through, and I only make everything worse?"

"Well, the idea is for you to open it, take command of the demon, and send it back. But for that, we need knowledge." Dax moves the book closer, placing it on my lap.

"What are you suggesting?" I ask.

"Hear me out. In order for you to learn how to take control of a demon and send it back through a portal, you will need to learn how to conjure. Taking control of this demon is not going to be easy. Wouldn't it be helpful to have a powerful king like Paimon on your side?"

I gulp. "Yeah, that makes sense. But, what about whoever commands Ozo?"

"We'll still need help from a demon king for that."

I nod.

"And we will be there with you every step of the way in case something goes wrong."

"Why can't one of you conjure him? Why does it have to be me?"

Ambrose softens his tone. "I am limited in what I can

and cannot do on Earth. My job is very specific and if I attempt to conjure a demon, it will lead to my permanent termination."

I swallow hard and then quirk an eyebrow at Dax. "How about you then, Dax Castillo, son of the great and powerful sorcerer Orlando Castillo?"

"Because I do not have my father's abilities, nor yours, as it seems."

"True," Ambrose cuts in. "It's time to put the power to good use."

I look down at my hands in the dim lighting of the library. "Why do I have this power? You hiring me wasn't a coincidence—was it?"

Dax stares at me.

"Was it? How did you know to call me? What do you know that I don't?"

Ambrose leans in toward Dax. "How are you going to get out of this one, Sherlock?"

Dax shoots him an angry glare. "Been watching my TV, have you? Oh, how fast they grow."

Ambrose scowls at him.

"Shut up, *both* of you. Answer my question."

Dax hesitates. "Addison, you've spoken very little of your parents. What was your father like?"

I cross my arms in front of me. "Why are you answering my question with a question? I told you already, they died when I was young."

"I think you and I both know that's not what happened. Amuse me. Think."

As thunder rumbles through the sky, I think hard of my childhood. I can't remember the last time I took a moment to reminisce. All I have is a garden notebook left to me by my mother . . . the beautiful blonde woman from my dream.

My pulse quickens and I dart my eyes from side to side. "I can't remember."

Dax sits back in his chair.

"Why can't I remember?" I sit back on the couch. "I always just thought something horrible must have happened, and my brain blocked it all out."

Dax falls silent again.

"Please, tell me what you know," I plead. "I can tell you know something about me I don't."

A loud, demonic shriek erupts from inside the family room, just outside of the library doors. "They're back. There's no time." Ambrose clutches his scythe.

"I have to go protect my dad, Addison. Stay here and practice. We don't have time to waste."

"Wait! What were you going to tell me?"

Dax opens his mouth to speak, but Ambrose grabs his arm. "Not now, we have to go."

Ambrose's scythe glows bright blue. "Addison, shut these doors and lock them."

"But what about you?"

"We don't have time; you stay here and learn how to open a portal. We'll manage."

"You'll manage? You could hardly manage last time!" But he was out the door.

"Just open a portal, they say. Like it'll be so easy! I have no idea what I'm doing!"

I grab the sliding mahogany doors and watch them leave, slamming them together as I catch glimpses of the faceless demons as they emerge from the walls.

I walk backwards until I slide back on the library couch, clutching the Goetia in my arms. The candle lights flicker on the walls and I close my eyes as shrieks and clashes echo from outside. My mind grows fuzzy. Every time I learn something new, my head gets bombarded with even more questions. Why can't I remember my parents? How did Dax know to find me? Is any of this real or am I going to somehow wake up in my old apartment from a long and terrible nightmare? I pinch myself. "Ouch." Nope, definitely awake.

I open the book and scan the pages.

Something crashing outside disturbs my concentration. I slap my hands over my ears, only moving them to flip through the book. I skim the pages on history and stop at one that reads, "Preliminary Definition of Magick."

"LOVE IS THE LAW"

AMBROSE

I nearly lose my footing as one of the faceless demons catches me off guard from behind. I swing my scythe around, hitting the necks of two unnatural beings in one blow, their heads coming right off. More of them surround me, and while my scythe is powerful, I am only one reaper. I spin on my heel, driving my scythe into a faceless creature's neck.

Nothing can kill me except dragon fire and the Judge's golden scythe. Even if I am gravely injured here and he sentences me to extinction, for the short time I stole away from the fabric of reaping, I have lived. So *what* if I become more human? I welcome it.

Addison's smile flashes in my mind. I could never abandon her after this. I won't leave until I know she is safe.

Another creature lunges toward me. I lose my footing and it falls with me as we land hard with a thud at the bottom of the stairs. I reach for my scythe, but something is wrong. It is no longer glowing. I grip it hard and concentrate my energy, but the weapon is dead.

I take the blade, without its power, and swing it to my

side. The faceless creature has already opened its hole for a mouth, showing its rows of teeth.

A high-pitched laugh shrieks from above. My powers have somehow been absorbed. I try to stand, but I cannot. Arching my head up, I catch a glimpse of the demon's red tongue and yellow eyes. How the hell does this demon have the power to absorb my scythe's energy?

Then, I think of Deacon. I promised her we could go home.

Now, as there is no way for her to make contact, she will most certainly return without me and report my actions.

Ozo drops down a flight of stairs and hangs over me. His yellow eyes glow, and I freeze . . .

"STRANGELOVE"

ADDISON

I focus on my breathing, releasing warm energy through my hands, as instructed by a book on meditation and raising energy. The Goetia says to raise a sufficient amount of energy in order to do a conjuring, which sends me down a rabbit hole of figuring out what it meant.

This is a complete waste of time. I open my eyes. How long has it been? More than an hour, surely! I listen out for the sounds of screeching or clashing, but the house is quiet.

I close the book and open the library doors. The living room is empty. As if nothing has happened at all. I walk over to the window and pull the curtain to the side. Dark clouds still lie overhead, with streaks of lightning bolts in the distance. A soft groan comes from the bottom of the stairs.

His voice strikes me like a punch to the gut. "Ambrose?" I say. "Is that you?"

"Addison!" he gurgles.

"Oh my god, I knew I should have been here." I sprint down the stairs to him.

"No, no Addison. I'm glad you weren't. My scythe . . . it's dead." I drop down on the floor next to him.

"What do you mean, it's dead?"

"It's stopped working. There's more," he says, struggling to sit up. "My power has been drained. I'm completely defenseless now."

"What does this mean?"

"I'm not sure. But without my powers, I'm useless."

"Well, not useless. You're alive." I smile at him and his cheeks redden. Do reapers blush? How human are they? His deep blue eyes flick down, and then up, locking me in.

His eyes stop at my lips and stares. I forget to breathe.

"What do you see when you look into my eyes, Addison?"

My breath escapes me. What a question. ". . . It's like I can see the endless possibilities of the universe . . ." I laugh. "Wow, that was so cheesy." I cannot believe I just said that! "What do you see in mine?"

"Hope."

I bite my bottom lip. Ambrose nudges himself up with his elbows and inches closer to me.

I don't move.

I let him come closer to my face until our lips are almost touching.

I close my eyes and my pulse quickens. My lips part and I'm about to lean in when a familiar snoring breaks the silence. "Fuck!" I say as I jolt back. "*Dax.*"

Ambrose is out of breath as he sits back. "Yes, we need to check on Dax and Orlando."

"And Marcelo." I stand and lend him my hands.

He grips my hand and shakes his legs. "I'm okay. The demon's paralysis is starting to wear off. I underestimated his power. Demons cannot overpower reapers, but whatever is commanding Ozo must be enabling him to do so . . . somehow."

I help him stand. "So, reapers are more powerful than demons?"

"Normally. We usually just respect each other," he says as he straightens himself up. Wisps of his hair fall on his forehead and I wish for all of this to be over so we can be alone and undisturbed. He lightly squeezes my hand and smiles. "Things are quiet for now, but we don't know how long it will last. Let's go."

"Give me a second to grab Orlando's medicine." I jog over to the kitchen to get it and we make our way up to the top of the third floor. The usual, steady snoring of the sleeping sorcerer echoes through the open-space area. I creak open the door and find Dax sitting at the edge of the bed.

"We're fine," he says, holding onto his father's hand. "I've just been afraid to leave his side." Ambrose and I walk silently into the room. "It felt like only yesterday when he was standing up on the boat, cleaning the deck after a ride while mother worked on the garden. It pains me to see him so lifeless."

I lower my eyes to Orlando and nod. "Of course. Don't worry, Dax. We'll save your dad." I straighten my scrubs and remember the nasty venom that dripped on my shirt. I feel like gagging.

"I did learn a bit about channeling energy but Dax, there's no way I'm strong enough to channel enough to open a portal. It takes sorcerers years of practice to do something like this. I'm not going to be able to learn it all in one night, let alone in a few hours."

Dax sighs and squints his eyes at us. Ambrose touches my arm with his fingertips and my breath grows shallow again. I move just a smidge to refrain myself from falling in his arms. I clear my throat. "Now, one of the books I read did mention that a sorcerer normally likes to use a magical instrument, like a wand, or a staff to help channel large amounts of energy from the ground. I think this may be of use for a beginner like me to complete a ritual such as this . . . Would your dad have anything I could use?"

Dax smiles. "There is something he used to use long ago; a dagger, better known as an athame. Unfortunately, it's locked away in a safe in the first-floor doll room."

My nose wrinkles. "All the way down there?"

"The key is hiding in plain sight, right on the door, but be very careful. I think I should stay here with my dad."

"Ambrose will come with me," I say, quirking a brow at him.

"I wouldn't dream of letting you go down there by yourself." Ambrose has been standing alert by the door, occasionally glancing at me.

"Hurry back up. The sooner we get this started, the better."

I nod and we walk out of Orlando's bedroom, shutting the door behind us. "Let's check on Padrino first; that way, I can grab a change of clothes. I'm dying to get out of these demon-venom-splattered scrubs."

I open up my bedroom door and step inside with Ambrose close behind me. My eyes stop on Padrino Marcelo, whose chest is moving rhythmically up and down in a deep and peaceful sleep. I open a drawer to find a pair of clothes. Ambrose watches my every move. I might not get another chance to confront him about us, so I decide to just go for it.

"Are we going to talk about the elephant in the room?"

Ambrose tips his head, hesitating to respond, and then looks around the room, confused.

I let out a laugh. "It's an idiom. Never mind. I mean, we . . . almost kissed . . ." I blush and a nervous laugh escapes my throat. "I'm so stupid. We were just attacked by a demon and this is what I'm thinking about."

Ambrose can't hide a smile. "Yes, we almost died. Addison . . ." His voice trembles just a little and I can tell he's nervous. "I've never done this before. Reapers are not allowed to have relationships with humans. It is considered . . . unnatural."

My stomach flutters. So that's what Deacon meant! I let out a sigh of relief, but at the same time, my stomach drops.

"So, what do we do now?" I say.

Ambrose inches close to me. "I don't fully believe in the Reaper Council laws . . ."

"Oh? What are you suggesting?"

He takes a deep breath and brings me in closer. My groin tingles as I breathe him in. His soft lips brush against mine, only tickling the surface, and I part my lips. Something about being in my room with Ava's grandfather sleeping peacefully on my bed makes this weird. I take a step back. "Rule breaker," I giggle.

He lowers his head. "So it seems. But we can't do this now."

It takes everything in me to let go of him, my fingers touching the fabric of his coat. I turn to Padrino and put my hand on his forehead, then take his pulse.

"He's okay, Addison. Let's go."

"Just making sure," I whisper. I grab a pair of jeans and a black shirt and quickly change in the bathroom while Ambrose waits in my room. Can I really have a relationship with a reaper? How would it even be possible? Why does he have to be so damn sexy? I pull the shirt over my head, check my hair in the mirror, and pull back my brown waves into a ponytail.

I step out of the bathroom and meet his handsome gaze. "Ready?"

He nods.

I reach over and pull my bedroom door closed behind him. When I turn, I spot a blue and yellow beach ball bouncing on the floor, making its way to us from the piano room, behind the chimney. "That wasn't there before, was it?" Laughter erupts from around us, a child's voice.

"Who's there?"

"Addison, I don't think—"

The ball bounces and lands right in front of the stairs. A child runs out of the piano room after it.

It's the kid again!

"How'd you get in here? The doors are locked. Are they opening again?" I move to the child. Ambrose puts his hand on my arm, holding me back. The boy takes the ball and throws it down the stairs before looking back at me, giggling.

Then another voice calls out, a young girl, only a few years older than the boy. "Hey, stop playing ball in the house."

I jump back as the girl comes out of nowhere and runs after the ball. "I'm serious, you're gonna get hurt and then it'll be my fault."

I cup my mouth in my hands, recognizing the girl from the other dimension.

"Wait, *stop.*"

The kids stop and look straight at me. This time, I notice something is off . . . something about their pigment. Their skin is discolored—almost gray. The girl has short curly hair. Out of nowhere, it hits me. I recognize the little girl now. The room starts to spin, and my heart flutters. I reach for my chest and fall to my knees in pain and confusion.

The little girl is . . . me. As a little girl. "Wait. How could —" I look up to catch the kids running down the stairs.

"We're sorry," the boy yells as they both disappear.

My mouth gapes open and no words can come out.

Ambrose joins me on the cold floor and wraps his arms around me. I lean into him, my eyes welling up with tears. How is this possible? Was that me, or am I imagining it? "It's okay, it's okay," Ambrose says. "The demon is trying to get inside your head. Are you okay?"

Rubbing my chest, I dry my eyes with one hand and catch my breath. "Yeah, I'm fine." But I'm not. "You saw that, right? I didn't imagine it?"

"I did, yes. You didn't imagine it."

My eyes round as I sit back. "A–are they both ghosts?" I shake my head. "This isn't making any sense at all. How can they be ghosts? That little girl looks just like me and I know I'm not dead." Calm down, Addie. He's right. I take his hand and he helps me to my feet. "You're right. It's just the demon trying to confuse me."

Ambrose nods and wraps his arms around me as we stand at the top of the stairs. I wrap my arms around him and squeeze tight.

"I have a feeling the demon is going to keep trying to confuse you. You have to stay strong, okay? Let's go get the dagger."

We head down the stairs lit by the moonlight from the windows. It is dark, but light enough for us to notice a shadow waiting on the steps. I tread carefully.

"Stay close, and just keep walking."

"For a reaper, you sure know how to make someone feel safe."

"That's more of my job than you know."

As we approach the end of the steps, I force myself to avert my eyes, but the figure is far too close for comfort in the small space connecting the mid-level steps.

I can't help but to catch a glimpse of what now appears to be a tall man standing very still. The man is wearing a top hat and tails, and his skin is pasty, sickly even. His eyes are shut tight and he's holding his hands down in front of him. A faint smell of rotting flesh fills my nose. It takes me a moment to realize who this man is.

"Oh, it's Dax." As the man opens his dark, hollow eyes, his flesh begins to rot. He opens his mouth to say something, but nothing comes out. I jerk back into Ambrose and scream. I twist my body and run straight into the Venetian room. Ambrose follows and closes the door behind him.

"What was that, the future?" My voice shrieks at the end. Ambrose hugs me again as I weep into his chest. "This is just too much."

The silence is broken by the clashing sound of lightning hitting the house followed by droplets of rain falling on the terra-cotta tile.

Ambrose rubs my back. "I know, it's okay. We have just one more room. Do you think you can do that?" I nod and take a deep breath. I can do this. There's no other choice. We proceed into the doll room.

In darkness, the room seems even more ominous. A cold draft sweeps past my face as I reach to light the two candelabras on the long table and shivers run down my spine.

A tiny tapping sound runs across the room and I hold my breath, remembering Dax mentioning scorpions roaming free in here.

We search for the dagger, but the entire room is covered in shelves, from the floor to the ceiling with dolls, apart from two heavily decorated double doors at the end. "I don't see any closets in here. Could it be behind those doors?" I say.

Ambrose picks up a heavy set of brass keys, dangling on a giant key ring from one of the brass handles. He takes a key and tries it on the lock. Wrong one.

I walk over to help when movement in the corner of the doll room catches my attention. I quickly turn my head, expecting there to be a scorpion or a moving doll, but the figures stand motionless, staring out into the room. I try hard not to look over at the Phantom of the Opera collection by the unsettling portrait of Dax staring down at us.

I swallow hard. The nightmare with the musical monkey and the screeching garden gnome will haunt me for the rest of my life.

"None of these keys work." Ambrose turns over the brass key ring in his hand. I turn and inspect the door.

"They're false keys."

"What do you mean?"

"Look at the keyhole on the door." I reach over and grab the keys from him. "It's a modern lock, and these keys are old." I dangle the decorative keys with my fingers. My eyes flick up and I stare at him. He's no longer paying attention to me.

"What are you staring at?" I look back toward the room.

"Did you see that?" Ambrose asks.

"No, what?" I look again; a shadow is cast on the painting. Hands connect to a body posed like ballerina. "It's probably just from a doll." My voice cracks a little.

A soft tune starts playing as the shadow begins to turn on the wall.

My eyes find the doll that matches the shadow's pose. It is a musical, dancing porcelain mime doll, beautifully adorned with black, white, and gold Italian masquerade clothes. I take a few steps toward it, mesmerized by the music.

"What are you doing?"

"I think I remember something . . . but I can't put my finger on it. I just want to get a better look." I inch toward it as it moves to its song. "I think I had a doll like this when I was little. But . . . I can't. My memory is so fuzzy." I squint hard.

"Addison . . ."

Why can't I remember? Then, I catch a glimpse of another shadow; this time the silhouette is on the wall next to me. This doll is hanging on strings and has long, pointy shoes. It kicks its heels together and I look right up at the marionette with the large jester's grin, holding an accordion.

I gape at the musical mime and stumble backward. Black blood begins to seep from the mime's now hollowed eyes. I back into Ambrose, who is still standing by the double doors.

"Ambrose?" I say. "Look." Each doll's porcelain head turns toward us, and they do not look like they want to sit for a friendly tea party.

Marionettes of all kinds: porcelain dolls wearing frilly Victorian dresses, boy dolls dressed in fishermen outfits, Venetian plague doctors holding instruments, others holding sharp staffs and tools that can be used as weapons. They contort their faces and stretch toward us from their usual inanimate positions.

I gulp.

Their expressions screw up and they move in for their attack.

Ambrose quickly grabs onto the lapis lazuli hilt of a sword on the wall. The shadows on the walls grow bigger and bigger as the dolls close in on us.

"Don't underestimate them Addison . . . dolls are hollow shells. Demons can fill them with whatever they please."

My stomach churns. "Okay, Dax said the key is hiding in plain sight on the door!" I look at the fake keys in Ambrose's hand. I don't know what it is, but something tells me there's more to those keys than we think. "Let me see those," I say, grabbing them from him. Ambrose moves in front of me, blocking the dolls as I try to figure this out. I try bending each key, but they're made out of metal.

"Addison, hurry . . ."

My heart pounds as I inspect each key. It has to be one of these, what else could Dax have meant? One of the keys has a skull symbol. I take it and a rumble in my hands surfaces through my palms. Woah, what the hell was that? A reflective glow glosses over the key and I squint at it. I don't know how I know to do this, but I twist at the top of it and tug. The top of the key snaps and I pull out a smaller key. A key that would for sure fit in the door.

"I got it!"

A dozen dolls jump to the ground and run at me. I jump back as some sprout sharp teeth, while others hold their weapons. Ambrose swings the sword, but the dolls fall back and jump at him again. The replica sword's blade is dull and can only be used to push them away.

I quickly turn the key in the lock. A sound clicks before the door opens. Inside is an oriental-inspired room with a set of couches, and katanas hanging up on the walls.

"Addison, this isn't getting any better. Do you see it?"

I dart my eyes up and down the room. "No, I don't even know what it looks like."

"Look for a *dagger*."

"There's a *lot* of daggers and swords in here." As I make my way around, a shiny red hilt reflects and draws my attention. Up on a mantle, there is a beautifully crafted dagger with gold engravings and a solid ruby hilt. It glows as if it is calling to me.

"I found it." I grab it with one hand and join Ambrose. All the dolls stop to look at me. I take one step forward and they jump back.

I hold onto the hilt and point the dagger at them. "That's right. Stay *back*." Once again, they jump further away. Ambrose and I exchange a glance. I move my gaze to the dolls again, but this time I shout, "Immobilize." The dolls fall onto their backs, lifeless once again. I stare at the dagger's ruby hilt. How the hell did I know to do that? Any of it?

I drop my arms down and let out a deep breath.

"Addison, you did it!" Ambrose says.

"I couldn't have done it without you, Ambrose." With all the adrenaline, I can't contain myself any longer. I turn to Ambrose, grab his head, and bring him close to me. His lips are soft against mine, yet cold, but I warm them as I lick the inside of his lips. He squeezes my arms as he embraces me. And I thrust him closer. Then I let go.

My breath is heavy and so is his. I want him badly but a kiss will have to do, for now. I reach for his hand and he grabs it. "Okay, now we can go."

He chuckles and moves his hair from his eyes. "Come on, let's get out of here. Before something else happens."

We step over the dolls and make it back up to the room, making a quick pit stop in the library to pick up the Goetia. Dax opens the door, letting us in. "Was everything okay? What took so long?"

"We ran into trouble along the way." Ambrose takes off his coat and undoes the top buttons of his shirt. Dax gives him an odd look.

"I've never felt hot before . . . It appears losing my powers, and being here so long, well, your humanity is finally starting to catch up to me."

I wrinkle my forehead.

"Don't worry about me. You have things to do." He gives me a soft smile.

I shake my head. "What happens if you become mortal?"

Ambrose shakes his head too.

"His age will catch up with him, and it will mean the end," Dax mutters.

Blood drains from my face. "We have to hurry, then. I got the dagger."

As I go show him the weapon, Orlando's bedroom doors swing open. Lightning rips through the torrential rain. Dax freezes again.

"Oh no, Dax?" I run toward him.

"It's started again, Addison. He won't be able to move."

"Shit, *again*?" I turn toward the open doors and gasp as shadows emanate off the walls.

"I think it's much worse now . . ." He points to my hand. "I think Ozo's been after the dagger."

I look down at my hand and see that the dagger's ruby hilt is glowing. "This was his plan all along."

"YOU CAN'T HANDLE THE TRUTH"

ADDISON

"Dax? *Dax?*" I shake my boss's shoulders, attempting to snap him out of his frozen state.

Ambrose puts his hand on my shoulder, edging me away from him. "This will pass. He will be fine."

"But I don't understand . . . why does this keep happening to him?"

I allow Ambrose to pull me away and I shut the doors, locking them. "It's time to set everything up," he says.

I nod and take a deep breath, feeling a chill run down my spine as I turn and face the motionless man, frozen in time. Behind him, Orlando is in deep sleep, completely oblivious to the world around him. Sweat starts trickling down my face, and the room spins.

"Addison? Are you okay?"

"Umm . . . yeah. I'll be fine." I stumble over and open the Goetia along with Aleister Crowley's *Magick in Theory and Practice* to help me set up a corner of the floor as an altar. I try hard to fight off the anxiety, gripping the athame tightly in my right hand.

Okay, breathe Addison, I tell myself, closing my eyes to

block out the world around me. I focus on grounding myself and raising enough energy from the ground up. Steadying my breathing, I become deaf to the sounds around me. The power rises and then dissipates. Why won't it work!?

A rush of wind blows my hair over my face as the doors of the bedroom swing open again. I know Ambrose is capable of protecting me, so I continue to focus, ignoring all the noise. I concentrate my energy on the dagger, seeing its glowing hilt in my mind's eye, and intense pressure surges through my veins as its power courses through my body.

Outside of the bedroom, the third-floor balcony doors bang against the walls. I open an eye and see Ambrose running to lock them. Strong winds fight him as he struggles to close the doors against the storm, but I have to stay put. Something happened to break the barriers the demon had set up, but I don't know what. I haven't done anything yet.

He comes back inside and tries the light switch; still nothing.

"Addison, my scythe is calling to me. That must be Deacon. Did you break the barriers?"

I flick my gaze up at him and shake my head, breaking my concentration. "No, at least I don't think so—"

A sudden flash of light momentarily blinds us as it passes over the floor and walls.

"What the fuck was that?"

"The spell is broken."

"But how?"

Ambrose takes out his scythe and dashes out of the room, slamming the door behind him.

"Ambrose!" I yell. I budge to get up after him but stop. He can handle himself. I bring the Goetia closer to me and read what to do next. I maintain my focus and picture a portal opening in front of me.

The double doors break open again, but this time Ambrose isn't near. Something is happening out there, but I refuse to stop. A heavy gust of wind comes through, throwing the Goetia across the floor. It is time to improvise. I run over to the doors and lock them again.

Behind me, Dax intakes a giant gasp of air. "What the hell is going on?"

"Dax? You're back!" I run over to him, enveloping him in my arms. "I don't know what's going on. I've been trying to block everything out and complete the spell. I guess the demon's warding broke somehow."

Dax remains rigid. "Addison . . . I think it's time you know the truth."

I knit my eyebrows together as I glare up at his dark, saddened eyes. I almost don't notice him changing.

"I don't understand . . ."

"Please, let me talk. I should have told you earlier, but your memory was completely wiped, and I was afraid—"

"What are you trying to say?" I back up slowly.

"I was afraid that you wouldn't believe me, and you would have never stayed. You've been under some sort of forgetting spell this whole time, Addison . . ."

I back myself into a corner as he approaches me, his clothes changing into a black suit with a black top hat. His eyes are sunken, and his flesh begins to decompose to resemble the figure I met on the staircase.

"How can this be? W–why are you changing? What are you saying?"

Dax takes off his top hat and shifts his head to reveal a bleeding, splintered skull.

"A few months ago, I was in a motorcycle accident. I

didn't survive, Addison," His sunken eyes become heavy with sadness as he looks at me. Without a moment to think, I scream in alarm and run out through the double doors.

"Go *back*," Ambrose yells. Ozo's tongue hangs out of his fanged smile as he focuses on the reapers. Ambrose takes hold of his glowing scythe, facing the demon. Deacon had joined him and was fighting by his side.

"He's dead. Dax's *dead!*" I am shaking, hardly believing what I am yelling. I spin around and Dax grabs my arms and pushes me back into the room.

"What are you doing?"

"Stay inside. Let them handle it." Dax grabs me by the shoulder in a sorry attempt at calming me down. "Addison, I'm not going to hurt you. I need to tell you something so please, listen." He stares into my eyes as he takes a deep breath. "I'm your brother."

I try freeing myself from his grasp. "What? You're *crazy*."

"I know, I should have told you before. I—"

"No, you were right. I wouldn't have believed you," I say, struggling free from his grip.

Dax releases his hold and stares at me. "Addison, we don't have time for this right now. You will remember. I know you will."

I remain silent.

"Right now, I need you to focus so we can finish what we've started. Our father's life depends on it."

I blink rapidly as he speaks. "Our ... father ..."

"He attempted to summon Paimon to bring me and mother back from the dead. A scorpion demon intercepted and took your memory away. He sent you away, but I was brought back somehow. I needed your help, so I thought about how to bring you back here." Dax is talking rapidly now. "Then I remembered you had been studying to be a nurse. It wasn't hard to hunt you down after that."

"Shut up. I can't listen to any of this. None of this makes sense!"

"Only you could break the curse. You're magickal, like father. That's why Ozo wiped your memory. He wanted you out of his way."

I look hard at Dax. Then back to Orlando.

"Think about it, Addison. Why do you think you can't remember your parents? Where did your notebook come from? I thought, by bringing it up before, it would spark some memories, but it didn't."

I bring my hands up to my hair and squeeze. "I don't know why half of my life is missing from my brain, okay? No, I don't remember my parents but that doesn't mean . . ." I close my mouth and shut my eyes. I'm not buying into this. "My mind blocked it all out because of some trauma that must have happened . . ." I say.

"I know my death must have been traumatic for you, Addie. But please listen, I was brought back. But you were gone. I looked everywhere for you, but I couldn't leave the house. I was trapped here. Months passed and, with my father's memory gone, I did the best I could until I found you, Addison. And when I did, well, you were even given a different surname. A name I found familiar because I remembered you liked it when we were kids. Brooke."

When we were kids . . . The children, the boy and girl playing in the house! Something doesn't add up and I can't shake it. "I saw myself, as a little girl . . . playing with the neighbor's kid . . . I thought it was the demon messing with me . . . but . . . How is it that the kid can play with her? With me, as a child?"

Dax nods. "The venom from the demon does something

to Dad . . . It's like whatever he dreams up comes to life. His memories come out to play. I tried to pass it off as the neighbor's kid. I didn't know what else I could say . . ."

I stammer, trying to take this all in. None of this can be true. But the dream I had makes its way into my mind . . . When I was a little girl walking in the garden, *this* garden. And my incredible power. This whole time . . . the kid was a ghost? My brother? No. I don't believe it. But either way, this demon needs to be stopped. I inhale and say, "Okay, fine. Let's finish this."

"There's just one thing."

"What?"

"You have to do this properly, using Dad's altar up on the roof."

"Are you serious? There's a hurricane outside. The timing couldn't be any worse."

"I'll be there with you."

I open the doors and make a direct left to the upstairs balcony terrace. Heavy winds and rain whip across my face. To my left is a cast-iron, spiral staircase leading up the terraced rooftop. We climb the stairs, holding on to the railing, fighting against the wind threatening to pull us apart. Memories flash in my mind as I brave the harsh winds up toward the roof. How Dax would carefully avoid being out in the sunlight, I guess to hide his dead pale skin. How he would disappear for hours on end without leaving the house. Ambrose isn't here for Orlando. He is here for Dax.

We make it to the top of the stairs and up on the roof.

"Over there." Dax points toward the altar in the far-right corner.

We crouch to avoid the worst of the wind and slowly move toward the stone slab. I hold up the dagger, gripped tightly in my hand.

"That's your dagger, Addison. It's yours, Dad gave it to you on your eighteenth birthday."

I stare at the glowing ruby hilt, trying to remember. A realization snaps me from my daydream. "Shit, we left the Goetia. I was struggling to conjure the portal, but it was all we had. What should I do?" I look back toward the spiral staircase and a loud screech tears through the winds.

The owl appears, slowly inching forward as the wind tosses him around the sky, clutching a leather-bound book tightly in his talons.

"*Crowley*," we both exclaim.

"This is the book he flew away with in the astral plane."

"I am always happy to see you, my friend," Dax says. Crowley draws himself close to Dax's shoulder and drops the book.

I open its pages and begin to read quickly. This is the right book. I can feel its power. I shut my eyes and once again, the energy rises in me. This time, it does not fade. I raise my dagger and begin:

Ancient dwellers of the darkness beyond; veiled, misshapen, and unloved

I call upon you now and make you this offering

You malignant and grotesque

You cold of heart and pitiful of mind

Take this offering and torment not my rites.

Be banished from here all ye irreverent.

Gates of the Cloaked One be unblocked.

For my own will be true

Hail to the masters of dark and of light!

Hail to the perpetual beings who for eons have cast!

I promise thee that my will be honest and true

I call upon Sethos! O' hail Sethos! Rise and protect!

The house shakes. "Addison. *Keep going*," Dax shouts.

"I alone summon thee here, myself and no other." A large gust of wind pushes me off balance and I drop to the terrace. Crowley shrieks as Dax runs to help me stand.

"Where's the dagger? I dropped the dagger." We crawl along the roof, attempting to find it through the sheeting rain, when a shadow appears in front of me. I arch my neck, squinting through the rain.

I gasp. "How did you get up here?"

Orlando has miraculously made it out of bed and up the stairs. He holds the dagger in his hand and continues the conjuring. I get up from my knees and join him at the altar.

I conjure thee for the purpose of your highest power.

Hear me O great King Paimon, rise from your home; come forth from your journeys!

I call upon thee, ye Great King; bringer of hidden secrets, creator of visions, and reanimator of the deceased!

I welcome thee with ye mighty dromedary! Come and walk here among us!

Come in your most natural form; sagaciously and graceful.

O' Paimon, I do summon you here! I do call on you alone! Rise from your home; come forth from your journeys.

Come and aid me in my rite; I ask from you a trade;

Sever ye the shrouds of matter and the thresholds of form.

Unbar the gates and the passageways wherein the spirit shall walk.

I shall in return giveth unto ye my eternal servitude until unworthy you deem me be . . .

I summon you, Oh Paimon, mighty King of the West—honor me with your presence.

The house stills. The rain stops, and the sky clears. I open my eyes. "Did we open the portal?"

"Look, there." Dax points to a dromedary, a single-humped camel walking through the sky. At first, it is nearly translucent, but becomes more solid as it approaches. A tall man with an ornate crown and burnt orange cloak sits on its back. The features of his face are effeminate, but his eyes are a piercing blue. The more I stare, the more I become fixated.

"Once again I am summoned to your bloodline. Why?" Paimon's voice echoes. He looks down at Dax. "Wasn't it enough that I brought you back for your father?"

I clear my throat. I'm not sure how to address such a powerful demon. "It appears, your greatness, that after Orlando—"

Paimon interrupts and leers straight into my eyes. "You are cursed, child. Yes, I know what happened here." With one thud of his staff, a giant white light encompasses the rooftop.

The house rumbles. I crouch down to the floor, expecting the whole building to fall. Early morning clouds clear and a sense of calm descends on the rooftop.

Heavy footsteps come from the iron spiral staircase. Ambrose and Deacon reach the top and lock eyes with the demon god.

"I'll leave you two to clean up the rest of the mess," Paimon tells them.

"Ozo's gone," Ambrose says while helping me to my feet.

I rub my head. "Thanks to Paimon."

Deacon clears her throat.

"Yes, but also to your friend Ava and Deacon who broke the spell on the house so you could conjure."

My eyes widened. "Ava is here? Where is she?"

"She couldn't stay away," Deacon says. "She's downstairs tending to her grandfather."

I let out a sigh of relief.

"Wait." Ambrose steps forward and slowly moves me toward Paimon.

I hesitate. "Ambrose, what are you doing?"

"There is something you still need to do."

My forehead wrinkles as I look at Ambrose, confused, then quickly realize he is talking to Paimon.

Paimon grimaces at me as he glares, and I stare back into his eyes. As his stare intensifies, my legs weaken and my heart strikes me with a strong flutter; I drop to the ground. Ambrose catches my head.

Memories flood through my mind. My mother's smile . . . the garden . . . the house . . . my younger brother. I open my eyes and grip onto Ambrose's arm, lifting myself from the ground. "Dax. I . . ." My eyes sting, and tears start to drop down my cheeks. "I'm sorry I didn't believe you." I rub my chest hard.

My brother embraces me. "Don't say anything. None of it is your fault."

Ambrose places his hand on Dax's shoulder "It's time."

Dax slowly pulls away from me.

"Wait. Does he *have* to leave?"

Ambrose walks over to me and dries my eyes with his finger. "Yes, Addison. He cannot stay here."

"A–and what about us?"

Ambrose clears his throat. "Addison, your brother and I will never be truly gone. Our spirits will always be with you."

My mouth drops as I peer into his eyes. "But it's not the same . . . You know it's not."

His gentle smile makes me want to lash out and cry like a toddler, but I hold it in. "I finally got to experience humanity and what it feels like to love—and be loved. I have you to thank." He leans in and kisses me on my forehead.

Dax wraps his arms around his father. "This is not the end, Pop. I love you more than life."

Orlando's eyes are heavy. "I know, my son. I have missed you so much."

"Remember, you still have Addison. She loves you." Orlando holds his son tighter.

"Don't go conjuring anything else up after we've gone."

Orlando gives a soft laugh. "I promise I won't."

"This isn't the end," Dax repeats, smiling.

Deacon opens the portal and Ambrose takes hold of Dax's arm.

"*Wait*, please." I run to Dax, gripping him tightly around the waist. "I love you, brother."

"And I you, sister. Thank you for everything. One day, we'll meet again."

I loosen my grip and watch as they disappear into the bright light.

The smell of jasmine fills the air and butterflies appear from the light, fluttering into the shape of a person.

My heart stops. There, in the distance, is my mother, smiling at Dax as he greets her.

"*Mom*," I cry as I start running toward the portal.

"*Stop*," Paimon roars. Orlando runs to me, grabbing my arms so I can't go any further.

"Let me *go*. I want to speak to her."

"No child, you *cannot* enter." Orlando brings me closer, comforting me until my tears slow.

My breathing evens out. "What happens now?"

"Now you must close the portal when I leave so nothing else comes through," Paimon orders. "You, Addison, were strong enough to conjure me. The power of your bloodline courses through your veins. You have the ability to call upon me and any spirit gone who still lingers in the realms."

"Who still lingers? What do you mean by that? There are realms?" But the demon has already turned his dromedary around, vanishing, leaving behind a thin gray film of dust that falls to the ground.

My legs quiver. I reach toward my dad, who is struggling to keep his balance. "Are you okay?"

"I'm fine. Let's go."

I take hold of my dagger with my left hand, taking my father's hand in the other. With my memories back, I no longer need the spellbooks. Together we channel our energy through to the dagger and the red ruby on the hilt starts to glow. Moments later, the portal turns in on itself and disappears from sight.

I turn to my father, the man who minutes ago I thought was my patient. This is all so surreal. "I can't believe I ever forgot you," I say. "I'll never let a demon take my memories from me again. Dad, I want you to know I'll always be here to protect you."

Tears well up in my father's eyes as he looks at me. It takes everything in me to refrain from wailing in front of him, and just letting it all out. Seeing my father cry sends needles through my gut. I have to stay strong for him. All this was to bring my brother back. How could I blame him?

"There's something I need to tell you," he says while clutching my hands. I take a deep breath as he stammers a bit. "The demon didn't take your memory away, Addie."

I tilt my head to the side, confusion fuzzing my brain. "I don't understand. Who did?"

"I did. It was me."

I let go of his hands and take a step back. My eyes fall to the floor. "But why ... Why would you do that?"

"Please don't pull away. You have to understand. I knew I would be putting you in danger if you had been here. The only way I knew to keep you safe was by taking your memory away and sending you to a life I knew you would succeed in. To be a nurse, to follow your dreams."

My mind grows hazier by the moment and my arms started to shake. "Keep me safe?" I don't want to start an argument with him now, not after I just got him back. Got my life back. But I dated a demon in disguise, for Christ's sake! My father was being fed on by a scorpion demon!

"I never should have done it, Addie, I'm so sorry." The sorrow in his voice makes me look up at him. His eyes are full of regret with the fear of losing me over this. Pull it together, Addison. My father made a reckless decision to save Dax.

"My plan was to bring you back the moment your brother returned . . ."

I take a deep breath. "I know, Dad," I say, my voice shivering. "I love you. We'll talk about it later, okay?"

He rubs his eyes with one hands and inhales.

"Let's go inside," I say. We turn to leave when one final jolt comes from my chest. My surroundings cave in and all I see is black as my head hits the ground.

"ROMANCE MACABRE"

ADDISON

One . . . *two* . . . *three*. I hold my breath and shoot a pill into my mouth, following it closely by water. Forcing myself to swallow, I screw up my face, cupping my hand over my mouth. Taking a deep breath, I hold the other pill in my hand. "Come on, Addie, you're a nurse. You can do this." I never was good at swallowing pills. It probably comes from my fear of suffocation, although after having my neck gripped by a scorpion demon, and a hellhound, you'd think I'd be over it by now. I close my eyes and count once more, pushing the pill to the back of my tongue, hoping it will be easier to swallow. I twist a fistful of my nightgown as I fight the urge to gag. Tears sting my eyes, but I get the job done.

I let out a long sigh, trying to relieve the stress that had built since I found out about my heart condition. An arrhythmia. Quite common, but still to be taken seriously. I guess my heart fluttering all those times meant more than just love being in the air. The jolts of pain should have been a dead giveaway though.

And after I opened the portal to summon Paimon, I hit

the floor. My heart couldn't take it anymore. I was rushed to the hospital shortly after. And now here I am, young as hell and having to watch over my heart. Just like my mother had to.

For me, death is always around the corner. First my mom died, then my brother, and now I'm dating a freaking reaper. Go figure. And I'm not afraid of dying, I just never thought I'd have to worry about my own mortality at twenty-one.

I slip into my red nightgown and loosen my braids as I admire myself in front of the mirror. I caress the satin fabric of my gown in my fingertips when a man's voice startles me from behind.

"You look beautiful."

I turn and reach for my shawl. There he is, staring at me with heated intensity, as he always does.

"What are you doing here, Ambrose?" My arms shiver from the cool wind blowing from within the portal.

"I wanted to see you."

My cheeks flush red as he stands before me, draped in his usual black but for me, and only me, he is wearing his sexy grin.

"Is this my Christmas present?"

Ambrose quirks an eyebrow. "Christmas?"

I roll my eyes, letting out a soft chuckle. "Christmas, it's a holiday, and tomorrow is Christmas day . . ."

His eyes twinkle with a hint of mischief as he slants his smile. He extends his hand. "Come with me."

"What? Now? Where?"

"To spend some time together. On my job." He extends his hand further.

"Are you sure this is okay?"

"I never said it was or it wasn't. I simply don't care. Are *you* okay with it?"

I glance at his hand, curiosity coursing through me. Go with him to reap people? Sneaking around behind the Reaper Council's back? Sounds dangerous. A smirk creases on my lips. I'd be lying if I didn't wonder what happens after a person dies. How do they react to him? Is he kind to them? A twinkle gleams in the corner of his eye and my fears leave me. "I'll learn to be. If it means we can spend time together." Without giving it another thought, I place my hand in his and follow him through the black portal.

My lips freeze, but I don't care as long as he holds me close to him. In what seems like a blink of an eye, we are on the other side.

"Portals are strange. I expected there to be some sort of a tunnel, or a bridge even, but no," I say while clinging to his arm. "For a split second, it's freezing cold, but then, you hardly notice it opening again. It's like stepping through a doorway."

"There is a bridge in between, but only when I'm jumping from appointment to appointment. If I take you there, we'd get caught by the Reaper Council immediately."

We land and I let go of him for a second and rub my hands together. "Where are we?"

His hood now covers his face, but he lifts his finger up to his lips, motioning for me to be silent. I don't need to wait for my eyes to adjust to the light as the all too familiar beeping of monitors pierces my ears and a distinct smell of iodoform fills my nostrils. We are in a hospital room.

In the center of the room, an old man lies on a hospital bed, connected to monitors.

I grip onto his hand. "Is he . . . ?"

"Not yet."

But then it comes. The sound of the flat line rings in my ears, and even though I never knew the old man, tears choke my throat. Seeing a frail old man on his deathbed reminds me of my father's old age after having just been sick in bed, although I didn't know how close I was to losing him. My pulse quickens as I let go of Ambrose. "But wait—why is he all alone?"

"His only son died in a car crash at the age of twenty-four, and his wife died only a few years later. There is no one left but him."

"But the nurses?" I scan the room. "Where are the nurses? Can't you prolong it a little?"

"Time works differently for us right now. They will come. There is nothing I can do, Addison." I look up at his stern face and then back at the dying gentleman.

I tilt my head to Ambrose. "Can he see us?"

"Only if we want him to. I can make it so only he can see us, and no one else can. Perks of the job. What do you have in mind?"

I walk over to the man's side and take hold of his hand. Even though his eyes are closed, and his body is still, he grips my hand one more time, right before letting go. Nurses barge through the door moments after, but they can't see me. I hold on tightly for the last moments of his life.

"Addie?"

A tear rolls down my face and I glance up at Ambrose. Standing beside him is the old man. I glance back down at the body and let go of his hand.

"It's time to go," my angel of death says to me.

The old man opens his mouth to speak, his voice cracking, as if unsure of how to accept his fate. "What's next for me?"

"I can't tell you, but what I can say is this: you haven't even neared the end."

The old man smiles at death and looks at me. "Thank you for holding my hand during my final breaths. It meant a lot."

I wipe away my tears and nod. We both grip death's hands on either side and walk into the portal. For me, the portal is black, but for the man, Ambrose tells me it is white, illustrating the new beginnings awaiting him.

I look down and find us standing on a bridge and there is nothing but black that goes on for miles. "Ambrose? I thought you said we'd get caught?"

Ambrose holds my hand up to his lips and kisses it. "Are you okay?" he says, wiping away a tear.

I let out a nervous chuckle. "Yeah, I'll be fine. I'm sorry. I know this is part of your job, part of life, it was just . . . Watching him die made me think of my father."

"He won't die alone, Addie. Not like that."

"I know, it's not that. I guess death just has that effect." I swallow and flick my eyes up to him. "I mean, not you, death. Just . . ."

"I know what you mean. Do you want to keep going?"

"Yes, I do. I feel like me being there for him helped him a little. Like, I had a purpose or something."

Ambrose nods. "You did a good thing holding his hand in his final moments."

We step into a yellow nursery room with an old lady rocking a baby to sleep.

I look around. "So, where did the old man go?"

"That is not for you to know."

"But I—"

"Shhhh."

The creaking sound of the rocking chair moving back

and forth gets my attention. A baby girl of about a year old is being rocked back to sleep by her grandmother.

"Oh no . . . is the granny going to die holding the child? She'll drop her! Can I wake her up?"

"You won't be able to affect those who are not in their final moments, Addie. And, I am not here for the old woman."

My vision becomes cloudy and a surge of pain hits the pit of my stomach. I flash my eyes up at Ambrose. "What? No . . . you can't!"

His voice remains calm as he places one hand on my shoulder. "I don't take the lives, Addie—I just help them cross."

I move my shoulder away from his grasp and pull my shawl around me. I know he doesn't kill them, but he is the only one in the room I can be mad at. I walk closer to the baby and look down at her cute little button nose. She is sleeping peacefully, and her grandmother is soon to fall asleep with the baby in her arms. Tears well up in my eyes, but I fight them back. The poor grandmother is going to wake up and the baby is going to be dead. The parents will be horrified! "I can't do this," I gasp. "I can't handle your job."

"Go on, Addie, it's time."

"What?"

"You can pick up the baby now."

I lean in and pull the baby's spirit away from her grandmother's arms, leaving only a tiny, cold corpse behind. I cradle the little girl in my arms. "Why, Ambrose?"

"The baby was born with VACTERL association. It was only a matter of time."

Holding the baby close to my chest, I hold back my tears. I am familiar with the condition, where a baby is born with an upside-down heart. Some go on to live until their teens but rarely ever live until adulthood. Ambrose leans in and takes the child from my embrace. I look back at the grandmother, who is still rocking back and forth, still unaware of what has happened. I walk over and kiss her on the forehead. What lies ahead of her will devastate her final years and the lives of loved ones around her. But at least the baby went in loving arms. I take Ambrose's arm and walk in through the portal with him again.

I fight against asking where the baby will go, and instead decide to ask a different question. "How can you bear it?"

"What do you mean?"

"Collecting souls. You've said so yourself: you've been different since you spent time on Earth, since you've been with me. You feel more. So, how can you bear the grief?"

He hugs me from behind and kisses my head. "The pain lasts for a second compared to the rest of eternity. Death is not the end."

I gaze up at him with glossy eyes and he returns my torment with a soft smile.

This time I find myself in a crowded park. The smell of fried bread and sugar fills the air. There is music and laughter all around. The cold of the portal on my skin melts away under the heat of the sun.

"Oh, which fair is this? Are we done for your shift?" My eyes scan the many vendors selling leather goods, goblets, and jewelry.

"I'm afraid not, my sweet Addie. Just this last one, I promise."

Out in front of them is a heavy-set lady at a table beneath a purple tent. Her curly black hair shows beneath her headscarf and she shuffles her tarot cards while waiting for a customer to appear.

"Is she the one? But she looks fine," I say, eyeing the woman for any sign of illness.

Ambrose stands silent as he watches. The lady continues shuffling her cards, setting them down on occasion to rub her left arm. As she reaches for her water bottle under the table, she starts gasping for air. With each heavy breath, the lady lets out a harsh, forceful moan.

She grips onto the table to try to stand but it comes crashing down and her legs can't support her weight. She lands on the floor with a heavy thud. A few passers-by see what is happening and run to her aid. Someone gets on their phone to call an ambulance.

Without hesitation, I run over to the lady and lift her head. I remember Ambrose telling me I can only affect the dying. The lady looks up at me, red in the face, with tears streaming from her eyes. She tries to speak but foam protrudes from her mouth. It is a heart attack; in the medical sense, a myocardial infarction. I hold the lady's head tightly. My mother had gone the same way, and now here I am, with heart conditions of my own.

Ambrose walks up behind me and places a hand on my shoulder. My throat thickens as he lets go and bends down with his scythe, easing the lady's pain. The dead weight of her head lets me know she is gone, and I gently set her down. He takes me into his arms. "You did well." I smile weakly and he nudges for me turn around.

I crane my neck to find the lady standing behind me.

"Thank you," she says, before turning to Ambrose and asking where he was going to take her.

"All I can tell you is this is not the end." He gives her his warm smile and extends his hand. The lady softens her eyes, trusting Ambrose, and takes his hand in hers. I follow close behind.

"One more stop before I take you back." We land on a field of light gray grass covered in frost. Crystals hang like icicles from sage-colored trees nearby.

"Where are we?" I ask as a chill creeps back into my bones. Solemn clouds embrace the pinkish-gray skies. My breath mists in the air and he wraps his arms around me.

"We are in between planes." He bends down and picks up a flower I have never seen before. It looks similar to a rose but the petals are sheer.

"What? Did you think flowers only grew on Earth?" he chides, a giddy smile pasted on his face. "This one will last forever." He takes the flower in his hands and presses his palms tightly together. When he releases his grip, the rose has transformed into a small pendant. He reaches for his pocket and takes out a silver chain and clasps it together. "And it'll glow whenever I am near."

He tilts his face away from the moonlight, hiding his skeletal figure, only wanting to show me his face in the flesh.

I reach over and bring down his hood. "Don't hide. I can handle it."

My pulse is steady as his hand goes from bone to flesh while he reaches for me and pulls me close. He wraps his arms around my waist and while the moon gleams behind him, I can peer into his deep blue eyes once more. He curls his lip, giving me a sly smile, and lifts his arm to spin me around. I laugh and we dance, with my red shawl trailing behind me.

He leans his head down and my knees grow weak as his lips meet mine. Warmth washes over me and my toes curl, silencing all thoughts.

"So why me?" I say as I let myself get lost in his gaze.

"Why you, what?" he says, smirking.

"Out of all the girls on Earth, why did you decide you wanted to fall in love with just an ordinary nurse like me?"

Ambrose leans in and whispers in my ear. "Ordinary isn't the type of word I would use to describe you, Addison."

"One more thing," I say.

"Anything."

"As I grow old . . . you'll stay the same. Will you ever fall out of love with me?"

Ambrose lets out a chuckle. "No, never. Aging means nothing to me, Addison."

The world unfreezes as he gently pulls away and I nibble on his bottom lip once more. Holding me close, he whispers in my ear. "Until next time?"

My pulse quickens. "I don't want to let you go yet," I say, although I know the night has to end.

"Nights like these can last for us forever."

A soft chuckle escapes me. "I can't wait." And that's when I finally understand: death is only the beginning.

"THE REAPER'S APPRENTICE"

ADDISON

Christmas day.

I walk in from the kitchen carrying two mugs full of my dad's very own eggnog recipe with a shot of brandy and laugh as he sits on the couch working hard at unravelling a ball of Christmas lights. I set the mugs down on the table, away from Crowley who is perched up next to him, entertained by all the movement. I grab on to one piece of the knotted cables and shake my head.

"This is insane," I laugh.

My father laughs. "I know. Someone should invent an unravelling spell. Anyhow, I'm almost finished." He shakes them a little, releasing them to the ground and setting them aside to pick up his eggnog. "Addison, why don't you go and check the closet in the hall near your room. There are some more Christmas boxes your mother had stored there with a whole Christmas town that goes under the tree."

In the past two months since my memory was returned, I have been settling back in with my father and accepting the memories that slowly seep back into my mind as I wander through the old house or practice alchemy with my father in the library. I still travel to Miami to visit Ava, who has been spending more time with her grandfather. He is still in recovery and doing a lot better.

Oh yeah, and I managed to get a job in a local hospital nearby the house.

I smile to myself as I stare up at the boxes on the closet's high shelf. A draft flies past me, sending goosebumps erupting through my skin, and I shiver.

"I wondered when you were going to show up."

"I was just here last night."

I turn around to meet my reaper's eyes. I take a step toward him and he takes me in his arms, kissing me gently on the lips.

Ambrose gives me one of his side smiles. "It feels strange, not hearing Deacon's constant complaining. Not that I don't miss having her around." Ambrose rolls his eyes up to the ceiling.

I let out a loud giggle. "Oh, come on. She wasn't that bad."

Ambrose chuckles. "Anyway, I am enjoying having my freedom back and she has decided to keep quiet about our rule-breaking . . . for now." Ambrose kisses me on the forehead. "So, are you ready for your Christmas present?"

A smile creeps across my face. "You got me a present? *You* went shopping?"

"Not quite. But I did request a new student, and my application was granted."

My eyebrows knit together as my nose scrunches up. This time, Ambrose takes me by the hand. "Come on, let's go to the living room."

Holding his hand, I follow him, my eyes big and round. "Okay. Oh, and you're just in time for my dad's special eggnog."

"What's eggnog? Is it like coffee?" Ambrose widens his eyes, giving me a lopsided smile. I shake my head and laugh as we walk toward the hallway.

"Hello, sister."

My jaw drops and I turn to see Dax standing in the hallway beside the Christmas tree. I take off at full speed, slamming into his chest. Tears stream down my face as I hold onto him tightly.

Dax laughs, kissing the top of my head. "I've missed you too."

I wipe the tears from my eyes and then look at Ambrose. "How are you here? I thought I'd never see you again?"

Ambrose walks to Dax's side, placing a hand on his shoulder. "Meet my new apprentice reaper."

"Does this mean you're here to stay?" I ask, my eyes hopeful.

"Not quite," Dax says. He glances at Ambrose. "My presence here on Earth comes with certain . . . conditions. But let's not talk about that. For now, I'm here and we're all together." He reaches into his pocket and pulls out a butterfly ornament. "Addison, this is for you."

I take the ornament from my brother and examine the fine silver detail. As I turn it around and watch the fine details in the butterfly's wings glisten in the light, the scent of jasmine fills the air. I am overcome with a sense of calm.

Orlando leaves the Christmas lights and moves closer to examine the ornament. "Dax . . . is this from . . ."

"Yes," he says. "She is always with you. She loves you both, very much."

I clutch the butterfly to my chest and close my eyes. I see a family, a mother and father, a boy and a girl all playing together in a garden. They are happy. They are loved.

Ambrose places a hand on my shoulder and squeezes. I

place my hand over his and gaze up at him. "Thank you," I say as I let myself melt into his warm eyes. Wrinkles form at the corners of his eyes and he says, "I'll always do everything in my power to make you feel safe and loved."

I lean in for a kiss as he wraps his arms around me right in front of the tree. Dax clears his throat but we ignore him.

I quirk an eyebrow just as Ambrose lets go of me to reach into his coat. "Is something the matter?"

He lets out a sigh. "I regret that Dax and I must already be on our way."

My forehead wrinkles and I rub my arms. "So soon?"

"I'm afraid so. People die every second and we mustn't upset the Judge. Especially with our new recruit as my student." He flicks a smirk at Dax who is lending our dad a hug goodbye.

"When will I see you both again?" I ask while walking to my brother to give him a hug.

"Before we go, I'd like just a quick word with my sister," Dax says, to which Ambrose nods. He nudges me to the TV area in the next family room.

"Dax, is everything okay?"

Dax rubs the back of his head. "Addison, I didn't have time to tell you before all this but . . . I don't know how I feel about you dating a reaper."

"Oh . . . I don't know either, if I'm honest, but it kind of just happened. You know? What's the problem though?"

"Well, for starters he's kind of old for you . . . Don't you think?"

I let out a laugh. "I haven't asked him, but I'm assuming at least a few hundred years or so . . ."

He chuckles. "I think you could do better with someone your own age, Addison. "

"Why does it matter, anyway?" I say, letting out a scoff.

"Age is just a number, isn't it? I mean, he's immortal. It's not like we have to worry about the older one getting sick or dying . . . and me having to take care of him, ruining my youth on him, or all the reasons why social norms look down on it. In some cultures, anyway."

"Fine then, what about experience? Aren't you afraid of the things he's seen in his life? You have so much life to live, Addie. He is . . . literally death."

My brow arches to the top of my forehead. "What experience? He's like the little mermaid when she first got her legs. Have you seen him eat? It's as if he's tasting food for the first time." My blood boils. Leave it to my brother to be a killjoy. "So what if he's seen death? He has perspective. I bet you could learn a thing or two from him."

He scoffs. "Yeah, I'm basically being forced to."

My mouth drops open. "Are you two not getting along?" Oh no . . . What if Dax hates being a reaper?

"No, nothing like that. To be honest, I'm growing quite fond of him. This is about you. I just want to make sure this isn't going to blow up later."

"Dax, any relationship can blow up. I mean, remember my last one? Carl was a demon in disguise!"

He pauses to think. "Alright, then what about when you get old?

"What?"

"Attraction fades. You'll be old and he'll still look the same."

I gulp. "I already asked him. He says he doesn't care about aging." At least that's what he told me last night, but how much like us is he really? "Dax, I have to follow my heart. And I'd really like it if you were happy for me."

"Okay, Addie, if this is where your heart truly lies, I'll respect it."

Ambrose clears his throat from the living room.

Dax squeezes me tight and pats me on the head. "Be good, sis. Stay safe."

"Always," I say.

Ambrose opens up a portal in our living room, sending Crowley's feathers into a fritz as the cool wind chills the air. Dax steps through first, leaving Ambrose behind for one last goodbye. My dad shakes Ambrose's hand and walks over to the kitchen to give us some privacy. My eyes fall to the floor.

Ambrose moves in close and I can't help but wish things were different. That he didn't have to go. That he wasn't a reaper with an enormous duty to the order of the universe. But if that were true, I wouldn't have my brother back. So, I should be happy he is what he is. I raise my eyes to him and he gently touches my face with both hands.

"Don't be sad, Addison. You know already I can always visit you. And I promise to bring your brother often."

I smile back, showing my teeth. "I know," I say. "I guess I'm just afraid of unknown circumstances happening. Like if your Judge decides he made a mistake about my brother. Or if you can't come back for some reason. Anything can happen."

"Anything can happen here too, Addison. I need you to trust me, and just enjoy the moment you have here on Earth."

"I know, and I do. But it's not like I can call you or hop on a plane to visit you. You're literally going into another dimension."

He pulls my face closer to his and plants his soft lips on mine. "I'll be back soon, Addie. I promise."

I watch as he steps into the portal, looking back at me one last time. I wave as he disappears into the vast darkness of the astral plane.

The only suitable thing to do after they leave is to watch Charles Dicken's *A Christmas Carol* with my father. We used to watch it together as a family when Dax and I were kids. Despite my brother being dead, I think my dad is happy now knowing death isn't the end, and my brother can visit us.

A cold breeze swooshes past me and I blink my eyes open halfway through the movie. Shit, I fell asleep. Flicking my eyes over at my dad, I smile to myself seeing that he has fallen asleep too. I take a blanket that's folded on the chair next to the couch and drape it over him.

I turn off the TV and make my way through the living room when a whisper comes from behind me.

"Addison."

Goosebumps break the flesh of my arms as I rub them furiously, spinning myself around. There's nothing here. It's probably just my nerves again.

I switch on the light and spot a black rose on my bedside table along with a note. I walk over and pick it up. The petals are glass-like yet soft. A lot like those gray flowers in Ambrose's private quarters. A smile pastes on my face and my stomach flutters. How romantic of him.

I pick up the note to read it.

Dear Addison,

Someday soon someone will enter your life

Who will see all the dimensions combined

Knitted into your bones. And they will help you rise to power. Until then, you will truly not know what it's like to be loved.

Love,

A

I read the note a few times over. Someone soon will enter my life? That's strangely ominous for him to say to me . . . Love A?

Blood drains from my face and I can't help but to think this letter isn't from Ambrose. Who's A? Dread sinks down into my gut as my eyes fall back to the silky, glass petal rose. Whoever wrote this letter has to be watching me from the other side.

EPILOGUE

"Well done, Paimon. Addison successfully used her powers through the dagger and I am finally free to roam Earth. And Ozo, my pet, did exceptionally well."

"And my payment, my liege?"

"Soon, Paimon, soon. First, I need to become Emperor of LLAPS. And there's only one way I can do it."

"Addison needs to open the gates with her dagger."

"You mean *my* dagger."

"Yes, of course, Azazel. I knew that. All of the weapons of the Astral Dimensions were forged by you."

I give him a nod. "You're dismissed, Paimon."

From the akashic waters of the astral veil, I outline Addison's face with my gloved hand. A loved family indeed. "Oh, Addison, I cannot wait for us to meet."

Turn the page for a sneak peek of '**Lying with Demons**'.

"AMBUSH"

DAX

My life changed when I was brought back from the dead. They say you never appreciate what you have until it's gone. For some, it's their partner, for others, it's a parent or sibling. But for me, it was not being remembered by the people I love. A year ago, I would sit at the corner of my sick father's bed while my sister tended to him. The only problem was, my sister couldn't remember I was her brother, nor that the man she was hired to care for was her father. And my father couldn't remember that my sister was his daughter, or that I was dead.

I learned then that everything comes to pass. Nothing is permanent, and those you love will love you unconditionally even if they don't remember you. No matter the reason, in the end, it is the heart that remembers when your mind is fogged, or in my father's and sister's cases, a spell that had been cast upon them.

Today, I watch as others go through similar pains. I wait in hospital rooms, sometimes a bedroom, sometimes even the street, while someone meets their untimely death. I watch as loved ones cry over them until it's time for me to guide them away from the life they've always known. It sounds morbid, I know. And it is. But don't get me wrong. For the first time in my life, I feel like I am making a difference.

I follow closely behind Ambrose as he leads me through to the next portal and into a quiet nursing home. "After this one, we can go visit your sister."

I shoot him a sideways look and nod. "I could use the break." I haven't always been fond of the idea of Ambrose dating my sister, him being a reaper and all. What kind of life could they have together? Reapers aren't allowed to have relations with humans, and a life of secrecy isn't what I want for Addison. But, as time passes, I have come to realize that Addison can handle herself. "So, who do we have here?"

The man has tubes coming out of his nose and is connected to a machine. "Clany Rogers, eighty-seven years old. Remember to keep an eye on the scythe meter. His time is up in a few seconds."

I lower my eyes to the inner blade of my scythe. There is a thin meter that measures the amount of time left for each appointment. Not all scythes have this though. Since I am new, and have become a reaper through unordinary means according to the Judge, this scythe is meant to train me. Each scythe has a unique insignia for the reaper it was crafted for. No one knows the height of a scythe's magick, but its primary purpose is, of course, the reaping of souls.

My scythe gives a soft blue glow. It is time.

"Little by little, you'll get the hang of when it's time.

You'll just feel it, instead of waiting for your scythe to glow. You're up."

I move forward as the man's spirit sits up in bed.

"Who are you?" the man says.

"I am here to tell you there is no more pain. And to guide you out of this plane."

The old man looks down at his body as the machine next to him flat lines. A nearby nurse walks in silently. "I am ready. My wife is waiting for me."

"That's right, Clany. This is not the end."

Ambrose takes his scythe and opens a portal, leading the three of us through. I lead the man to the left, where I can see a young woman with shoulder-length hair wearing a red dress. The old man's wrinkles fade away as he transforms into a younger version of himself. He looks back at me and smiles. I nod and wave him off.

"Does that feeling ever get old?"

"What feeling?" Ambrose asks.

"The feeling of having accomplished something beautiful, in reuniting loved ones, and in easing the pain of someone's death."

Ambrose puts his hand on my shoulder. "I think you feel it differently than I do because you were once human, and I have always been a reaper. But no, it doesn't get old. Shall we?"

I tuck my scythe inside my jacket. "Ready when you are."

I take a step back to give Ambrose some room. We stand on the cold and dark bridge that was created by reapers to allow a gap for when they guide a recently deceased to their pathway.

Ambrose takes out his scythe and holds it out in front of him.

I quirk an eyebrow "Bit theatrical, don't you think?"

"Shhh." Ambrose waves at me to come closer.

"What's wrong?"

"My scythe isn't opening the portal."

A fog descends on the bridge. I take out my scythe. "Mine doesn't open portals yet. What do we do?"

"Something is wrong," Ambrose says. He chafes his chin and turns his scythe around in his hand, inspecting the blade. "I was given complete clearance; it can't be because of me."

"Well, what else has the power to shut down a reaper's scythe?"

"To my knowledge, nothing." He lowers his scythe and peers through the blackness. A flickering light coming from his scythe catches my eyes, except—it isn't blue.

"Ambrose?"

"What?"

"Look at your scythe."

Ambrose widens his eyes, peering down at his scythe as it flutters red. "Oh shit."

My eyebrow arches to the top of my head. I rarely ever hear Ambrose cuss. Something is definitely off.

"This has happened before but . . . I thought I fixed this." It flutters a few more times before the glow strengthens, burning his hands. Ambrose drops his scythe and a portal opens in front of us.

"Do we go in?" I ask.

"Watch out!" Ambrose yells as two figures take hold of my arms from behind. Still in shock, I quickly bend over, flipping one over his head. The second one clings onto me and bites my arm. I yell as pain surfaces down to my bones. Demons continue to pour from the abyss. Tall, pointy-eared creatures that resemble Anubis stand on their back legs, their glowing red eyes in dog-like faces staring back at us.

Sharp fangs overlap their lips, protruding along the length of their muzzles.

We're surrounded. I grip my scythe hard and swing at as many as I can before a hot sensation hits my palms. My scythe burns my hands as it too changes from a blue glow to red. I drop it and start swinging as hard as I can with my fists, but I can't take them all at once.

One of the figures, a larger hooded demon, reaches down and collects the two fallen scythes.

"Who are you?" I hear Ambrose say. No answer comes. Only heavy breathing from the creatures holding us both down. I watch in horror as the hooded demon uses Ambrose's scythe to cut him slowly from his throat down to his stomach. He cries out in pain as the demon then pushes him through the portal.

I jerk and kick as these creatures swarm around me. A hand wearing black gloves appears and holds the glowing red scythe up to my neck.

"Hmm, you're different."

"What do you want? Who are you?" my voice croaks before I too am dragged through another portal.

Demons kidnapped my boyfriend . . . and took him straight to hell.

Not exactly something I can file a police report for though, so into the fiery depths I go.

Except . . . apparently hell is a labyrinth now.

Perfect.

Prison guard? Check. Tortured souls? Check. Shadows lurking in the walls and demons waiting to attack around every corner? Check check and double-check.

When they said love could conquer all, I wonder if they counted damning myself to the underworld.

Available everywhere they sell books.

The Judge thinks imprisonment can subdue the Angel of Death. He's an expert at underestimation.

Unfortunately, my ticket to freedom is a screeching, child-stealing demon. Do I dare lull her into submission, just to help my betrayer of a father? Even if it means exposing my deepest, darkest secret?

Desperate times call for desperate measures.

Buy now

A MESSAGE FROM AMBROSE

FREE BOOK

Hello human,

This is Ambrose. This is my first time using one of these devices, so please bear with me. I'm typing fast before Deacon catches wind I'm reaching out to you. I fear there's more at stake here than meets the eye. I didn't want to tell Addison this, but Ozo wasn't fooling me.

"What's that Deacon?"

She's coming. I have to hurry. I fear there's a bigger plan at play. And after that letter signed "A," . . . something bad is coming. I don't have time to get into details but one way you can find out is by reading my story. Yes, I believe the author called it . . . Defying Dragons? No, that's not it. Defying Demons! That's it. All you have to do is join the virtual mailing list and download it for free.

And remember . . . This is the only way you'll be able to read my backstory about how I got into this mess, just don't let any demon get out of the pages! Good luck.

Get the prequel free when you sign up for Killian's mailing list at http://killianwolf.com/

ACKNOWLEDGMENTS

I'd like to thank Cuban coffee for not only giving me the jolt of energy I need to start writing every day, but for also inspiring my character to have a caffeine addiction as well.

First, to my husband, and my most cherished proofreader. Your patience and support in letting me follow my dreams has meant the world to me as we go on this author journey together. The many nights we spent on the couch while you read my work, helped me with edits, and sacrificed time together while I wrote another book does not go unappreciated. And after all that effort, I had to go unpublish them and rewrite the series. I love you to the Death Star and back.

To mom, thank you for inspiring me at such a young age to write and for introducing me to *Star Wars*. Thank you for continuing to proofread my work, even though I'm past thirty. When I was five years old, you handed me the novel *Jurassic Park* and encouraged me to read the entire thing, all 500 pages of it, with your help of course. From there, my expectations could only go higher. You not only got me interested in science, but science fiction and fantasy as well. Because of you, I knew that I could always follow my dreams, and I'll never stop.

To dad, thank you for your continuous support in everything I do. You taught me to practice what I'm not good at and to never give up. That little girl who was afraid to take a jump with her dirt bike made a different leap to become an author. Thank you for always being there for me. I know I can always rely on you.

To Abuelo, my sole inspiration for book one of this series. Thank you for your vast, detailed imagination and your love for wizardry. Your architectural designs, trapped doors, and hidden closets made me grow up in a world that not many others get a chance to see. I still remember sitting at the kitchen table with you while you helped me create my very first wand out of a branch. You inscribed runes on it and drilled a charm at the top. You forever inspired me to live a magickal life.

To my editor, Claerie Kavanaugh, where do I begin? You have done so much more for me than just edit my book. With each edit, you brought me invaluable lessons that I can apply to the next books and short stories I write. Not only was I lucky enough to meet an amazing editor, but a wonderful friend as well. Thank you. I couldn't have done it without you and I look forward to working with you for the rest of the series, and many more after that.

To Hunter Groupie and your endless support, critique, and general awesomeness. Having you as a friend and reader has made me feel like a real author. I can't wait until you publish your first novel so that I could return the favor and show you the support you have shown me.

To my Axen Club accountability partner, Josh Malina, thank you for your encouragement and helping me battle imposter syndrome. I keep my Axen Club notes by my laptop to remind myself of my goals and how far I've come.

To Summer Benito, you were the proofreader I needed when I didn't have one. Thank you for coming to my rescue and being there for me. You're a superhero and don't ever stop believing in yourself. I look forward to reading your story someday.

To Bianca Cagigal, no matter where in the world you go, I always think of you when trying to make a joke in my writing. Your wittiness and cleverness know no bounds and sometimes smack me right in the face, figuratively.

To Liz Kormesser, your continuous friendship and support has given me the stability I need to continue on my journey as an author.

To Ash the Silent, both your worldly and otherworldly wisdom speaks to me as a conscience on my shoulder. Your teachings of the runes, ogham, and Sabbatic philosophy has inspired me in many facets of this series and they will stay with me forever. Thank you for your love and support, and for always believing in me.

And finally, thank you all my readers. Without you, this wouldn't be possible. Thank you for taking the time to buy *Escaping Demons*. I hope you enjoyed the first book of Addison's story and want to continue on her journey with me.

THANK YOU!

Thank you for reading *Escaping Demons.* I hope you enjoyed Addison's adventure as much as I loved writing it. If you did, I would be grateful if you could leave a review on the site you bought it from. Reviews mean the world to authors.

If you would like to receive updates on all my new releases, please join my mailing list at http://killianwolf.com/. You will also get access to my books at a discounted launch price when they first come out, along with an exclusive sneak peek or short story just for you.

Get in Touch!

Please feel free to get in touch with me at:

http://killianwolf.com/

You can also join the party at my reapers and demons Facebook group:

https://www.facebook.com/groups/killianwolf

facebook.com/killianwolf22

twitter.com/killian_wolf22

instagram.com/killian_wolf

pinterest.com/killianwolf22

goodreads.com/killianwolf

bookbub.com/authors/killian-wolf

amazon.com/Killian-Wolf/e/B07WHFB8FW

Killian Wolf is a Miami, Florida, native who enjoys pirates, rum, and skulls as much as she loves writing about dark magick and sorcerers. She holds a Bachelor of Arts degree in Cultural Anthropology and Sociology and a Master of Science in Environmental Archaeology and Palaeoeconomy.

Killian writes books about obtaining magickal powers and stepping into other dimensions. She lives in England with her husband, a tornado of a cat, and the most timid snake you'd ever meet. When she isn't writing, you might find her at an archaeological dig, rock climbing, or sipping on dark spiced rum while working on a painting.

HOUSE PLANS

Paradise House

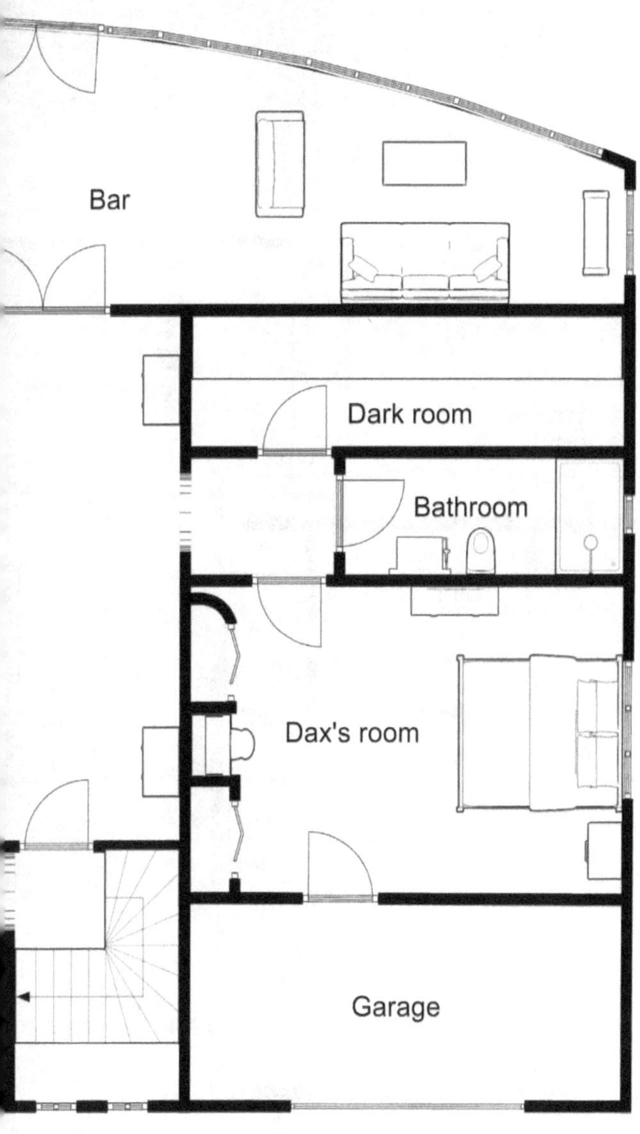

First floor

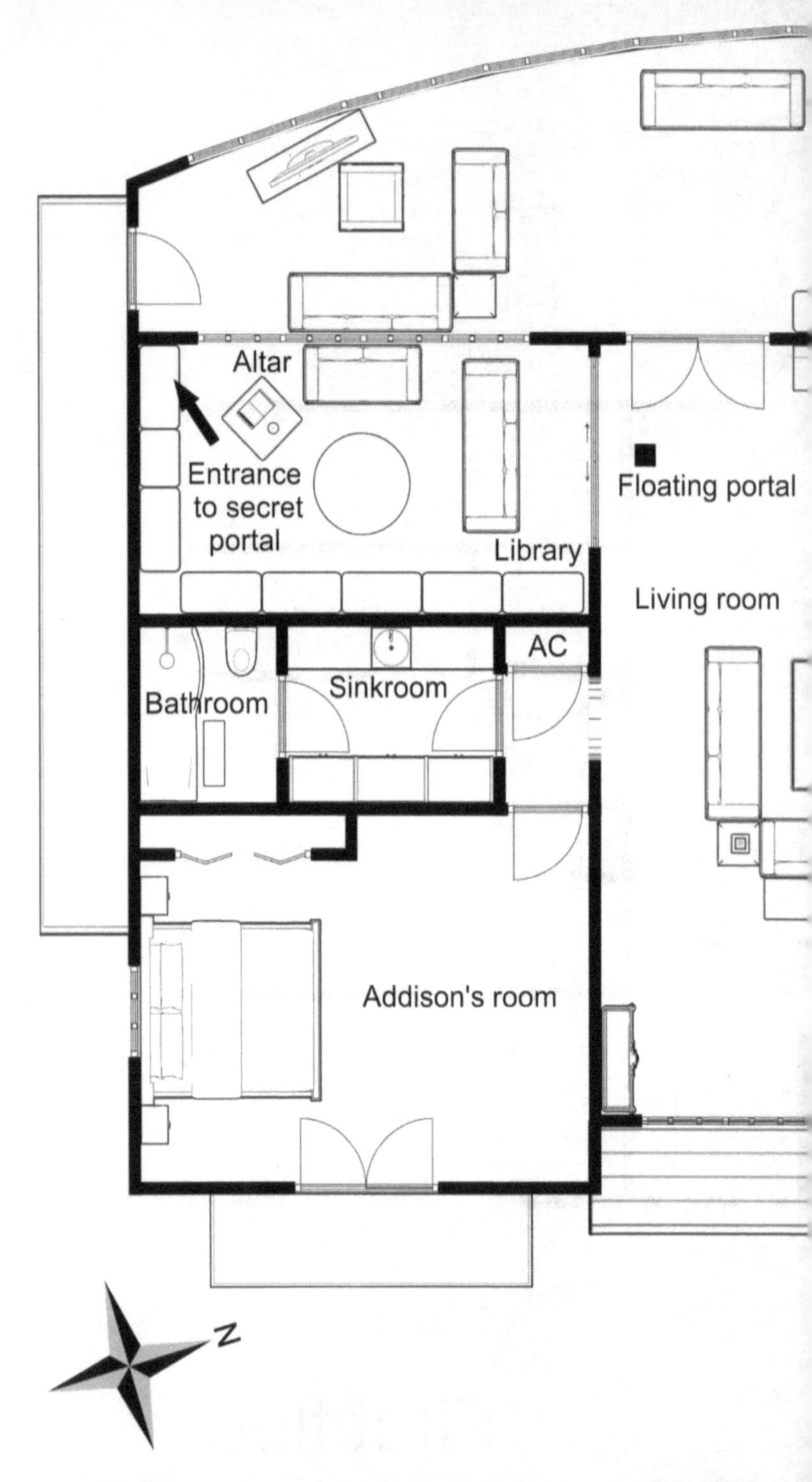

Altar
Entrance
to secret
portal
Floating portal
Library
Living room
AC
Bathroom
Sinkroom
Addison's room
N

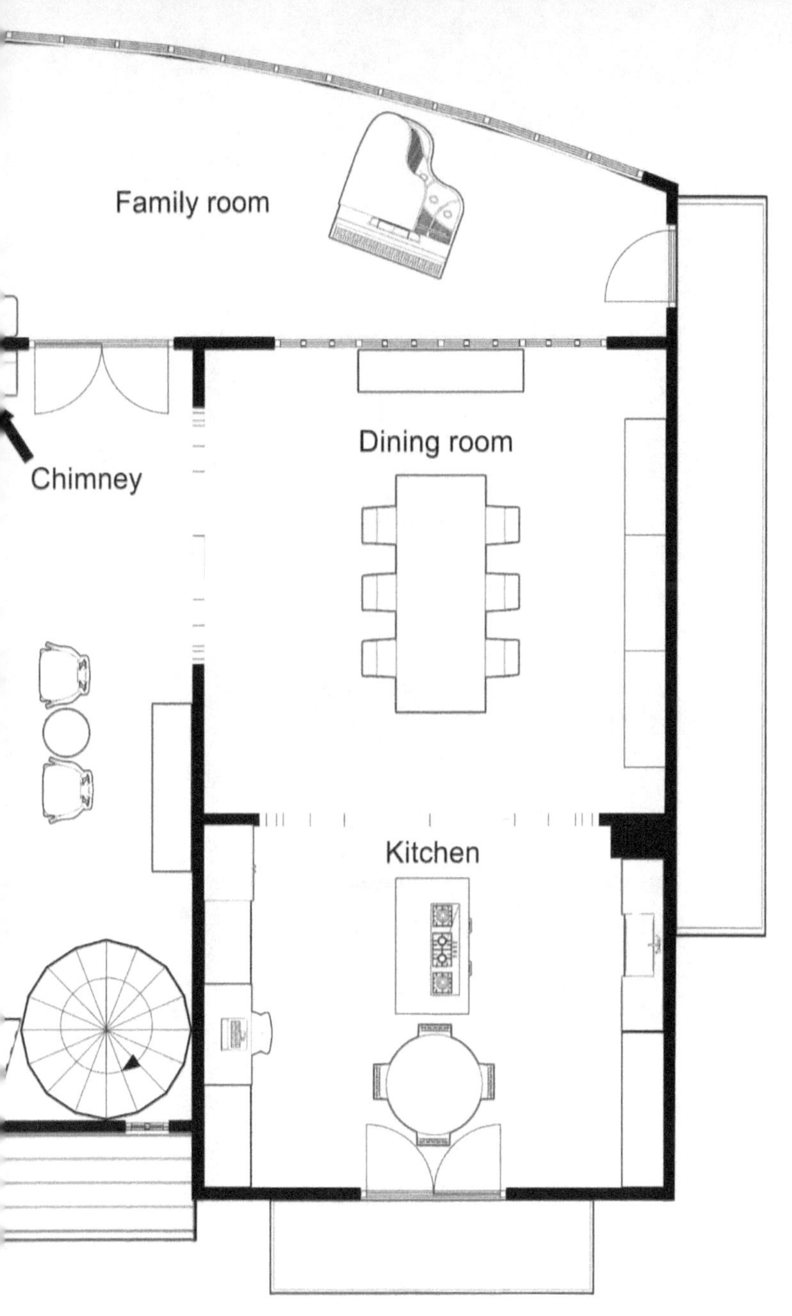

Family room
Chimney
Dining room
Kitchen
Second floor

Stairway to
the roof
Orlando's master
bedroom
Orlando's
closet
Wife's
closet
Trapdoor
Master bathroom
N

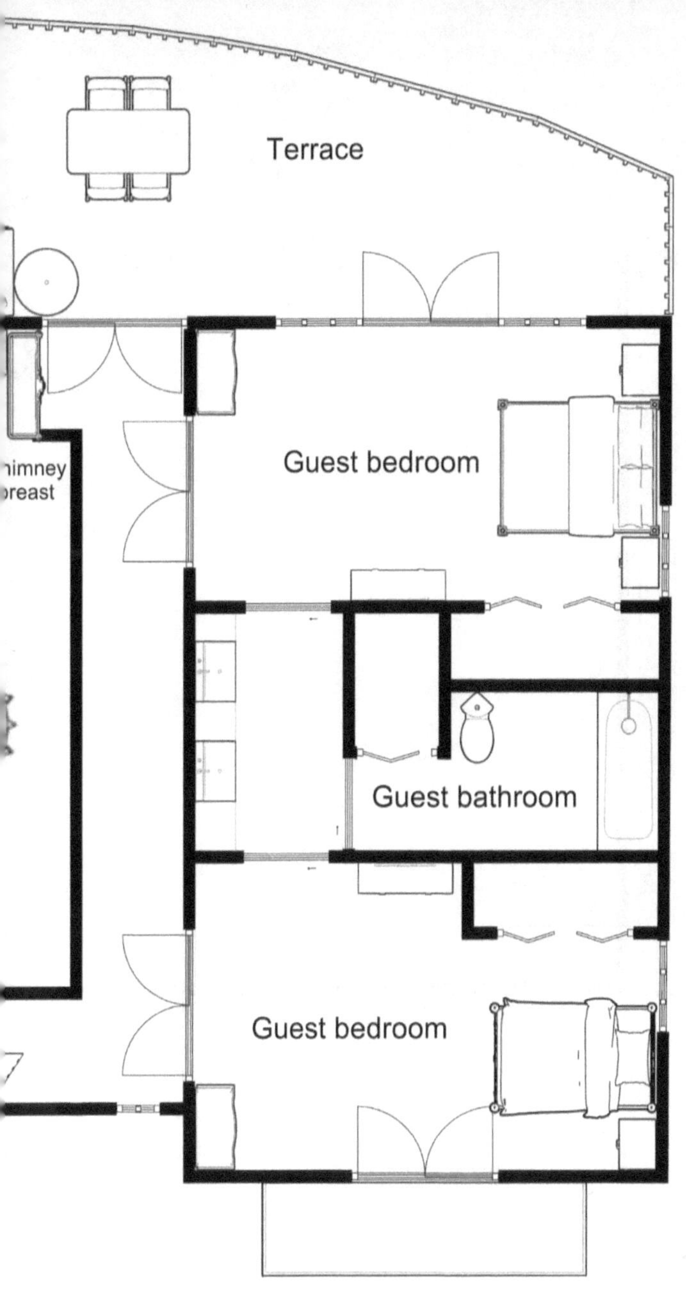
Terrace
Guest bedroom
Chimney breast
Guest bathroom
Guest bedroom
Third floor

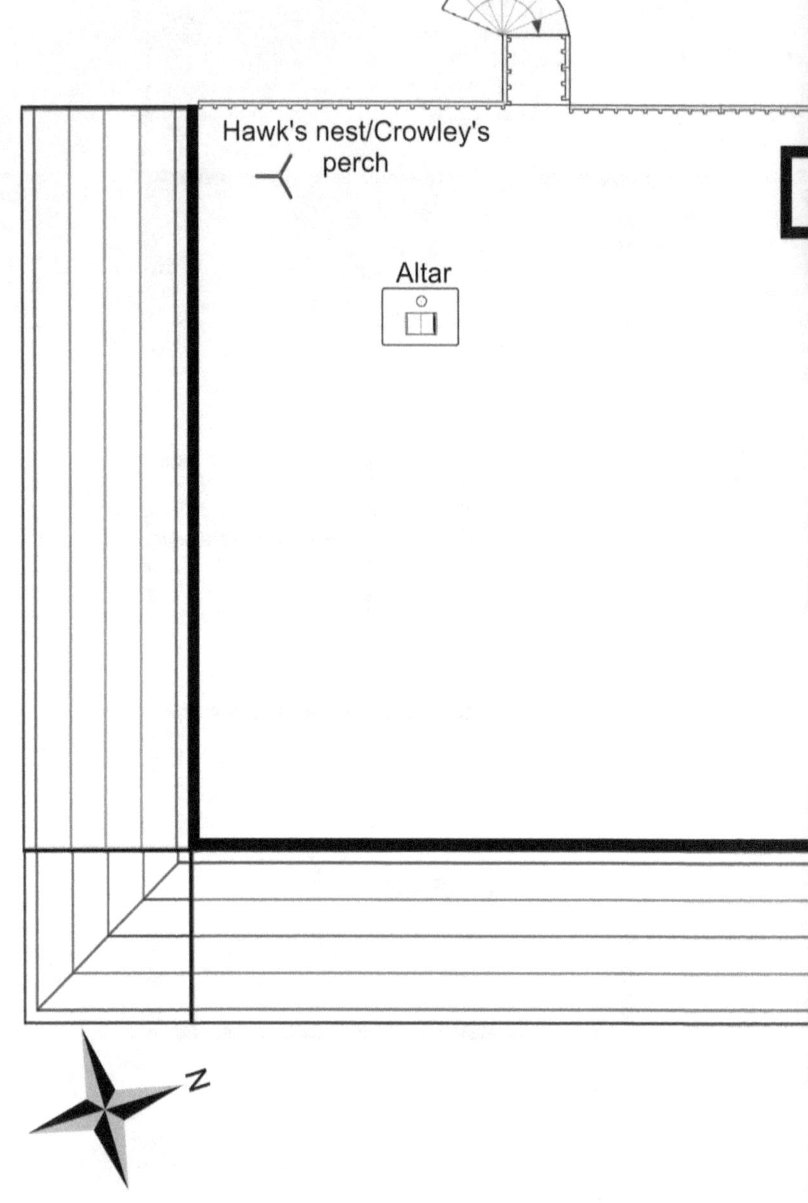

Hawk's nest/Crowley's perch
Altar
N

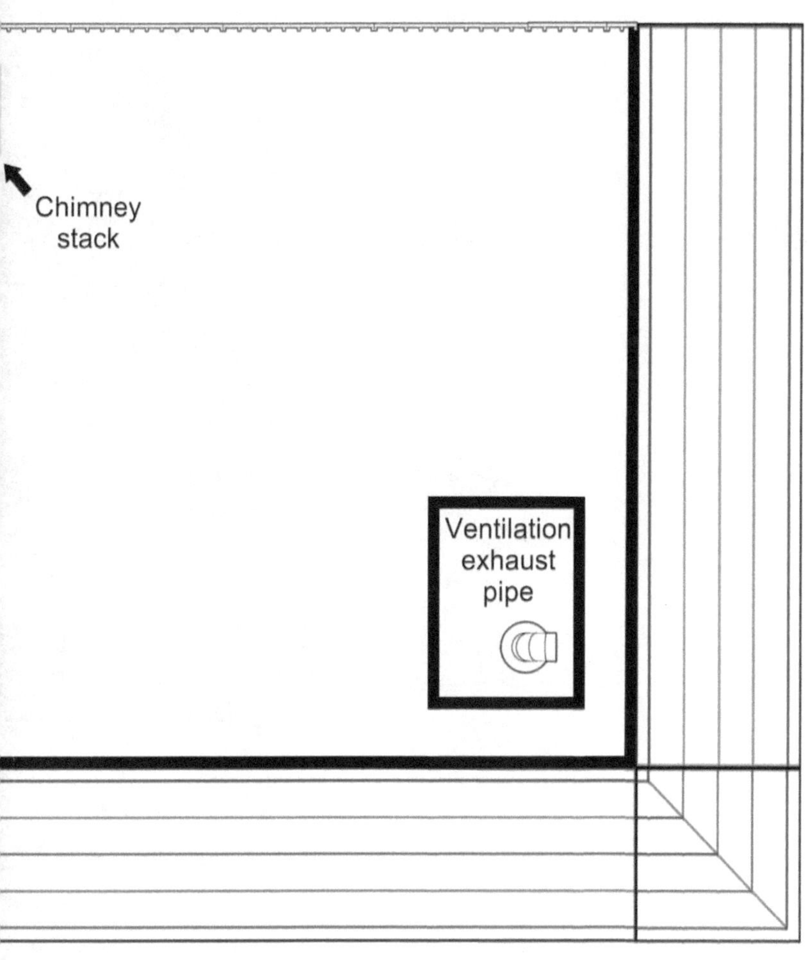

Chimney stack
Ventilation exhaust pipe
Rooftop terrace

GLOSSARY

akashic level: *The akashic level is considered a neutral zone where demons are not meant to enter.*

akashic water: *Eternal and universal knowledge is stored here.*

astral plane *(also known as the fifth dimension, astral world, astral dimension): Realm of existence where spirits go after they leave Earth. Also known as the "in between" or space between physical realms. It is divided into two halves, higher and lower levels.*

astral projection: *The ability to leave one's body and enter the astral plane in spirit form.*

athame: *A small dagger used for magick and ritual purposes. In paganism, it acts as a wand, but possesses the element of fire rather than wind. It can act as a magickal tool to channel one's energy while carrying the magickal attributions of the dagger, including any sigils or stones it possesses.*

Babalawo: *A priest in the Santeria religion who can channel prophecies from the Orishas.*

Book of Shadows: *A magickal practitioner's personal spell-*

book, containing their secrets and handcrafted spells. Much like a journal or diary but for magickal purposes.

cascarilla: Chalk-like substance made from finely crushed eggshell used for means of protection and banishing in Santeria.

curse: A negative form of spell intended to do a person or place harm.

demon (demonio in Spanish): An entity born in the lower level of the astral plane which has tendencies for evil. Some feel they are often misunderstood.

dromedary: Also known as an Arabian camel. A type of camel that only has one hump.

egregore: A life-form created by the brewing of negative human emotions over a long period of time. They eventually become poltergeists if allowed to live for too long.

Enochian: Divine language spoken by dwellers of the astral planes.

Enochian sigil: Enochian scriptures bound together to form written spells, often used by demons or sorcerers.

Goetia: Grimoire on the practice of demonology.

Grimoire: Text that holds magickal spells and incantations, including but not limited to the creations of talismans, servitors, and the conjuring of entities.

lesser-lower-demon: Demon with little intelligence, akin to pets or thralls to higher-level demons.

LLAPS (Lower Levels of the Astral Planes): The bottom half of the astral dimension. The energy source of all negative forces, and the birthplace of demons.

Lukumi: Liturgical language of Santeria in Cuba.

Magick: Magic spelled with a "k" was first written in the early twentieth century by Aleister Crowley to differentiate the difference between "magick," as in to give energy direction, and "magic"s as stage tricks.

Ochun: Deity or goddess in the Yoruba religion, one of the

Orishas worshiped in Santeria. She is known to be the manifestation of the Yoruba Supreme Being and the goddess of love and fertility.

Orisha: *Spirits in the Yoruba religion sent down by the higher divinities to guide humans on Earth.*

Odu: *A divination reading in the Santeria religion by method of using cowrie shells.*

osorbo: *The negative side to a reading, meaning obstacles and misfortune.*

Egun: *In Santeria, this is the spirits of one's ancestors. This can be a deceased loved one, grandparent, parent, etc.*

portal: *A forced breach into the astral dimension.*

reaper: *Operative dispatched to collect souls for the purpose of guiding them to their path. They are stationed in the akashic level of LLAPS, near the higher astral levels.*

sorcerer: *Practitioner of magick, often known to conjure, create servitors, and open portals.*

Santera/Santero: *Practitioner of Santeria.*

Santeria: *Afro-American polytheistic religion developed in Cuba between the sixteenth and ninteenth century. It is a blend of the Yoruba religion of West Africa and Catholicism.*

scythe: *Tool used by the reapers to open portals, collect souls, and connect with other reapers. Reaper lore suggests that the original scythe was once used in war and can channel energy in either direction. The golden scythe, the scythe used by the Judge, is the only scythe powerful enough to kill another reaper.*

servitoire: *Life-form created by the concentration of a human emotion for the purpose of serving a sorcerer/sorceress.*

sigil: *A symbol crafted by a magickal practitioner intended for a specific desired outcome. These symbols are often private to the practitioner, encompassing a particular scripture or blend of different scriptures, including ones that can be made up. It is often difficult to break a sigil if a different practitioner of magick cannot* decipher the sigil, especially when it has been sealed with blood magick.

spell: *Energy given direction, often but not always in the form of a spoken word.*

toque: *Drumming ritual in Santeria involving the deities.*

www.ingramcontent.com/pod-product-compliance
Lightning Source LLC
Chambersburg PA
CBHW051641180726
48284CB00006B/1818